DISMANTLED

Dismantled   Yara Greathouse

Also by Yara Greathouse

Girls on Top Series
Unavoidable
Dismantled

Southern Comforts Anthology
Tequila Sunrises Over Georgia (July 2015)

Other Standalones:
Broken Mirror (September 2015)

Dismantled   Yara Greathouse

DISMANTLED

by
Yara Greathouse

A Girls on Top Novel (Book 2)

(Terri)
"Live your life full of chances and void of regrets."

(Thank you for reading!
Yara Greathouse)

Dismantled   Yara Greathouse

DISMANTLED

Girls on Top Series, Book 2
Copyright © 2015 by Yara Greathouse
Published by Yara Greathouse, LLC, yarawrites@hotmail.com

All rights reserved. Without limiting the rights under copyright reserved above, no part of this publication may be reproduced, stored in or introduced into a retrieval system, or transmitted, in any form, or by any means (electronic, mechanical, photocopying, recording, or otherwise) without the prior written permission of both the copyright owner and the above publisher of this book.

If you are reading this book and have not purchased it or won it in an author or blogger contest, this book has been pirated. Please delete and support the author by purchasing the book from one of its many retailers.

This is a work of fiction. Names, characters, places, brands, media, and incidents are either the product of the author's imagination or are used fictitiously. Any resemblance to actual events, locales or persons, living or dead, is entirely coincidental.

The author acknowledges the trademarked status and trademark owners of various products referenced in this work of fiction, which have been used without permission. The publication/use of these trademarks is not authorized, associated with, or sponsored by the trademark owners.

FBI Anti-Piracy Warning: The unauthorized reproduction or distribution of a copyrighted work is illegal. Criminal copyright infringement, including infringement without monetary gain, is investigated by the FBI and is punishable by up to five years in federal prison and a fine of $250,000.

License Notes: This ebook is licensed for your personal enjoyment only. This ebook may not be re-sold or given away to other people. If you would like to share this book with another person, please purchase an additional copy for each recipient. Thank you for respecting the hard work of this author.

Cover Photos: (Female & Couple) Erin Dawson Photography
http://www.erindawson.com/
(Male) Andreas Gradin/Shutterstock
Cover Design: Rebecca Berto, Berto Designs
Editor: Janie Thornley

DEDICATION

To all who have had the strength to hold on tight when the unexpected happens and to our friends who helped put us back together when we have fallen apart.

Dismantled   Yara Greathouse

PROLOGUE

Traxx

Life can spin you off its axis when you least expect it with something as simple as a knock on the door. Yes, it's possible. It happened to me.

I used to take life for granted. Girls for granted. I never cared what happened after we had sex. I use the word "sex" on purpose, instead of using the friendlier "seeing each other," because that's the absolute truth. Girls were just objects for me to use. I would pick up a new girl with promises of a good time. I was always honest about what I wanted. I never lied to get them to do the things I needed from them.

Sometimes I asked them out, we grabbed dinner then headed to the bar or the club to drink and dance. Other times, I would just pick them up at the bar or at the club. Either way, I always end up in their bed. Sex and satisfaction were the ultimate goal. They got as good as they gave. I never did the "getting to know each other" crap – what's the point? Show 'em a good time and leave 'em. And leaving them I did. As soon as I was finished with them I cut all ties. No thank yous, no repeat performances, and most of all, absolutely no further contact. Like I never even knew them. Cruel? Perhaps, but it was a necessary step for me. I'm not proud of it and some days I hate myself for the person that I used to be.

For the past couple of years, I've been a bit confused. My heart belonged to me. No one has been able to reach in and grab it. I wouldn't let them. I stayed closed in, with walls higher than the Empire State building. Why? You will soon find out. There may be – possibly - only one exception. There's this girl I have some... *feelings* for. Her name is Ciara Collins. I have known her for over two years. She is absolutely off limits. She is also absolutely fucking perfect. What's the problem, you ask? Well, she is Brianna's bestie, and Brianna is Colton's girl. Colton's my best friend. Brianna and Ciara are like sisters. It's complicated, to say the least. My best friend has put her off limits due to my incredibly terrible track record. I can't say I blame him... I've managed to stay away but it's been hard as hell. She is beautiful. I want her. When we spend time together with our friends, nothing makes me happier than her smile and her laugh. When her deep blue eyes look at mine with so much understanding and care, I feel like I have a chance to be normal.

Normal. Who am I kidding? The asshat I used to be never thought there would be consequences with the girls I slept with because I made sure they understood how a night with me was going to work out. Everything was clear from the get go: sex and a clean break. Nothing else was supposed to happen. That is, until something did and this one thing rattled me to my very core. My entire world started to spin in the opposite direction. Complete, absolute chaos and despair. No one should have to go through what I went through.

I know, I know... I'm a pig and I deserve it. Well, sometimes things are not as clear as they seem. Try not to judge me – yet. Get all the facts and then make an informed decision. I bet you cannot possibly imagine everything that takes place in the following pages.

If you want to know the cause, effect and the rest of the story, stick around and continue reading. This book is about to get real. My name is Traxx Maxwell, and this is the story of when my life was dismantled by a stranger and how one tough girl and my friends fought to put me back together and helped me become a man.

Ciara

The very first time I saw him, I knew deep in my heart he was pure, undiluted trouble. Did it matter? No. There was nothing I could do. The word attraction is defined as "the electric or magnetic force that acts between opposite charged bodies, tending to draw them together." That's exactly how I feel about Traxx Maxwell, and I'm almost certain that he feels the same way about me. When we are together we levitate towards each other, and from the moment my blue eyes met his gorgeous brown ones, I have not been able to stop thinking about him.

For over two years I've tried not to let him get to me. It's impossible. Every time I close my eyes, it's his intense gaze that I see looking back at me. His deep voice caresses me in my dreams. If I'm being kissed, it's his lips I picture lightly grazing mine. I have been warned by my best friend Brianna and her boyfriend Colton, more times than I care to think about, to be careful. Traxx is in the business of breaking hearts. Not on purpose, mind you, but he has never been in a relationship. He believes he is a manwhore or love 'em and leave 'em kind of guy. When I see him putting the moves on some girl who catches his eye, it hurts, because I want it to be me he's giving his attention to, but I have to hide those feelings. I'm just patiently waiting for him to be ready to find something other than a quick fuck. I'm in no rush. I know the real Traxx. The one he only lets me see when no one else is around. The one he tries so hard to hide. I like that version of Traxx. *My Traxx* is genuine, caring, smart and funny.

You can say we are good friends. We laugh. We talk. We joke and hang out in the same circle of friends. Does he like me on another level? I think so. I just don't know how much. I've noticed that when I go from one room to another, his dark eyes follow my every movement and appreciate everything they see. Other times, when I catch him looking at me, his lips curve into a half smile and he quickly looks away. Also, when I bring a date to meet everyone, Traxx's body tenses, his happy smile goes away and a forced one takes over. The look he gives him... it's like he's sizing him from top to bottom, as if trying to decide if the guy's good enough for me. And as soon as he gets a chance, Traxx comes over and starts asking me questions to figure out how I really feel about my date. Can we say *Alpha much*?

Then, one unexpected day, hell broke loose; which we now refer to as "the incident." After that, things as they used to be were no more. Actually, they got worse. Traxx is starting to fall into a person that we no longer recognize. There is a darkness moving within him. I know that he needs us more than ever. He's pushing everyone away. I need to prove to him that it's okay to let others into his heart. I have fought for many important things in my life: my country, my family and my friends... but I believe saving Traxx will prove to be the battle of my lifetime.

CHAPTER 1

Traxx

It's a nice fall evening today - cooler than usual, but warm enough that I can drive my truck with the windows down. At the red light, I smile at the pretty girl driving a sporty car next to me since she's trying hard to get my attention. If she only knew… I have girls throwing themselves at me at every place I go. Even on social media, girls I don't even know are constantly trying to get inside my pants – and I love it. I never have to worry when I need to hook up. Somebody's always a phone call away. "One Night Traxx," that's what they call me and what I'm famous for. I'm not proud of that, but the idea of giving my heart away scares the crap out of me.

As I pull up to my driveway, I press the garage door opener that's clipped to my visor and notice that my best friend and roommate, Notso, isn't home yet. Given that we have plans tonight, I have to get in touch with him to make sure everything's still in place. I also need to call my other best friend, Colton, to make sure he and his girlfriend Brianna are also coming with us. I need Brianna to come along because her BFFs Ciara and my cousin Keagan tend to go wherever she goes. Those girls always do everything together and they're more like one of the guys... They fish, hunt, shoot targets, anything we want to do they are always game to do with us, and I hate to admit it, but sometimes they are better than us boys. I've known Brianna and Ciara going on three years from our college days. They used to be roommates in the Army and got along so well, they decided to continue to be roomies after they got out.

Ciara... She's the smartest, most beautiful, sexiest girl I've ever met. I think there's this mutual attraction. When I see her and get to spend time with her, I'm happy. That is until some random guy comes by and talks her into dancing or even worse, hangs around and won't leave her alone. It puts me in a fucking bad mood. The worst thing is that I can't do anything about it – she isn't mine. I can't claim her. I've never been anybody's boyfriend and I wouldn't know where to start with that. Ciara's one of the good ones. If there's one thing I'm certain of it's that I don't deserve her, and she probably won't want anything to do with me after watching me interact with girls the past few years. Besides, I'm not sure that I can trust her or any girl for that matter. The moment they know they have you, they will stomp on your heart and take it, leaving you heartless, which is something I already know too well.

I start to pull out my tie and unbutton my shirt with one hand, and with the other I'm calling Notso.

"Hey man. I wasn't able to get away from work early enough, I'm just now leaving the office." I hear him say as I place my tie on the back of one of the kitchen's chairs and grab a cold beer from the fridge.

I hold the phone between my shoulder and my ear. "Have you heard from Colton yet?" I ask, using my most inconspicuous voice.

"Not yet, but I spoke to Keagan earlier and she said the girls were also coming with us."

After twisting the top, I take a long swig and do a quick fist pump in the air. Playing it cool, I respond casually. "Okay, that's fine."

"When are you going to stop being such an ass? You need to ask her out already!" Notso says loudly into the phone.

Not surprised that he can read my mind and knows the real reason behind my question, I answer him. "You know why."

"Then stop being such a man whore. That shit's gonna flip on you someday."

"Yeah, right." I laugh to myself because I really wish I could just turn it off. "Look, I gotta make some calls to lineup a girl for tonight. I'll…"

Beep.

I hear the sound of call waiting. "Hey, Notso, hold a sec while I see who's calling. It appears that pussy is coming to me instead of me having to fetch it." I laugh loudly and click to the other line. "Hello?"

"Who's this?" A girl asks.

"Hold on, you have it backwards. You called me. How about you tell me who you want to talk to and perhaps we can go from there." This shit annoys me to no end.

"Is this Traxx Maxwell?" Must be a damn telemarketer.

"Yes, but I don't need…"

She cuts me off immediately, "I'm not selling anything. You need to come open your front door. I'm outside, waiting."

What the hell…? I click off that phone call and click again so that I have Notso on the phone. "Man, some girl is saying she's outside waiting for me to open the fucking door."

"Who's this chick? Did you bring some tramp to the house and forgot to tell me? I thought you never let anyone know where we live."

"Hell, no! You know better than that. Stay on the line a minute, let me get rid of her."

I move quickly to the front door. As I'm looking at the door, all I can think about is that this better be a joke. I open the door in a rush. A brown hair girl is looking at me. Her hair is a mess. She has dark shadows under her eyes. She looks rough. Disheveled. I don't recognize her. "May I help you?"

She stares at me like she's willing me to say the right thing. I stare back with a hard look. She has some guts to show up at my place. And how did she get my address?

"Hi Traxx… by the way you are looking at me makes me think you don't recognize me."

"You are right, I don't. What do you need?" I don't mean to be rude but damn, I don't have time for this shit.

She looks away and starts laughing hard. When she looks back at me, she is once again serious. Her expression goes from happy to neutral, to… pissed. What the fuck? "Well?"

"Of course you don't remember. You are 'One Night Traxx.' Isn't that right?"

I smile uncomfortably at her. Where is she going with all this? She can't be pregnant. I always use protection and check carefully when I remove the condoms to make sure no accident has happened.

"You think you are some kind of god who gets to use girls left and right without repercussions, don't you?"

Shit.

I give her my best smile. "Look, if I was with you, I'm sure we had a great time. But I don't bring girls to my place and as you already know, I don't do repeats. It's always a one-time thing. I'm sure that I told you that before we hooked up. So, if you'll excuse me, I have things to do…" I start to close the door on her face when I notice some resistance, at which point I look down and see a dingy pair of black Chuck Taylor's on her foot blocking my door. Still frowning, I hear a loud click. My eyes slowly move up away from the shoes so I can tell her to fuck off right to her face, only to realize she has a cocked revolver pointed at *my* face.

"How about you let me into your house? Right. Now."

Fuck!

"Okay, no need to be harsh. Take it easy." I can hear Notso on the phone asking me what the hell was going on. I don't want her to take my phone away. Without putting it to my ear, I raise my hands on a pose of surrender and speak a little louder than usual. "Whoa! Is the gun really necessary? My roommate will be home soon and you may scare him with that thing. Let's go ahead and keep it relaxed. We can talk without you pointing the gun at my face."

"Is that what you think? That I've come here to 'talk'? You're fucking dreaming!" She takes one of her hands from the gun to her head and grabs a fistful of hair. She's pulling so hard, a bunch comes out and she doesn't even acknowledge it. While the girl is mumbling to herself, I hear Notso on the phone, saying something about not spooking her, because he is calling the cops right now. I wish I knew what the average response time for the local police is nowadays. Fuck me! The room is suddenly so terribly hot and I feel heavy sweat beads forming on my forehead.

With the dark silver barrel staring at me, my mind briefly drifts to think about all the shitty things I have done in the past. I also think about my mom, how I don't want her to see my body without a face. My dad. My brother. My friends. As the images cloud my vision, Ciara's smiling face is a constant next to all the others. Simultaneously, I'm also trying to come up with a way out of this mess. The girl is steadily mumbling and whispering to herself, shaking the gun every which way – I wish I knew her name… Isn't that what they say in situations like this one, to appeal to their human connection? If that fails, can I try to overtake her?

"Why don't we sit down and just talk through this situation like adults." I take one step towards her. She looks at me, with tears in her eyes that have started to overflow and fall delicately on her cheeks. She looks lost and so sad.

"Don't you fucking move one more inch! Adults? What the fuck is an adult to you! You treat girls worse than trash! Use them and leave them! What kind of fucked up human being are you? Why do you do that?"

If she only knew why…

It was the beginning of 8th grade. I was looking forward to seeing my friends after the summer break. As I caught up with them, I noticed that I was a bit taller than most. Taller and heavier. I was happy to be that way, because it meant my chances to grab a good position for the football team were really good. The happiness didn't last long. During lunch on that first week, a swarm of girls came to my table, where I was eating with my friends. I vaguely remembered the girl leading the group as somebody from elementary school. She wasn't all that pretty and her family had lots of money. There was always something about her eyes that kept me away.

"Hey Traxx – How was your summer?"

My friends at the table started to giggle, which embarrassed me. I didn't like being the center of attention.

Barely glancing at her, I answered with a muttered "Fine."

The giggles got louder from the guys and I noticed the girl's face turning red. She looked back at the other girls around her, took a deep breath and asked "Do you want to hang out sometime?"

Giggles were starting to turn into laughter when I looked up at my friends. I wished for a hole in the ground that I could crawl into.

"Not really." Was all I had to say. Two small words. These simple words made my experience in middle school pure hell.

"Why not?" She asked me and sounded a little upset.

My friends were not subtle with all their giggling. I didn't know what to say to her. I was not into hanging out with girls. Shrugging my shoulders at her was the action that lit the match of her anger towards me.

"You think you are funny, don't you? Well, I promise you that I'll be the one laughing from now on. Remember, you had your chance."

Just like that, I became the target of the Queen Bee and her minions. Every day I was taunted, pushed around and made feel like a nobody. My height and size were no longer something to feel proud of as it became the point of all their cruelty. They even got some of the guys from the team to pick fights with me. I had to learn to fight the hard way — I didn't have much of a choice on that. The mental anguish I had to endure those years because of their bullying almost broke me. If it wasn't for Colton having my back and being my friend regardless of anything that they did, I would have lost my sanity.

I learned that I could not trust girls. They are crafty and use their powers over boys to get them to do anything they want. They pushed me to be this way. I hate the thought to let any girl near my heart. They don't deserve it. They don't deserve me. Thankfully, the torture ended when I entered High School, as those girls ended up attending a different school from mine, but the damage was done. I was brainwashed and scared to get close to anyone of the opposite sex. So, I switched the tables and started to take from them. It made me feel powerful and in control.

At that moment, this girl's voice brought me back to the here and now.

"I was supposed to be THE ONE! The one who finally gets the guy of her dreams. We were going to date for a couple of years, then one beautiful Valentine's Day spent in the Caribbean you were going to ask me to marry you, because you had come to realize that you could not live without me. At that point, I would cry and say yes. After a one year engagement, we were to have our dream location wedding in Bali. We were going to read our very own vows professing unending love for one another, followed by the best honeymoon ever. We couldn't wait to start our very own family: three kids, two boys and a girl. Together we were going to buy a dog and be absolutely happy. Now, thanks to you, all of it it's ruined. You... YOU ruined it all! They all think I'm crazy and that I was lying to them!" She raised her hands to her head and squeezed hard against her ears, as if trying to keep something or someone out. Then she slaps her flattened hands on her temples over and over again.

What.the.hell?

"You are a selfish motherfucking asshole, you know that? You only think about what you want and damn the consequences!" She is yelling and starts to pace. Nope, I'm not calming her at all. It seems I have gotten her more agitated.

"Look, I'm truly sorry for whatever I did to you. I just don't do relationships and I prefer casual sex, that's all."

"I know that! I've seen you around, always picking up a girl and fucking her and then never have contact with them again. That's why I'm here. I refused to be ignored by the likes of you."

What.the.fuck?

"I'm sorry, can you please tell me your name?"

"I don't know what for, if you don't remember it, why do you want to know now?"

"Well, because I was obviously careless to have forgotten your name." I really hope this works. I take a deep breath and give her my best smile. "Because you came here – to my place - to see me and whatever the reason, it's important to you. It's only fair that we communicate by using our names. Don't you think?"

She gives me a confused look. "I guess... My name is Marcy." She scratches her head with a child-like quality. She still looks confused, but has not loosened her hold on the gun.

"Good, that's really great, Marcy. Thank you. Now, please tell me what brought you here today." Her brown eyes suddenly frown, and suddenly her stare becomes cold and dark. I feel chills going through my body and I realize this is a life or death situation.

"Months ago, you saw me having fun with a group of people. There were smiles from afar, a few drinks and a lot of flirting. We were attracted to each other…" her voice lowers a bit, so I think she is calming down. "… then we have the most passionate night together. I still remember the way you touched me." Her free hand moves over her breast and continues down until she reaches her pelvis. Her crying eyes are pinned to mine and I notice with her free hand she is touching between her legs. Oh, man. This girl has lost it. "It was pure heaven. Hours later you had your fill, got dressed and left. Didn't even say goodbye."

"Look, Marcy, I'm sorry. That's just the way I am. What else did you expect me to do? I'd explained that I stay away from relationships or any type of commitment…"

"Shut up! Shut your nasty, ugly, lying mouth! You have no right to say *shit* to me! You have not earned that right! You actually think I'm pissed out of my mind because I wanted a relationship with you?"

She laughs and sounds like a crazy person. She pulls on her hair again and starts pacing from one wall to the other. What the fuck should I do? Damn it! I just need her to keep talking. If she's busy talking, maybe she will be too busy to start shooting. I lift my hand to wipe the sweat from my forehead, as I feel it dripping down the sides of my face and down my back. "I mean it, Marcy, I'm sorry that you feel this way. I was very clear…"

"Oh, yes! *Very* clear. I've got you now. I have all your fucking attention, don't I? Do you want to try to run out like you do after you fuck somebody and then I can shoot you in the back? Or should I shoot your miserable dick off instead and see what kind of dating life you would get then." She moves the gun down a bit. "Your problem is not that you bed too many girls. Your problem is the way you treat us after the fact. Like we don't exist. What kind of shit is that? I may be an easy lay, but I'm a human being. I have feelings. Don't you understand that you cannot make someone the center of everything for a few hours and then act like they never existed? It makes the other person feel bad, like they are worthless… In this scenario the only worthless person is you! YOU!"

She screams and her words make me flinch. I can actually feel her pain. I should not care, but deep inside somehow I do care. Even though it is obvious Marcy's mental state is not well, I had something to do with this final result. And I do feel bad. I'm not mean or hateful, and at this moment I wish I could, some way, somehow, lift some of the burden off of her.

When she's done screaming, she takes a step forward and raises the gun until it's pointed right between my eyes. Her tears are heavy now. She's really upset and I feel… I actually feel bad for her. To top it off, I have no idea what I can do to help ease her pain and her hate. Sympathy has never been my forte, nor can I imagine the way she's feeling because I haven't been in that situation. Ever. Regardless of what I choose to do, I feel as if it'll fail.

"Please, don't do this…" My eyes divert to the door because I suddenly hear sirens and realize the police are finally coming our way. Shit!

Her head tilts towards the door. "Is that the police? How…" She is looking around everywhere within the room, then, she notices the phone still in my hand. "Is that phone on?"

I swallow hard but choose not to answer.

"Cut that shit off and put it down!"

I slowly show her that I cut off the phone and crouch down placing it carefully on the floor.

"Get your ass back up! Who the hell was on the phone?"

As I slowly get up, I try to explain. "It was my roommate. Look I'm sure we can work something out. If you put your gun down and leave my house, I won't press charges. You can disappear and go about your life. Move away, start anew, and don't ever sleep with pricks like me *ever* again." I am pleading to her shamelessly. I don't want to die this way. I can hear the sirens very close now. Come on, COME ON!

"No! I'm going to do this! You are going to pay the price to know what it's like to damage somebody's life. All my friends saw me leave with you that night! They think I'm trashy and worthless! They look at me differently now. My own family feels sorry for me. They constantly whisper and talk to each other, they are talking about ME! My life's ruined – can't you see that? You ruined me! You can't use people and expect them to be all right with that! Do you understand how hard it is not to be wanted by anyone? It's over, Traxx. From this moment, your life as you know it, it's no more! No one will want you, either."

This is it! The police are going to be here a few minutes too late. I see the pain and torture in the tears brimming from her eyes. I truly feel pain for what I've done to her and to so many others. I really am scum. Whatever happened in my past that shaped me into this substandard human being is irrelevant. I realize a little too late that what those girls of my past used to do to me, have nothing to do with the girls of my present. Years of feeling betrayed, humiliated and - most of all – hurt, are thrown on my face as I think of things that I've done and come to regret. Why couldn't I see things clearly before? I should not have taken it out on them. I'm too late for that now. I can't leave this world and not face up to what I did to this woman…

With sorrow and sadness in the recognition of my faults and the knowledge that my life was about to end, I look at her one last time, eye to eye, while I whisper the words she should have heard long time ago. "I'm really truly sorry for what I've put you through. You didn't deserve it. I'm sorry for the past, I am sorry for the here and now. My heart has been cold and closed for so long, it takes an incident like this to make it feel again." I laugh dryly. "And... I'm feeling you. I'm feeling your pain. I'm feeling your despair. Most of all I'm feeling your need to put an end to it all. I understand, because some years ago I was you. My heart was destroyed and at that moment I made promises to myself that led me to be someone I never expected. I had to make choices that had me treating people in the worst possible way."

In that moment, I knew that by looking for ways to protect myself, I had become one of them: a person who caused pain to others, a bully and a hater of my own accord. I loathed the person that I'd become. "I wish you can find peace within you soon and that you can move on. Live your life the way you should, with dignity and respect. I'm sorry that you were a victim of my terrible behavior. I deserve this." I feel tears coming down my face as I close my eyes and wait.

Suddenly, the most painful, haunting wail is coming from the girl. My gut twists and turns as I pop my eyes open and look at her. What befalls next, plays in front of me in slow motion. She's screaming while turning the gun away from my face, to placing it against her temple. I blink once, twice and when I realize what's happening, all I want to do is to stop her. I lunge myself towards her and reach with my arms as far out as I can, but I was never close enough. By the time she's only a step away, her finger pulls the trigger. I'm crying out "No!" when a rain of warmth touches my exposed skin, wets the front of my shirt and hands while the coppery smell fills my nostrils and my brain produces nothing but sadness and regret.

Like hitting a wall, I stop cold long enough to see her lifeless eyes looking at me and her body slowly falling to the floor while I'm falling to my knees. At the same time, policemen enter the house bursting through the door and as I look at them coming towards me, I've come undone and my world finally fades black.

Marcy Smith (four months ago)

Tonight is going to be *the* night. I can feel it. I take my little black dress and lay it on the bed. Looking at the shoe rack that hangs over the door, I look for my sexy black shoes with the rhinestone covered straps. My long brown hair is full of soft waves for extra sexiness. I have applied dark eye shadow for a "smokey" effect. Going to my bathroom, I start to remove the rollers. The medicine cabinet catches my eyes and I play tug of war in my mind: open it – don't; open it – don't.

Finally I decide to open it. My medicine bottle sits there, staring back at me. I rub my finger lightly on the label. It has been exactly three weeks since I decided to stop them. I hate medication and the way they make me feel as if I'm trapped inside my mind, unable to express myself. A prisoner of my inner thoughts. I need to be free. I'm aware of my symptoms and will go to the doctor if they start to manifest. In the meantime, I'm happy.

I skip-dance to my closet and glance to make sure the door to my room is locked before I step inside. I have placed a curtain on the far wall. My fingers itch to touch it and move it out the way so I can admire my masterpiece. I reach and slowly reveal the picture mosaic behind it. *Traxx…*

I have been following him for weeks since that day at the pharmacy, when I came around the corner and bumped into him and all the items I was carrying in my hands fell inside his shopping cart. As I picked up my things, I noticed the giant box of condoms labeled "Lifestyles KYNG." I felt the hotness travel all the way up to my face, making me blush.

"Is everything okay, miss?"

I could not help it. I had to take a quick look at his package and yes, the guy was well endowed. "Yes," I smiled, "everything is great. Sorry about bumping into you, but I'm just going to take my things and be on my way." The smile he gave me melted my panties and I suddenly felt exposed and curiously,

I also felt beautiful. To have his total attention for a couple of minutes was the highlight of my day. A female voice came around and bumped me out of my happy place. Then I saw her, blonde, stylish and beautiful. Figures.

"Traxx, did you find the ice cream I want? Oh, hi there." She looked at him and then at me.

"Ciara, this is...."

"Marcy."

"Marcy. We just accidentally bumped into each other and she was gathering her things that fell inside the cart."

I manage to smile a little and waved with a couple of free fingers.

"Okay, see you around Marcy."

That was the moment I realized he wanted to see me again. I had to make it happen. I followed him to her place and waited in my car until he came out and I could follow him to his place. It's been weeks, but I have documented everything in tedious detail. My mosaic wall can attest to that. And tonight... Tonight I am ready to make my move.

Ciara (Present day)

Today I was at the receiving end of one of those calls you really never want to get. The sun had started to set as I was getting ready to go out and have a careless evening with my friends. Notso called to tell me that an armed woman had shown up at his place and had locked herself inside the house with Traxx. He was still on the phone as I grabbed my purse, keys and headed to my car.

I'm used to keeping control of myself even as the worst type of situation comes my way thanks to my past years in the Army, but I would be lying if I said I was not shaking inside. Many scenarios were going through my mind. My friends are my family. Traxx is one of my best friends. I care deeply for him and I also harbor an inner desire that we could be more than friends one day. I buckle my seatbelt and take off doing sixty in less than four seconds.

As I shifted my car through the backstreets of our town, everything's a blur. I brush my right eye with my hand, to realize a lonely tear was running down my cheek. Dammit! Please let him be okay. In less than five minutes, I enter the subdivision, slowing down only when I see blue lights flashing on top of at least three police vehicles. There is a fire truck and an ambulance on the street as well. I park as close as I can, as I get out of the vehicle, I feel my feet moving faster as I approach the door. My heart is also beating fast. It's like a drumline has taken residence inside my chest. Suddenly, a policeman stops me by grabbing my arm. I try to shake him off.

"Excuse me ma'am, but you cannot go in. This is a crime scene."

"Please, *sir*, remove your hand."

"I can't let you through quite yet. The paramedics and the coroner are on the scene."

"And who, exactly, needs the paramedics?" If he doesn't take his hand off me, he may need to call his own paramedics. Asshole.

"That is confidential information, as the *incident* is being investigated."

I look around to see if my best friend, Brianna is around here. She could get through to this guy. I'm sure Notso called her too, especially because she's a cop. But it's dark already and all I notice is the eerie sound the tree branches are making against the wind. Is that an omen of bad things to come? Turning to the other side of the street, I spot Notso's truck. I excuse myself and shake the policeman's hand off of my arm and start to move towards the giant blond guy who's like my brother and whom I trust without hesitation. As I get closer to him, I notice he's talking to a guy who looks like a detective. I also see Brianna and Colton approaching from the opposite direction.

"Notso! Please give me an update."

"Ciara… He's okay. Traxx was not hurt. Physically, at least. This is the detective in charge, Cutter Hall. He was asking me a few questions since I was on the phone when all of this went down."

I looked at Detective Hall and extended my hand in order to introduce myself. "Detective… I'm Ciara Collins. Can we please get an update on what's going on? By that time Brianna and Colton had reached us, so I introduced them to the detective.

"Detective Hall, I'm with the local police department," Brianna showed her badge. "Can I please get a debrief on the incident and the current situation?"

"Sure, Officer Gilmore. Please follow me."

As the detective was turning, I touched his arm. "Detective Hall, can we please see Traxx Maxwell?" My eyes and voice were pleading.

Looking at me with compassion, Detective Hall replied in a low, sympathetic tone, "Sure, Ms. Collins. As soon as the paramedics clear him, I will send Ms. Gilmore to come get you guys. But please, know that there is a chance he may have to be taken to the hospital for further treatment. Some people are unable to come out of shock right away. It takes them some time. Keep that in mind."

I nodded and forced my hand to release him. I crossed my arms in front of me to act as a barrier for any bad news that may come our way. I felt Notso's arms wrap around me and I let his familiar cologne soothe my fragile soul. Notso knows my feelings for Traxx. He knows how I have not been in a serious relationship for months... No – correction – years, because I keep hoping that Traxx will see me differently. That he would want to take a chance with me - to let me love him. Now who knows what's going to happen? Everything could be in turmoil, the unknown.

Colton paced the street and shoved his hands in his now messy hair. He stopped and looked at me. We were both at a loss for words. "Ciara... He is a tough ass, he will be fine."

Looking at him, I gave him a small smile and whispered "I know." Notso squeezed me harder. We heard steps come our way from behind us. I glanced back over my shoulder and saw Keagan, Traxx's cousin and one of my best friends, approach us.

"Where is he?" She immediately asked.

I was sure that Notso has been updating her via text messages until she was able to get here.

Keagan came to me and hugged me from the opposite side where Notso was holding me.

"He's still inside. The paramedics are with him."

"Dear God!" Keagan inhaled deeply and her trembling hands came up to her face to wipe the tears that had escaped her eyes.

"The good news is that we don't think he was hurt, well, at least not physically. Let's think positive and hope for the best."

Suddenly, the front door opens, we see Brianna and Detective Hall coming out and behind them is Traxx, covered by a blanket and with a paramedic on each side. I turn and escape from Notso's and Keagan's embrace.

Brianna stops in front of me when she reaches our group, and grabs my arm while giving me a sad look. I gently push around her so I can see Traxx, calling after him.

"Traxx!"

Slowly, he lifts his face to look at me. My eyes grow wide, when I notice his cheek and neck peppered in red. Instead of his usual cocky smile, I see sadness surround all his features and his brown eyes are sparkless, similar to the darkness found in a hollow tree. I gasp loudly and use my hand to cover my mouth so the scream that wants to escape stays secure inside.

"Can we go with him?" I asked the detective.

"Ciara... It's better if I drive you." Brianna says close to my ear. I look at her and shake my head from side to side.

Detective Hall looks at me and says "I will be escorting him since our crime scene investigation team needs to gather evidence from his clothes and body, before he can be released."

I nod to make sure he knows I heard him. My tears are on full cascade mode now and I can't speak. Traxx looks like a different person. He may not be physically hurt, but the Traxx I know is missing at the moment.

"Come with us, Ciara. I'll take you to the hospital. Give me your keys, Colton will drive your car there."

I can't move. I stay standing there like a statue, watching the paramedics help Traxx inside the ambulance and close the doors behind him. Then, Brianna being true to her impatient self, pats down my jean's pockets, but can't find what she's looking for.

"Colton, she must have left the keys in her car. Can you go check? If they are there just text me and I'll meet you at the hospital."

With a head nod, he is on his way.

"Keagan, will you be okay to drive?" Brianna asks.

"I'd rather ride with one of you, actually."

Notso immediately offers to take her and soon after we're on the move to our vehicles. Colton's text came in as we were buckling our seatbelts. We have to wait a bit before we can start driving, because some of the patrol vehicles and other first responders have started to clear out and move about the street.

"Are you going to be okay?" Brianna asks me.

"I think so." I manage to whisper but knowing Brianna, I know she's got something on her mind. "Why do you ask?"

"Well, you have never been a 'crying it out' kind of girl. So I was wondering what's up with the river of tears you've got going on this evening. No bullshit, please."

"I care about him, Brianna. What do you want me to say?"

"I think you more than just 'care about him.' Tell me."

Taking a deep breath I start to voice my thoughts. "I'm scared for what this is going to do to him. He was messed up before, you know how he never let anyone get close to him. That's not normal. I can't help the way I feel about him. I have always wanted it to be more between us, but stayed away because I didn't think he was ready. Now, after this experience, I'm worried and scared that he will push me away even further. I don't know. My head's just rambling around all the possibilities. Bottom line is that I'm nervous about what tomorrow and the days after will be like."

Brianna lets out a sigh. "Yeah, you are right. But he's not alone. He has us. You have us. We will figure it out. You'll see."

I wanted to believe her. I really did – and even with all my doubts, I hung tight to her every word and kept quiet until we arrived at the hospital.

Traxx

I feel numb. I want to be angry. I want to feel sadness. I wish I could yell and scream and smash some things and throw others out the window. But all I feel is blank. My brain is not helping me make things happen. It's like it's tied or tethered to something stronger than itself. It still creates thoughts but it's unable to act on them.

The investigators swabbed and collected what they needed from my skin, hair and nails, took my clothes and gave me one of those half robes that cover your front and has the back wide open letting your ass get some air. The nurse came in and gave me some pills. I think she said they will help me rest. I don't want to rest. Like a never ending nightmare, every time I close my eyes the scene replays in my head causing my body to shake. I feel cold, so I pull the covers higher up.

The nurse tells me there are a lot of people in the waiting room, wanting to see me.

"Do you feel up to some visitors?"

Nope. "Sure." I don't know if I'm going to be able to deal with the pity looks that are about to come my way. I slowly lay my head back on the pillow.

I close my eyes and visualize the one person that can help me build up some new memories. The one person whose innermost goodness can take away a slight amount of the bad I have inadvertently created. I also need my roommate. There is no way I can go back to that house. No way in hell. The thought of stepping foot in that living room makes me tremble.

Keagan opens the door and leads all my friends inside my room. They stand around my bed, all eyes on me. Keagan squeezes my hand and leans over to kiss my cheek.

"Hey, Traxx... we are so glad you are ok... How are you feeling?"

I shrug my shoulders. "Tired, I guess. They gave me something to help me sleep." My eyes naturally look for *her.* I see her move from behind Keagan, flashing her sweet smile at me. Her warm hand touches my arm and soothingly strokes it.

"Traxx... it's so good to finally see you. We have been waiting outside for you to be ready. We want you to know that we will take care of everything."

Colton chimed in, "Yeah, man. No worries. You and Notso will stay with Brianna and me for the time being. Tomorrow we are going to your place to pack everything." Brianna smiled at me and starts talking.

"We will put what you guys don't need at this time in a storage unit – I know a great one, nearby Ciara's place, climate controlled and accessible 24/7. Ciara and I keep some… *stuff*… there." She gives Colton a knowing look and he looks at her with a crooked smile. A couple of years back, Brianna, Ciara and Colton had to face off with some bad people and Colton had told me about all the weapons that Ciara and Brianna had stowed away in storage. It didn't surprise me, given they were Military Police while in the Army and Ciara was a weapons expert.

Then it was Notso's turn, "I'll start looking for an apartment tomorrow. It will do us good for a change of scenery." I nodded in agreement.

My friends were staring and expecting some kind of sign that I will be okay. I'm not sure. How can someone get over what I witnessed today? Suddenly it's hard to breathe. I feel nervous and agitated. I close my eyes and concentrate on the warm touch of Ciara's hand on my arm. I change the rhythm of my breathing to match her hand's movement. My chest is no longer tight, and I feel more relaxed. I believe the medication has started to work. I hear my friends discuss their taking turns and staying with me until my release. I don't want to think about anything. I decide to just give in to the pull my mind is feeling. Slowly the voices just fade and I let the silence and blackness wrap around me.

CHAPTER 2

Traxx

I'm not sure if I should be here or not. It wouldn't feel right either way, I think. Ciara and I stand back to the side. I'm glad the day it's pretty and full of sunshine. There was so much darkness in Marcy's life she deserves to have light and brightness in her death, at least. The pallbearers gather at the back of the hearse, in order to pay their respect by handling and supporting the weight of the casket. The family plot is in a nice area, with big shady trees, towards the back of the cemetery.

"Are you sure about this, Traxx?"

Ciara's whisper pulls me away from my thoughts. "Yes. Thank you for coming with me. The guys just don't get it."

"Well, I really can't say that I do get it, but I was not going to let you come here by yourself." She looks up at me and smiles. I like her smile. It's always genuine and it really highlights her natural beauty. She continues, "Brianna and Keagan would have come too, but they couldn't get out of work."

After I was released from the hospital, Notso and I took residence at Colton's and Brianna's place. They had promised that I would never have to return to my house and luckily I haven't had to. They are the best friends a person can have. They also had the place professionally cleaned and listed it for sale with a real estate agent. I didn't expect it to sell for a long time, given what happened there, but that's the thing about a good location – sometimes people don't care about the history of the home as long as a new floor and a couple of layers of paint can cover it up. I'm sure whoever bought it has a morbid sense of humor.

I haven't been in the mood to go looking at homes for sale. My mother offered to come to town and take me with her or to take care of it by herself, but I haven't felt up to that, either. To tell you the truth, the little I have felt lately has been drowned in whiskey. Notso has been giving me space. He could go buy his own place, if he wants, but he feels he's not ready to commit to that or live by himself. I'm sure that Keagan wouldn't let him be alone much, but I really don't want to think about that either. So we compromised to rent a house for six months to a year and then we will figure out what to do. Timing has not been on our side, because we can't find anything nice to rent that can be considered affordable.

A couple of weeks later, Notso tells me he has rented an apartment. He said he was talking to the Manager at the apartment complex where Ciara and Keagan live and that they were running a special that could not have been passed up. Out of pure coincidence, the apartment is located in the same building as Ciara's place, but one floor up from her. I have not decided how I feel about that. Sometimes it feels like too much pressure to be "on" and have a somewhat happy face for my friends and family when all I want is to lock myself in a room and never come out.

We hear the priest starting his sermon. Everyone became very quiet and still. The priest's words were gentle and reassuring. From my position across the crowd, I could see an older couple which I assume was Marcy's parents. The lady was inconsolable. Perhaps I should not be here. Looking at the sad crowd makes me feel guiltier. Everyone is constantly telling me that it is not my fault. When Detective Hall came to visit to tell me I have been cleared from the investigation, he also mentioned they had discovered that Marcy had a past that consisted of many visits to a mental care facility and she was unstable. She also had a history of inconsistency on taking her medication, which had caused her more problems than given her benefits.

That was obvious to me during the short time we were in front of one another, but I can't help to think "what if?" What if I had just gotten over the fear of being hurt by a girl? What if I would have not dated and used girls only to satisfy my male ego? What if I would have been a couple of seconds faster in my reaction when I saw her pointing the gun to her head? Could Marcy still be here trying to muddle through life in her own way, just like the rest of us? One thing is for sure, if I had made better choices I wouldn't have to see her die again and again every time I close my eyes.

When the service was over, I noticed Marcy's parents looking at me. I wouldn't know what to say since her daughter died because of me. I feel Ciara's hand taking mine, and she gently pulls me away, as if she knows the thoughts that are going through my mind.

Once we are in her car, she looks at me and softly asks if I'm okay. I nod, but inside my head, my own hell is burning me alive.

Ciara

We were able to drag Traxx out of the house in the hopes that he would get distracted, even if for a couple of hours. We are all at Twisted, our favorite bar, sitting at a table, chatting and waiting for the band to start playing. The guys are watching a live game on the bar's TV. Well, I guess I should say that Colton and Notso are watching. Traxx is at the bar, drinking, yet again, a barrel of alcohol for what seems to have become his go-to reality escape. Girls come by the bar and hit on him constantly, but Traxx politely declines all their advances. He won't even look at them. There is no interest on his part, he hasn't gone out with anyone yet and to make matters worse he keeps himself in a perpetual bad mood.

"Brianna, it's been a couple of months since Marcy's death, and I'm truly worried. I know we all agreed to let him deal with it on his own for a while in the hopes he will snap out of it but I don't think he knows how to deal."

She nods to acknowledge my comment, "You are right. He's not doing well. Colton finally agreed to speak with him and tried to get him to go see a counselor or psychiatrist, but Traxx was not very happy about it. He pretty much told Colton to shove it – you know where – and left the room. Also, Notso told Colton that Traxx has nightmares almost every night and he wakes up screaming, soaked in sweat. He hasn't been able to rest."

"Crap. That makes me worry even more. I really don't think he can snap out of it all by himself. He has taken it hard, which is good, because that may have been the bomb that forced him to change the course of his life. I'm just afraid that the new road he has taken is not better than the old one. Before, he would hide his real feelings behind a string of lovers, and now he hides his feeling behind countless bottles of alcohol. I think he needs help and I think I know how to help him."

"You? I'm afraid to ask. Please tell me you are not going to try to cure him with retail therapy? That doesn't work for everybody, you know? Especially with guys."

"Ha! Real funny! Says the girl who likes to work out everything at the gym pounding something, or better yet, someone."

"Hey! I resent that comment! A good round of sparring helps release the tension and the feel good hormones."

"Endorphins, you mean?"

"Yeeep. You know my tongue doesn't quite work after a few drinks."

"Why is it that I think you actually get to feelin' good because you get to kick somebody's ass in the ring, and not because you are 'exercising'?"

She looks at me and rolls her eyes to the back of her head, her lips break into a small smile. "Whatever." She gently hits my upper arm with her fist.

"All right, Knuckles, we'll leave it be for now, okay?"

Brianna earned her nickname from me, Knuckles, because while in the service, she re-arranged a guy's face who was trying to sexually abuse her. She hates it when I call her that. She's also very particular about always carrying a self-defense weapon or aid. Now that she is a cop, she normally carries her gun and something else. I believe today's selection is a pair of chopsticks, holding her hair's messy bun in place. These are not the feeble kind found at restaurants. Oh, no… these were special ordered from Chinatown, California. They are made from ultra-stiff carbon fiber tubing. They are non-metallic, extremely strong, rigid and way lighter than fiberglass. All of us girls have a pair, courtesy of Colton Hensley, Brianna's beau. When they first started dating, he thought we were kidding about her skills in the ring. By looking at her, she is toned like a girl who works out regularly, and certainly not like a girl who can kick your ass. Since then, he found out the hard way that a girl doesn't *need* to be a body builder to be strong, and the most important thing about self-defense is skill. But I digress…

"Brianna, I think I have to do something. I just cannot sit back any longer and pretend he is going to be okay… And it would be so much easier if I knew you guys agreed with me. Do you think you can have my back on this?"

"I always have your back, you know that!"

I smile, because I know it's true. The same way I always have her back. "Yes, sweets, I know you do."

I get off the barstool, come around and give her a half hug, just as we hear the band starting to play a Jason Aldean cover song.

"Well, sweets, I've got to go and convince a very brooding, sad and regretful man to dance. I've got my work cut out for me…" I wink at her and leave her shaking her head and slurping on her margarita… Need to remember to do a shot of Patron before we leave. It's been a rough month.

Traxx sees me coming and makes a point of looking away. This elusive action stops me in my tracks for a few seconds. I can tell this will be more difficult than I thought. I straighten my shoulders and with newfound resolve, I move forward towards him.

I stand next to him. I'm a lot shorter than he is, but since he is seated on a booth, our eyes are pretty damn level. He already knows how determined I can be, so he won't be able to ignore me for long.

Just as I thought, a minute or so later he looks at me and for just a second his eyes seemed to spark… And as fast as it flicked, it was gone, but it's in there *somewhere*. I just need to find it.

"What do you want, Ciara?" Hmm, he is trying to pull the a-hole act. He's gonna need a lot more ammunition to get rid of me.

"I'm here to inform you that your 'cry me a river' card has been revoked." I lift one of my eyebrows at him.

"Who the fuck gives a shit." He stares back at me, challenging me to go on. His eyes are ardent and furious at the same time. I place my hand on his upper arm, an unexpected move that causes him to flinch. While he takes a quick look at my hand, I hold his arm steadfast. I get close, really close, to his ear.

"Nice act, it may work on the bar flies that keep coming your way, but it sure as hell will not work on me. I know you better than that. I also know what you need. I have answers for you, Traxx. I have answers to all those questions that have been swirling in your head for weeks now. But these answers are not free. There is a price to pay." He looks at me like a lost puppy who has found a new owner, and I know he is intrigued.

"What do I have to do to get these answers from you?"

"Well, there will be a lot of things you have to do. I can help you, Traxx. But you have to let me. It's time to move on. Please note that I didn't say forget. Marcy wanted for you to destroy your life and you are doing exactly what she expected you would do. You are letting guilt consume you. It's time to find a way back to the living, Traxx. Aren't you tired of wallowing?"

"I don't know what to do, Ciara... I feel like I shouldn't be happy ever again."

"I know... and there will be plenty of time to talk about it. For right now, why don't you take your friend – me – to the dance floor and help her spin around a few times?"

He takes a deep breath. "I don't think I feel like doing that, Ciara."

"That's problem number one – you are thinking too much. Let's stop thinking for a few minutes and just enjoy the fact that you were spared, you're in the here and now, and you need to do something with your life. Something meaningful that will help even out the field of shit that you've been dealt. I have some ideas and I will help you out of the mess you created for yourself. I promise. The only thing you have to do is trust me. You know *me*, Traxx. It's *me*. I'm your friend during the good, the bad and the ugly. It's not easy, but we have to start somewhere. So, here goes:

I'm going to take your hand and lead you to the dance floor – don't look around at anyone but me. You are going to concentrate on the music, and just us. Let me carry the burdens of your mind, if only for a little while. You'll see - it will all be okay. Trust *me*, Traxx."

I look at him directly in the eyes, and try really hard to convey security, friendship… *love*. Traxx gives me an uncertain, confused look. I don't let him dwell on my words. I move my hand slowly but firmly from his arm down to his hand. Then I apply a tight hold and start to move away from the bar, never looking away from his eyes. When he starts to move towards me, my heart dances in happiness, and a small smile appears on my lips. Traxx reciprocates with a tiny small crooked smile, and a concerned look. But he is moving with me towards the dance floor. This is a small victory with a giant jackpot.

Traxx

This girl… Ciara's words spark something inside of me. Something unfamiliar and at the same time, something wanted. I know she's persistent and when she sets her mind on something, she won't leave it alone until she gets her way. So I go with her to the dance floor and do like she says, let her worry about my situation for a little while.

I chance a look at my friends, and they are all staring with a surprised look on their faces. Yeah, this is not like me at all. I'm finding out that it feels good to act differently than I used to.

"Quit looking at them." I hear Ciara whisper in my ear. "Look at me." I do as she asks.

"What do you want now, Nibblet." I call her Nibblet from time to time when I act like she is irritating me. She reminds me of a corn nibblet, with all her blond hair and petite size. But in that small package, she packs a huge personality, full of kindness and goodness.

"Ugh! I told you I hate that nickname!" She tries to be mad, but I see a smile across her face. She really likes it when I use that term of endearment with her.

"If you hate it so much, why are you smiling?"

"Because it's actually nice to hear it again, coming from your lips. It's been a while."

"Yes, it has… You are right about something, Ciara. I want to move on. I have been thinking a lot about the type of person I was, and one thing I know is that I want to do better with my life. I don't know how, and I need your help with that."

"Yes, I can help you, Traxx. But first, you have to heal. You can't do anything or help anyone when your life is out of control. And I can help you heal, but I need to know that you mean it when you say you are ready to change."

I take a deep breath and think about it for a minute. I don't want to revert back to being a senseless manwhore anymore. I want to do something good, but I don't know what and I also don't know how to move on from the incident with Marcy. I have returned to work, and even if I keep as busy as possible, images play in my head at unexpected times throughout the day and especially at night. Yes, I want to change. I don't want to help create any more situations like the one with Marcy.

"Yes, Ciara, I'm ready and I need your help, because I really don't know how to move forward with my life."

"Well, there is no magic formula or a practical plan. And it won't be easy, either. We are just going to have to take it one day at a time. For now, though, we just need to concentrate on being part of the living, and enjoy this dance." She lowers her head on my chest and I place my lips on top of her head and inhale her scent. I don't recognize it but she smells so good and sweet – like a promise should. I smile lightly and hold her tighter. Nibblet is going to be my beacon back to life and reality. You'd better believe that I'm going to hold on tight and not let go.

Ciara

Getting Traxx to stop drinking and to live in the moment – even for the length of a few songs – it's like a mini victory. When I was in college we studied a lot on Suicide Loss Survivors, but that applies to people who have lost a spouse, family member, friend, colleague, neighbor, client or co-worker... Traxx's situation is different; he was a Suicide Witness Survivor, which means he was witness to the self-inflicted violence and death of a person. There are different ramifications for behavior between those two, so I have been reading up on that so I can be of help to him. The fact that he has not wanted to go see a specialist is bad. The fact that I'm in graduate school for a Psychology major is a plus. I'm not claiming to be an expert, because I'm certainly not one, but I may be the only person that can steer Traxx in the right direction, without him even realizing it.

"What are you doing?" My friend and roommate Keagan comes into the room and interrupts my thoughts. Brianna used to be my roommate, but she moved in with Colton a few months back. Notso and Traxx had to move out of Colton's place then, and ended up living together in the house Traxx had bought.

"I'm researching about Suicide Witness. My textbooks don't delve in the subject as much, so I talked to some of my professors and they lent me some books."

"Hmm... Do you think it's going to work? You helping Traxx, I mean?"

"It has to. I don't know what else to do." Keagan gives me a sad look.

"Have you eaten?" She asks.

"Not yet. I had coffee and toast earlier, but I'm hungry. Got anything in mind?

"I spoke to Notso a little while ago, and we are going to get a bite, pizza I think. Wanna come with?

My mouth waters before I can even answer. "That sounds really good, actually." Let me change out of these yoga pants. Give me ten?"

"Sure, take all the time you need. We aren't in a hurry. Besides, Notso was going to try to talk Traxx into going. Traxx is a little out of sorts lately."

"Why? Something happened?"

"I'd say… Traxx got a phone call from my cousin - his brother Wyatt, the one who lives in Texas, remember him? It seems that my uncle Logan is worried about Traxx and asked Wyatt to transfer from the Dallas office to the one here in Pristina."

"Permanently?"

"Not sure, but how can you pass up to keep your job and move to a beach town on daddy's dime?"

"Yeah, I can see that… Why do you think he's not happy about Wyatt's visit?"

Keagan thinks about it for a minute before answering. "I think he may feel like his dad wants to check up on him and meddle in his life. I know my uncle can be very overbearing at times."

Keagan's and Traxx's dads are brothers. So I know Keagan has the inside scoop to what's going on. "Now that I think about it, the last time Wyatt came to visit, they had a bit of a competition going on."

Keagan laughs heartily. "A little? Those two idiots have been competing against each other since they were kids. Having different mothers didn't help a bit. Maybe Wyatt can bring a little distraction for Traxx."

"Do you know when is he going to get here?"

"Not for a few weeks. He's trying to tie up some loose ends with some clients in Texas first."

Okay, I'm glad I have a few weeks with Traxx before he has to deal with his brother. There's a knock on the door.

"I'll get it! Ciara, you go ahead and get ready."

"Mm'kay"

As I'm putting on some jeans and pull on my ankle boots, I can't stop thinking that maybe Wyatt will be a welcomed distraction. It will remind Traxx of some good memories they have shared. I put on an off-shoulder blouse on top of my tank top, and quickly brush my hair. I apply some neutral eye shadow, put on mascara and finish up with a nude lip gloss. Ready in less than... well, I guess I was closer to fifteen, but I did clean up really well.

"Okay, I'm ready..." As I walk down the hall into the living room, I stop cold and think my eyes are betraying me when I see Traxx looking straight at me.

"Traxx... what a nice surprise!" He looks at me with a puzzled look on his face.

"Yeah, I was hungry. Hope you don't mind."

"Oh, sorry – that's not what I meant... You shaved, and... got a haircut, you look nice."

He rubs his jaw with his palm. Smiling, he replies, "Yeah, it was way overdue. I wanted to be able to look in the mirror and recognize the person looking back at me."

Although Traxx usually had some stubble, he had quit taking care of his appearance for several weeks and had let his beard grow, which would have been cool if he at least would have groomed it, but it made him look disheveled and lost. I guess it was a reflection of the way he felt inside. This is a good thing. I smile at him and nod.

"Good, then. As I was saying, I'm ready if everyone else is."

Notso is the first to get up. "Let's go! I'm starving!"

I laugh. "Does that mean we are headed for an 'all you can eat" pizza buffet?"

"Nah, that was during my broke days. I make good money now and I don't mind spending it on my dear friends at a "classy" pizza place." He winks at me.

"Wow! What a big spender!" I laugh at his antics. "I like it when others pick up the tab, I'm going to eat so much that you won't even recognize me!"

"What does that even mean? That instead of a bowl of salad and one slice you are going to eat TWO whole fucking slices? Pleazzze, girl, just don't."

Everybody's snickering at this point. "I don't know, Notso. I may feel hungry enough to forget the salad and eat a whole pizza! What you got to say to that?

"Dang, Ciara, you got me! I'll believe it when I see it."

As we get to his truck, I don't really need help getting up in it, but I let Traxx help me up and Notso is assisting Keagan. The truck has a lift and I like to see guys show their Southern manners. "Do you care to place a wager, Mr. Winslow?" I look at Notso expectantly. We are best friends and he knows that I'm a competitive bitch when I need be.

"Do you think I'm stupid? I know you well, and you get some kinda' crazy when it comes to bets."

"Party Pooper!" I yell at him crossing my arms in front of me. Traxx looks at me smiling, then at Notso, and frowns.

"Notso, what the hell?! Look at her tiny size, for goodness sake. You actually think she can eat a whole pie? You chicken shit!

Keagan and I are smiling from the back seat. I may not be able to move after, but I will eat a whole pizza if it's going to make me some money. Not that I need the money, but it's a matter of principle. Notso knows me well enough he recognizes he will lose his money. I'm sitting right behind him on the driver side of the truck and I can see his sky blue eyes looking at my sapphire blue ones… He's getting ready to fall for it… three, two, one…

"I'm betting low because I feel I'm just throwing my money away. If you eat a whole pizza, that will get you a crisp $50 – if you leave even a small bite of crust, I win. Deal?

"Ha! Yeah, deal! Sucker!" We laugh like we are kids, carefree and teasing one another as we drive towards the restaurant.

Traxx

I'm sitting here at the table feeling a lot of pride in my Nibblet, as she is polishing off the last slice of the cheese pizza that Notso ordered for her. It's the first time I feel...*free* since the incident. I have been living in my own condemned hell, sort of a way of punishing myself for what happened. It's my way of assuming some kind of responsibility for what Marcy did. It doesn't mean that I no longer feel guilty, because God knows I do. Guilt consumes me. If I was able to get to her just few seconds sooner... Well, but today... today it's the first time I get a glimpse of what my life could be once I learn to forgive myself and heal.

Ciara winks at me as we start chanting: "Go! Go! Go!" as she is chewing the last bite. The last swallow, then a sip of her Diet Coke and she leaps off her chair with her hands up,

"I did it! Pay up, Notso! Woohoo!"

On an impulse, I get off my chair and go to her lifting her in a big bear hug. "You did it, Nibblet!"

"Uh! Don't squeeze me too hard, I don't wanna blow!" She looks at me playfully, "You are going to have to roll me out of here. I'm so full I can hardly breathe and I don't think I can walk, either!"

Her laugh has always been something that makes me feel all warm and gooey on the inside, not that I have ever told her that. Our relationship has been somewhat strained in the past, probably because of the mixed feelings I have for her. Since then I have learned that life is short, and although I had mine on pause, I'm ready to put it to something good. Ciara is right, though. I need to work on myself and get better before I can concentrate on others.

Notso gets his wallet, pulls some money out of it and hands it to Ciara. "I knew I should not bet against you, Ciara. You have a very determined, competitive streak. Jesus! I'm still trying to figure out where in the hell you put all that pizza?"

"Unfortunately, I can't tell you where I put it, but I can tell you where it's going to go unless I go for a walk and try to exercise some of it off."

Keagan chimes in, "Yeah, it's probably going to go straight to your ass or boobies. Hell, every time I gain one ounce that's where it all goes."

"I fail to understand why that's a bad thing?" Notso tells Keagan with a flirty smile on his face as I give him a dirty look. She's my cousin for fuck's sake!

"Okay, y'all head on to the truck while I settle the bill. Traxx, you may need to carry Ciara." He says as we see her struggling to stand up.

"I'm okay, I can walk. I just lost my balance for a second. Here you see? It's all good." She turns around and starts to walk to the door. Keagan and I follow her. As we reach the truck, Ciara lets out a huge burp, surprising me and a couple of strangers walking by the truck at the same time.

"Girl, we aren't at the hunting land. I'm not used to you letting it rip in the middle of civilization." Keagan's laughing at Ciara's antics.

"Keagan, I can barely breathe – I need to make room for all that food! It's hard enough to fake it in front of Notso, but I'm not going to fake it in front of you." Ciara is rubbing her stomach.

"Okay, you and I are going for a walk as soon as we get to the apartment." I tell her raising my eyebrow so she knows I mean business.

"Okay." She says breathily and nods while rubbing her tummy one more time, and I find myself wanting to get there as soon as possible.

The ride to the apartment is quick and as we get there I'm amazed that I actually managed not to think about Marcy for the last couple of hours. And it never fails, the moment that I start to think about her, I feel guilty.

We get out of the truck, and I noticed Ciara starts to walk towards the apartment, I grab her hand and pull her the opposite way. "Oh, hell no! I know you are pizza-drunk right now, but I'm not about to let you lie down and sleep these calories away. Plus, if you go to bed, it means I would have to go home and be bored. So we are going to go on a walk, like we talked about."

"Really, Traxx, you pick this moment to be a 'follow-through' kind of guy, seriously? I'm too full to do anything, plus I have my cute boots on and they are not made for walking."

"Stop being a wimp, Ciara. Those boots are low heels and I've seen you dance the night away with some shoes that are three times higher than the ones you have on right now." She pouts at me and looks at Keagan and Notso while they are walking away. Keagan turns towards us and winks, "It's true Ciara, go walking. You'll feel better after a while."

"Fine. Let's go." She tells me in a very grumpy but cute way.

I smile to myself and pull on the little firecracker's hand. "Have I ever told you that you're funny when you're irritated?"

"That's a juxtaposition. How can anyone be funny and irritated at the same time?"

"I don't know. You just are."

"Whatever. How have you been doing lately?" She looks at me expectantly. I can see where this is going. The apartment complex is rather large and there is lots of time to talk while we walk. She said she would help me, so I guess I better be straight with her.

"It's rough, especially now that I'm trying not to drink so much. I'm starting back at the gym tomorrow. You should come with me."

"With my crazy schedule between work and school, I have to fit in exercise here and there. I don't want to promise that I will go with you and then not be able to follow up."

"I understand. It's cool." We are walking into the playground and she sits on one of the swings. I automatically walk around and start to push her.

"Traxx, how are you sleeping?"

"Not very good, Ciara. I still have nightmares almost every night."

"Do you have trouble falling sleep?"

"Not really. I just wake up screaming, re-living the moment, you know?" I push harder and she is swinging higher and higher. She swings her legs like little kids do. "When will the guilt stop? I feel guilty all the time. Will I ever get over it?"

"I'm not sure you will ever get over it, but I can assure you we will find a way to get you through it. It's normal to feel guilty about feeling good. You have to remember that it was her choice to end her life, not yours. It's not your fault."

"I don't know, Ciara. If I had not treated her like I did…"

"You don't know that. We have no way of knowing if it would have been different for her. If it hadn't been you, it may have been someone else. I'm not going to be all cliché and tell you to stop feeling the way you are. You have to work your way out of there on your own, one step out of time. I will help you."

"Promise?"

"Yes, Traxx, I promise you that. Now come around the swing and catch me – will ya'?"

There she goes with that sweet smile. How can anyone say no to that? I walk around to the front and she throws herself off of the swing, right into my arms.

We are laughing hard, looking at each other, becoming aware that we are both almost out of breath. I can smell her crisp, clean perfume. I can smell her minty breath. I look at her eyes and she looks back at mine. When I lick my bottom lip, she's intently looking at it with want and I notice her smile is gone and I see her swallow - hard. The wind is blowing her long blond hair all over the place. Suddenly, it becomes obvious that our playful embrace its more than that. I am painfully aware that my body's crushing hers and for a few seconds I become lost in her warmth. It feels good. Really good.

Ciara realizes what is happening and taps my shoulders to bring me back into reality. I slowly and carefully release her until her feet are steady on the ground. I keep one hand on her waist, and with the other hand I take some of her fly-away hair and tuck it behind her ear. And because I love to torture myself, instead of putting my hand inside my pocket, I lightly brush my knuckles on her cheek and jawline. I see her intake a deep breath and notice her pulse is going really fast. She is looking down, but as I finish touching her, she looks up at me – what is that I see? I swear I saw a flicker of *something*. It's probably just pity and I'm reading into it way too much. I'm probably the biggest ass she's ever known. Why would she care about me?

"Why?" I ask her and nobody in particular at the same time.

Ciara takes a step away from me. "Why what?"

"Why do you care so much?" I'm not sure I need to be asking her this. I don't even know why I'm doing it.

"Why wouldn't I? You are our friend and at the moment I'm the most qualified to help you out of all of us."

"You are the most qualified? So… I'm only a case study to you? A subject for your graduate course work?"

"No Traxx, that's not what I meant."

I turn around and start to head back. I can't stay here. "It really doesn't matter, I should have known better." I can't help but sound angry, because I am. What would I think that she actually cares for me in any other way?

"What? No, wait…"

"Never mind, Ciara. I get it." My mind is telling me to stay, let her explain things, maybe I got it all wrong. It wouldn't be the first time. But my pride, my pride was knocked down a few notches and it's telling me not to bother, to keep walking. So that's what I chose to do.

Ciara

"No you don't. You don't get it at all." I whisper to myself, ensuring Traxx cannot hear me.

As I start to head back to my apartment, I try to think about what just happened. I know I have feelings for Traxx, and at times it *seems* he has feelings for me. Does he? Is Traxx Maxwell capable of really caring for someone other than himself? Maybe what I saw was just gratitude. Yes, that's probably all there is to it. Right now, he's mad at me, but overall he's just grateful that someone cares about him – someone other than the guys.

Everything was going so well today. He seemed happy for once. Then I say the wrong thing and poof – it's all gone to the shitter. Do I have what it takes to help him out? He's definitely not a case study, but this is new territory for me and I have to tread carefully.

I hear my phone's text alert go off. I reach to my back pocket and pull it out.

Keagan: Where are you?

Ciara: On my way back

Keagan: Ok. We saw Traxx come back by himself but he wouldn't talk to us. I got worried.

Ciara: I think I said the wrong thing. He's pissed at me.

Keagan: Hurry back. We'll talk.

Ciara: Almost there.

I rush back to my apartment, to find out Notso has already left. Immediately, I walk to my room to change out of these tight jeans and back into my yoga pants. I need to breathe. I also put on a comfy sweatshirt, grab my e-reader and a Diet Coke and set to relax on the couch. Keagan comes out of her room and sits across from me.

"I'm ready. What happened?"

I better skip all the more 'gushy' details and go straight to the point. "I'm not sure. I said something about me being the only one who can help him and he accused me of treating him like a research project... It wasn't pretty. I know that his emotional state is all over the place, but I don't see him as a science project. I see him as someone who needs help to alleviate the stress and sadness he's going through. Based on the research that I've done, it is obvious that he will go through mood swings, irritability and bursts of anger, but it's still hard to be at the receiving end of those."

"Wow, I bet that was difficult."

"Yes, he's going through every day from dark to light and on repeat. I bet he's at home drinking to drown everything. That's his way to deal."

"I can text Notso and find out."

Keagan's red hair is in a messy bun, and not covering one of her blue eyes, like she normally styles it. It's almost weird to see her like this because she always has her hair down. "No, don't worry about it. He is safe at home and he needs to be able to drown out his feelings somehow. As of yet, I have not figured out a way that he can release his frustrations, so I don't have any suggestions for him other than ask him to go to the gym, and I'm still so full of pizza, if I exercise it's not going to be pretty."

Keagan giggles. "Okay, let's just have some quiet time and read, then."

"Yeah. Let's." Even though I want to get lost in the pages that I'm reading, my mind is only getting lost on my thoughts of Traxx, what he means to me, what he's possibly going through inside his head and how in the world I'm going to help him. Me. Am I over my head? Yes. I know it and my friends know it, too. Maybe if I can get him to progress one little bit, maybe he will agree to see a specialist. Living in denial won't help him either, but as long as he keeps moving forward, it's a lot better than moving backwards. So, I will continue to try and build new memories that hopefully will push the bad ones aside.

Traxx

As I'm walking up the steps towards the lobby, I see Notso and my cousin on the balcony, laughing carelessly and it only pisses me off even more. They try to get my attention as I'm climbing the stairs, but I just ignore them. I really don't feel like talking to anyone right now.

I unlock the door to my place, and walk straight to the bar, grabbing the bottle of Jack Daniel's as I come around the corner. I don't even bother with a glass, hell no. I wrestle for a second with the cap, which gives me pause. Am I sure I really want to do this? I need something to quiet down the screams inside my head and the pain inside my chest... I take a huge gulp and the heat rolls down my throat slowly... burning...

Then the guilt comes and it's overwhelming. I want to scream. I want to cry. I want to hurt myself. Instead I look at the bottle in my hand and before I can take another drink, it flies out of my hand across the room and against the wall. I'm on edge, on fire, in pain... A scream comes out of my mouth just as the tears start rolling down my cheeks. It's too much, I don't want to feel anything anymore...

The door opens and I see Notso coming towards me.

"Traxx, what's going on? What are you doing on the floor?"

I'm on my knees, looking down. I wipe my eyes before I look at him. I try to speak, but can't. Nothing's coming out. I'm overwhelmed by something greater that I can even understand. Am I going crazy? My heart is beating too fast, I don't think it's normal. Just then, a ringing inside my ears starts and slowly it's getting louder. Too much, this is a lot more than I can take. I can't breathe. I CAN'T BREATHE! My body is checking out and I'm falling back towards the darkness. Falling back where I belong. I see Marcy's image prompting me to follow her. She says it's good in the dark. She says the pain will go away. So I go.

"Traxx! Oh my god! Fuck!"

The last thing I see is Notso getting out his phone and calling for help.

Ciara

I hear my phone ringing as I get comfy on the couch with my book. It's Notso.

"What's up?"

"Something is really wrong with Traxx, he's not responsive and it looks like he can't breathe!"

"Crap! It's probably a panic attack! I'm on my way… Try to calm him down and regulate his breathing…" I look towards Keagan, who's wondering what's going on. "Come on Keagan, its Traxx!" She jumps to her feet and is following me closely. We're running to their apartment upstairs, taking two steps at a time. I open the door and find Notso kneeling beside Traxx, who has been able to regulate his breathing a little. I kneel in front of Traxx and notice his pupils are still a bit larger than normal. His skin is cold and clammy. Not good.

"Hey, loverboy, let's get you better. Why are you trying to scare the crap out of us?" I smile at him. He's able to focus on me briefly and I can see that he's scared. "Everything's going to be ok. You need to concentrate on your breathing. In through the nose and out through the mouth." His panicked gaze lifts to meet my eyes. I smile at him to give him confidence even though I'm shaking on the inside. My hand moves over to his arm, and I rub him gently, soothing him with my softly spoken words.

"Imitate my breathing. Slowly. Yes, that's it. Can you feel your heart slowing down?" He gently nods at me. Keagan is right behind me, asking if he will be okay. I turn to look at her and nod. "I think so…" I look back at Traxx, "can you talk to us?" I get another nod. After a few minutes, he seems almost normal. "You look better, what happened?"

"I'm not sure. I'd rather not talk about it."

We all look at each other, a little dumbfounded.

"Traxx… You have to open up. How are we going to help you if you keep us away from what's happening to you?"

"I don't need help."

"I beg to differ." I give him a hard look.

"What do you know about what I'm going through?" He's becoming agitated again. I decide not to push the issue.

"Look, I didn't mean to upset you. We're worried, that's all. How about you go rest for a little while."

"Traxx, you don't need to be so rude. We are your friends and family. You've gotta know that we only want the best for you." Notso chimes in.

"Perhaps I need to give Uncle Logan a call… Maybe you should go visit them for a little while, get away from here for a few days…" Keagan is trying to reason with him.

"No. That won't be happening. I don't need my parents hovering over me. I just want to be left alone." Shakily, he gets up off the floor, walks to the counter, grabs his keys and leaves the apartment. We stay in the middle of the living room, sadly looking at each other and feeling uncertain of what to do next.

Traxx

As I'm driving aimless through the streets, I'm trying to make sense of what's happening to me. Although I'm not the person who pulled the trigger and killed Marcy, I do feel somewhat responsible. The guilt is on one side pulling at me. On the other side, I have these crazy visions reliving those horrible last moments of her life over and over again. She did say that I was going to pay the price and she was right. I'm living in my own private hell day in and day out.

Sitting at a red light, I'm waiting for it to change from red to green, when I hear a sound that completely transports me to a different place and time.
Bang!
I'm back in my old living room, looking at Marcy pacing back and forth, not knowing what to do. She lifts her gun and points it at my face, and just as she is getting ready to pull the trigger a horn brings me back to the present. I shudder and make myself move my

foot from the brake to the gas pedal. As my truck advances on the road, I'm trying really hard to leave all the bad memories behind. I know deep in my heart I will fail miserably. Life is never that easy.

After driving for who knows how long, I find myself in front of Colton's place. His truck is here and Brianna's car is not. Perfect. I take a deep breath, jump down from my truck and go up to the door when I hear some noise coming out. I'm not sure if it's the TV or the Xbox. It doesn't matter. I ring the doorbell and follow with a loud knock on the door. I see his shadow through the hammered glass getting closer as he approaches to open the door.

"Hey, man, took you long enough. Notso called." Colton says as he opens the door wide enough for me to come in.

"I drove around for a while, trying to clear my head."

"And? Did it work?"

"Not sure." He goes to the kitchen and comes back with a couple of cold beers, handing me one. I take a long swig. I realize how thirsty I am as I feel the coolness going down my parched throat.

"You better start talking, unless you want Brianna to get on your case. She's on her way home, and you know how persuasive she can be." Colton raises his eyebrows at me as his voice lowers as if she was already in the house listening to our conversation.

"Fuck." If you see Brianna, you would not think she was an expert fighter who excels at personal defense maneuvers. The girl's beautiful and made of solid muscle, without looking like a giant bag of steroids. She has been training all of us in their basement, which was converted to a gym, and she always wins. Her beauty will distract you while her hand and feet will get you. The girl packs a mean-ass punch.

"Get on with it. Or deal with her." Colton laughs softly because he knows firsthand I have no prayer when it comes to Brianna. She will beat it out of me. Thinking of my best friend's feisty girlfriend who has a heart of gold, does makes me smile. A couple of years back I could have lost both of them, when someone from her past came after her. It was completely unavoidable. Colton, Ciara and Brianna confronted the guy and his men, thankfully coming out on the winning side.

"Fine." I tell him everything. The anger, panic attacks... the visions. I'm positive he can hear the fear that's rolling around my voice. As I speak these truths to Colton, I realize it makes me feel a little better.

"Do you think I'm going crazy?" I ask him while looking at him eye to eye.

"No. I think there are a lot of things you need to work out. And you already know I think you should get professional help."

"Well, you also know I'm a stubborn fuck who doesn't listen very well. I don't want to go to a doctor. I think I can work it out myself."

"Ciara thinks you are dealing with some kind of PTSD." He says pointedly.

I take a deep breath. "Probably so, but it's not going to make me change my mind."

"I want to understand why."

"The truth?" Colton nods. "I'm scared that a doctor will commit me to some kind of institution."

"Come on! Traxx, that's fucking ridiculous! The only way you would be committed is if you show that you're going to harm yourself or others. Be sensible, would ya'?"

"It is what it is. I don't want to talk about it anymore. Can we play a game until Brianna gets home?" He looks at me incredulously, but grabs one of the wireless remotes and hands it to me.

"Fine. I'll drop it for now, but I better start seeing some kind of progress or else we will be the ones taking you to the hospital. I'll be damned if we are going to stand by and watch you lose control of reality and your life. Not happening."

I nod at him and start playing the game. I know he's right. I have to find a way to work out this guilt and regret I feel inside.

CHAPTER 3

Ciara

I'm just getting home from work. Being an Assistant to the most popular psychologist in the state is not always fun. It's busy as hell most of the time. My family was against it. They feel I should finish my graduate course work and then join a practice. Some days I think I should have listened to their advice, but on the other hand, I really enjoy being completely independent and I appreciate that I can do whatever I want.

I enter my apartment complex's parking lot and right away I notice Traxx's truck sitting in the same spot he left it days ago. It pisses me off immediately. Since his panic attack I haven't seen or heard from him at all. He's been in his room probably feeling sorry for himself. It's time for him to get rid of his demons and it's time for me to shake things up a bit.

I practically run towards the building and up the steps, high heels still on. Opening the door to my apartment, I go straight to my room to change into some workout clothes. Keagan is not here yet, so I go on to the guys' place by myself and knock on their door. I wait patiently but there is no answer. I pull out my cell phone from the arm band holder, and I text him.

Ciara: I'm knocking on your door. Get your ass up and come open it.

Traxx: Go away.

Ciara: I have a spare key. I was trying to be respectful, but obviously you need a good ass whooping. I'm coming in. Be ready (meaning make sure you've got some clothes on!)

Just as I'm looking for the spare, I hear some shuffling and the lock clicks open. I look at this *thing* that has opened the door... Traxx resembles the Big Foot guy from the beef jerky commercials; my face gets all twisty - I can't help it - and he realizes that my facial expression is a bit distasteful.

"Oh, wow! You smell terrible! When was the last time you showered?"

"Mmm... I can't remember." He says with a sleepy voice.

"What have you been doing these past few days?" I cross the threshold and come inside his place. There's crap everywhere, when I turn around to look at him he's got his arms full of clothes and a couple of empty beer bottles in his hand.

"I took some stuff and I have been sleeping it off, pretty much." He shrugs his shoulders like it's no big deal.

"Sooo, you drugged yourself in order to slip into oblivion for who knows how long? And you think that's ok? We will talk about this later... right now you need a shower – you have some skunky smell going on..." I grab the clothes and the bottles from his hands and arms and start pushing him towards his room...

"Oh, Dear God! It's worse over here... Smells like something rotten died in this room... Get in the shower, I'm going to air it out." I start to crack open the windows.

"Can you put these in the dirty laundry, please?" He starts to pull down his flannel pants and stands in front of me almost naked if not for his undies. I already know he's shameless! But then I hear myself inhale a huge gasp of air as I take notice of his muscled body...and the rippled abdominal 'V.' Lord, help me! The asshole notices my reaction and he chuckles. Chuckles! My bad mood immediately evaporates because I can't even think of the last time I heard him laugh. I turn around so I'd stop staring, and get busy pulling the bed sheets off. One last peek at his natural tanned back, and I smile. He chuckled. There is hope for him yet.

I move from the bedroom to the living room, which looks a lot more presentable without stuff scattered everywhere. I also start the laundry and spray some room deodorizer to mask some of the funky smell that's still hovering around the place. I hear Traxx come out of his bathroom and a few minutes later walk into the living room. I hand him a bottle of cold water.

"Thanks. The place looks so much better." He says to me. He is wearing gym shorts, a muscle shirt and running shoes.

I smile at him. "How did you know what to wear?"

"I saw what you were wearing. I figured you were coming to either make me run or go to the gym." He's still showing me the 'I don't give a shit' attitude, but I press on.

"Which one do you prefer?"

"Let's go to the gym. I'm not ready to start running. Maybe we can warm up with some exercises and then take a run."

I look at him incredulously. "Well, I must say that I'm surprised that you are so complacent. I'm so not used to this side of you, Traxx."

"Let's just say I know how you girls can be. Too headstrong when you get your mind set on something. I don't have the energy to deal with that right now." I see a hint of a crooked smile start to show on his handsome face.

"You've got that right, 'cause I wasn't going to put up with your bullshit today." I raise my eyebrows at him. "Now, start moving." I start pushing him gently towards the door.

"Hey! You are manhandling me!" He says in a girly voice with a sarcastic tone.

"Don't make me show you manhandle, I may be shorter than you but I can still take you!"

"Hmm… That sounds good! Promise?"

"Ugh! You are impossible today!" I look like I'm aggravated but in reality, I'm super happy that he is finally in a good mood.

We reach the car and after he gets in he pushes the seat all the way back. I forgot he's got some long legs. "Do you have enough leg room?" I ask him.

"Yeah, it'll do." He suddenly gets serious. "Thanks." He says to me in almost a whisper. I nod back at him. There's no need to say anything else. I know why he's thankful. Which means that what I'm doing is right, for now, at least.

Traxx

Seeing her in front of my door was like smelling sunshine in the early morning. Even though the sun is setting and night is approaching - even after everything that has been going on in my life - she still has that effect on me. As we walk to her car I realize that when I see her smile, it's like the best high anyone can wish for. My heart rate accelerates, my stomach drops and nothing in the world seems to matter anymore. It all takes a backstage to her.

She's anything and everything I will ever need. I recognize that now, but it's too late for me to act on it. I'm all messed up and have done so many wrongs it will take a lifetime to right them all. The sad thing is that she has no idea of the way I feel towards her and I would never tell her. She deserves better. But if she wants to throw some 'scraps' of attention my way, I'm going to take them. I will *gladly* take them. These good memories will help me get my shit together later, during the times that I feel the pit of darkness calling for me.

She catches me looking at her. "Where is your head right now, Traxx?"

"Right here."

"You look like you were anywhere but here."

"Nah. Just thinking."

"Okay. That's a danger zone all on its own." She laughs gently. "Why don't you find me a song – did you bring your phone?"

I pull my phone out of my pocket and grab the plug she's handing me. As I'm looking through my playlist I find a song that she is definitely not expecting. As soon as the clapping starts, she looks at me open mouthed and surprised.

"Oh, no! You didn't!"

"Yes, I did!"

"I expected some hard rock, but this… you gonna have to sing with me now! I love 'Uptown Funk'."

"Oh, hells no! I'm not going to be one of those people…" And just as I say that, Ciara starts singing along to the upbeat music, and she is so happy it is contagious, so I start to play-dance like a maniac and she is singing – off key, as usual – but we definitely don't care. By the end of the song, we are both singing and car dancing with the rhythm of the music until we pull up to the gym's parking lot.

Ciara

"That was fun! Now, come on, champ. It's time to get serious and pump some adrenaline through your body."

"Do we have to?" He asks me with a sad face.

"What are you, five? Come on! The last one inside the gym will have to cook dinner tonight!" As soon as he realizes what I've said, he scrambles to get out of the car. Since I was already out, I slam the car door, turn around and book it towards the door of the gym, hearing him pounding the street behind me, but I'm in good shape and I give it all I've got, not daring to look back, finally reaching the door a mere few seconds before him.

"Dammit! Those little legs can move!" He says with a hint of a smile and it makes me giggle.

"This body has nothing but power!" I fan my hands from head to my knees and then point at him, "Don't you forget it! And now you need to start thinking about what you will be cooking *us* for dinner." He rolls his eyes at me as we enter the building.

We work our way around the machines, doing set reps and alternating between working our upper body and then the lower body. It's a light workout, definitely not serious. Traxx's mood has definitely improved, and that makes me happy. From time to time I notice

Traxx giving others a dirty look, and I wonder what's going on in his head. About forty five minutes later, we are sweaty and suffering from the 'feel good' kind of tired.

"Wanna jump on the treadmills for a little while? Or the ellipticals?" I ask him.

"I think my ass has been kicked around enough for one day – no elliptical. Let's go to the treadmills."

Since it's a little late, the gym doesn't seem as full as it was when we first got here, and we are lucky to find two treadmills side by side. The moment I step onto the treadmill's belt, I notice one of my shoelaces is undone, and I get on my knee to tie it. Traxx gets on the treadmill next to mine and starts pushing the buttons to get it going. As I'm finishing with my shoelaces, I see a pair of very large feet stand in front of me. I follow the hairy legs, strong tattooed arms, huge torso, until I reach the face of perfection.

"Hi, Ciara. Remember me?"

"Blaze!" I stand up to give him a hug. Traxx looks back with a questioning look on his face. I choose to ignore him for a moment as I would like to see his reaction if I show some interest in a guy.

"How have you been?"

"Super busy. After college I started my own business creating custom computers and network systems for other companies."

"Really? That's awesome! I'm just finishing my graduate coursework and I'm working assisting Dr. Ramos, here in town until I finish." He has come a long way from the hacker he used to be when we were in school. Even though he does not look like it, the guy has a genius IQ.

He gives me a once over, "You are looking just as pretty as I remember, tell me again why we stopped hanging out?"

I would have thought that Traxx's neck was going to break by the way he moved it so fast in order to look at us. "Because we didn't have any more classes together."

"That should not have happened."

"Blaze, don't be silly. You were dating that girl, with the jeweled necklace tattooed on her neck, remember? Besides, we are better as friends anyway and you know it."

He seems to think about it for a few seconds, "Oh, yeah… That was a few chicks ago."

"I'm afraid to ask how many is a few, Mr. Casanova." I smile at him.

"Well, it doesn't mean that we can't hang out sometime, as friends, of course."

"Of course." My eyes drift to Traxx, who's stopping his treadmill and coming over to stand by my side.

"Hey Ciara, what's up?" He nods towards Blaze.

"Hey, Traxx, meet my friend Blaze Debrecht. Blaze, this is my friend, Traxx Maxwell." They shake hands and give each other a thorough check. Men, ugh! When I look at Traxx, he's frowning.

"Are you ready to go, Ciara?" He sounds aggravated. I look at him curious to know what happened to change his mood.

Blaze looks at me and smiles. "Well, I was just going to get started on my daily routine workout." He 'bounces' his pecs while looking at me. "Call me sometime, Ciara. I don't have a business card on me, but you can google my company – Debrecht Systems – or find me through LinkedIn or Facebook."

"Has your number changed since college, Blaze?"

"Nah, it's still the same."

"Then I think I still have it stored in my phone." I smile at him.

"Good deal, then. Hope to hear from you soon." Blaze winks at me then looks at Traxx and extends his arm out towards him. "Hey man, nice to meet you."

Traxx nods his way while shaking Blaze's hand, then looks at me. "Ready?"

"I guess so. I thought we were going to do the treadmill for a bit."

"I don't feel like it anymore."

"Okay, let's go." We walk quietly towards the car. If he thinks he's going to flip flop his moods without talking to me about it, he has another thing coming.

Traxx

We get in the car and I'm struggling to keep my irritation contained. The little exchange inside the gym was just a quick realization that there are other guys, *normal* guys who are going after Ciara. And here I am, trying to exorcise my very own demons, holding a place at the very end of that line. Why do I even think that I can compete? That I can pull my shit together in order to have a chance with her? For years I've wanted her to be mine, but I was always too chicken shit to give into this thing between us, to try and have a normal relationship, preferring to keep her as my close friend without stepping over the invisible line. And now, now it's all fucked up. I've got to fix myself before I can pursue her like she deserves.

I don't have to look her way to know that she is looking at me. Studying everything I say and everything I do. It's unnerving. I love it when she does it, but still. No wonder I'm all fucked up – I'm a walking contradiction. The irritation comes back tenfold and I finally lose it.

"What?" I practically growl at her, but it doesn't faze her, I can tell because her facial expression stays the same.

"Grouchy much? Obviously, something has crawled up your butt. If I didn't know any better, I would put my money on Blaze talking to me being the cause of your current aggravation. Am I close?"

I close my eyes and take a deep breath. Then I lie. "Nope. Not even close."

She turns her whole body towards me, and I wish she was already driving so she couldn't put all her attention on me and read me like a book while I'm stuck inside this box on wheels with her. "Talk to me, Traxx. I care about you and it kills me that you hold everything in."

"Please, let's just go."

Her mouth opens as if she is ready to say something, and I guess she thinks better of it because she closes her mouth and turns around to face the steering wheel. Putting the car in gear, she starts to pull out of the parking place when she hits the brakes and puts the gear back in park. "You need to learn to communicate what's bothering you, you know? All the stuff that's inside your head can make you or break you. If you don't let them out, those things are only going to feel heavier and more difficult to handle. When you finally decide to let the barriers go, you will feel better. I promise." She raises her hand and grabs my chin, forcing me to look at her. "Sometimes sharing your pain helps the hurt and the guilt become more bearable. *You* need to feel that way. *I need you* to feel that way."

I choose not to answer. How can I tell her that over two years ago I met the one person that has captured my heart, but she's too good, too perfect and I don't deserve her? How do I tell her that I have wanted to be able to love her for years now, but that our own best friends don't think I'm capable of feeling real love and all they thought was that I was going to hurt her? And that I have had to witness her being wooed by other guys who actually get to hug her, kiss her, hold her at night? On top of that, all I have at night is an empty bed and nightmares of a person I made feel so miserable, she decided to end her life instead of putting me out of my very own misery. How can I tell her all this? I just can't. I can't. It will make her realize how worthless I really am. I'm just not ready for her to know all of this.

Her voice softens, "I know it's hard, but we need to start somewhere."

We drive in silence and I can sense her patience waning down. My insides feel like a blender in high gear, mixing and pureeing all the feelings going through me, leaving nothing but a dark mush that nobody wants or cares for. I try to portray a calm state. I remember the breathing exercises Ciara taught me the other day, so I crack the window open and start to let the air in through my nose and out through my mouth.

I think she is able to pick up on my anxiety, and I can feel her hesitate before she asks me a question.

"Is it helping?"

"Yes." *No. I'm too fucked up. I need you instead.*

Closing my eyes, I concentrate on the fresh air coming through the window, the smells of the street – barbeque, saltiness of the nearby sea, tacos – I can 'visually' feel the blender that's inside my body and mind starts to go into a lower gear, until it finally slows down to a stop.

"Yes, it helped."

She smiles. "Good." And changes the subject, "What are you cooking us for dinner? I'm starved. Do I need to stop by the store?"

"No, we are good. I think I have an idea of what to make." I smile back at her and I'm grateful the darkness was not able to claim my soul this time.

We get to the apartments and as we round the stairs to the 2nd floor, she turns to look at me.

"I'm going to stop by my place and take a quick shower first. Then I'll come eat dinner with you, okay?"

"Sure. See you in a bit." I continued to climb the stairs to the third floor. I open the door to my apartment to find it empty. I sigh loudly and place the keys on the silver dish resting on top of the entry room table. It's the same silver bowl that catches all kinds of things. I find myself wishing that this bowl could catch all my mixed up thoughts and feelings, so that I could just drop all my worries in it until another day that I'm ready to deal with all of it.

I go to my room and take my clothes off, leaving them right where they fall on the floor. I don't even have the energy to pick them up. I look at my bed languidly, wishing I could just lay there and give in to the blackness once again. In the blackness there are no noises or voices, it's quiet and I feel a little bit of peace, at least until Marcy invades my space. I shake my head from side to side and make the image go away – for now.

    I walk to the bathroom and start the water. I turn it to the hottest setting possible. I step in and let the heat and steam take care of all my worries. Perhaps it's time to put more hours into work. Maybe if I keep busy I will be able to put all of this aside. Although, I still won't know what to do with the guilt. The guilt can be overwhelming. At times, guilt also turns to anguish. I wonder if Marcy felt this way. I take my scrubbing sponge and I place a sizeable amount of shower gel on it and after rubbing it in, I start to clean my skin. I scrub, and scrub, and scrub until my skin is completely red and somewhat swollen, but I still feel dirty – filthy. I can't clean up because the filth is on the inside. It resides within me. I wonder if I bleed, would my blood be filthy black instead of the traditional red? For the briefest moment I contemplate exploring the color of my blood and how would it look like when it oozes outside my skin, after it makes contact with the air. Maybe the blood can reflect how I feel inside and if I let it out, everything bad will go out with it.

    I'm in front of the mirror with the towel wrapped around my waist and I realize I don't even know when I got out of the shower. I have my pocket knife on my right hand and a small cut on the inside of my left arm. A smooth breeze comes through and gently touches my skin, causing goose bumps. I look at the mirror once again and then I hear her, she's calling my name, enticing me. *"Everything's better in the dark. No one can find you here."* Marcy whispers in my ear on a daily basis.

Dropping the knife in the sink, I clean the cut and cover it with an extra-large Band-Aid that I find under the bathroom cabinets. I take a step away from the mirror and walk back into the bedroom to take out something to wear. As soon as I put on a t-shirt and pull up my shorts, I hear the doorbell. Thank goodness she's here. My own little piece of sunshine. I know that while she's here I won't have to worry about Marcy, because Marcy only comes around when I'm alone.

"Coming!" I yell, loud and clear towards the hallway. I comb my hair with my fingers, once, twice and wipe my hands on my shorts as I walk towards the front door. Before I open it, I take a deep breath and push down all the crazy things that are swarming inside of me. "Perfect timing! I just got out of the shower, too. Please come in." Ciara steps in, dressed in yoga pants, a tank top, and wet hair. *Fuck me.* She has no makeup and she's simply beautiful.

"You clean up good, Traxx." Her face has a happy smile while she's looking at me.

"I could say the same about you. You not only clean up good, but you smell great, it reminds me of wildflowers… Remember couple of years back at my Uncle Logan's land? When we ran across a tall field full of red flowers and we all got off the 4-wheelers and were trying to take pictures and selfies and you girls were freaking out because you thought a snake was going to bite you? Remember?"

"Yes! And then Colton screamed bloody murder and ran out of the field screaming 'something bit me!' and us girls started to scream like crazy and jump all over the place until we were able to climb on top of the vehicles – we were scared shitless!"

"Bahahaha! Yeah! And we have pictures to prove your valiant efforts that day!" I start to poke her on her side, tickling her, and she's laughing and trying to walk away from me. All of a sudden, it hits me – like a cinder block encounters a glass window: abruptly, frantically and heavily. I have a tender feeling all over me, making me want to hold on to Ciara and keep her close to me. I want to feel her skin next to mine. I want my lips to find hers. I want, I want... *I want her.* I haven't wanted anyone in weeks. Hell, it's been months. Why now? Why her? The one person who deserves better than me. I'm nothing but fucked up. My mind and my life are in pieces. No one's going to want to share the burden I carry, this affliction that I can't shake because it's rapidly becoming a part of me. Would she want me? No... NO! She deserves better. I have nothing to offer her. Nothing but broken and unmatched pieces of my so-called life.

The realization is like a gallon of cold ice water poured on top of my head. It makes me stop in my tracks immediately. Ciara frowns and looks at me. I don't know what to do with this information. I can't process it at this moment, so I file it away in my mind, to pull out later and try to make sense of it. I catch her looking at me, and I quickly turn around and head into the kitchen. I force the mask to come down and cover the real thoughts going through my mind.

"How about breakfast for dinner? I can make pancakes or breakfast tacos. Do you have a preference?"

"Mmm, let's go with pancakes. And bacon. Please tell me you have bacon or sausage?"

"Yes! I have bacon... And I have sausage, but I'm not sure you want *this* very special kind of sausage right now." Looking at her, I wiggle my eyebrows as I take the bacon out of the fridge, and pull out the box of pancake mix, milk, and eggs out of the fridge. Turning towards the cabinets, I find a flat griddle.

"Gross!" She says while she smiles. Is that a bit of red on her cheeks? Ha! I'm going to remember this tidbit for later. I don't think I have ever seen Ciara Collins blush before.

"What happened to your arm?"

I don't need to look to know she's asking about my self-inflicted wound. "It's nothing. Just a scratch." Then I give her my most charming smile hoping she drops the subject.

She looks at me – through me – causing me to purse my lips into a very tight line. I think she gets it because she nods and changes the subject. Good, at least for now.

I proceed to cook for her and we engage in mindless conversation for the rest of the night. Before she leaves, she tries to convince me to go with her to a "surprise" outing next weekend, of course, I want none of it. All I want is to wallow in my sorrow, alone.

"I don't like surprises," I tell her for the fifth time, but it's falling once again on deaf ears.

"You would like this one. I promise!"

"What and where is the surprise?"

"Well, if I tell you, it won't be much of a surprise, will it?"

She's absolutely excited over this, and since it's impossible to continue to deny her, I amusingly agree. Even though I know what I really need to be doing is walking away, far away from her. Away from *this*, but I can't, I just can't. The world's a much darker place when she's not around. Then, I hear it. Deep inside the psyche of my mind, I can also feel it happening. A little piece of my dismantled life moves against its will and falls back in place – exactly where it belonged. Perhaps there is hope for me yet.

CHAPTER 4

Ciara

    This week has gone by rather slow. They say when you are busy, time flies, but I find that it doesn't always hold true. It certainly didn't happen to me this week. I have been working like a dog, and every day as soon as I get off work, I drive to the library to do research for my thesis, and I can feel the seconds dragging by, like a sand clock which never gets full. Time just goes and goes and the days drag and drag.

    Today's finally Saturday and although I turned down two guys who were offering hot dates, I consider myself to have a scorching one tonight because Traxx and I are going to hangout and then we are going to meet everyone else later on for drinks and hopefully some fun at "Twisted," our favorite bar. Some people would think that I'm taking advantage of him while he's weak, but I don't see it that way. If we don't keep him away from his dark mind, he will go there and never climb out. My plan is to show him that life goes on. That it's okay for him to be happy and not think about the bad. Once he starts healing and he is more tolerant of the incident and comes to terms with the knowledge that Marcy didn't kill herself because he forced her, but because she was not thinking rationally and was unable to make good choices, then we can work on the steps to make him feel his life's valuable and worth saving, after that, he can help others heal.

I go online and set everything up for our outing. Then, I send Traxx a quick text to let him know what time to be ready and what to wear. I hear the front door open, when I peek out of my bedroom door, I see Brianna and Keagan.

"Ciara, where are you?" I hear Brianna call from the distance.

"I'm in my room. Come here." I smile when I hear my bestie Brianna. I don't get to visit with her a lot because, well, she moved out and her being a cop comes with crazy hours and too much work. As soon as I see her, I give her a huge hug.

"Hey, sweets! What an awesome surprise!" I smile at her.

"I know, although the other day I clocked you doing thirty miles over the speed limit, and it was so tempting to pull your ass over, just to see your pretty face and perhaps give you a ticket. Month end's coming fast and I still have not met my quota."

My mouth shapes into a huge 'O' and I take a deep breath, "Hell no, you better not give me a ticket! I probably can't afford it! I also don't wanna be the new poster girl for the jail flyers - that's just not my style!" We start laughing carelessly.

"Number one, you and I know you're lying about not being able to afford it, and number two, I guess orange is *not* the new black for you... Nah, don't you worry your pretty head – I wouldn't do that, but you should slow your ass down a little because another cop would have gone after you, for sure."

"Yes, ma'am." I give her a mock salute with my right hand's index finger touching the corner of my eyebrow. "I will try to watch out for my lead foot. What are you up to?"

"Colton went to take the truck to get the oil changed, so I figure I can catch up with you guys. I found Keagan coming in the parking lot at the same time I was pulling up to your building." She looks towards Keagan who's been busying herself in the kitchen since she walked in and then she looks at me. "How are things with Traxx?"

"Ugh! That boy gives me whiplash! One day he's great and then all of a sudden something clicks and his mood flips to a total opposite version. But I have been studying the possible triggers and I think I can identify a few of them."

Keagan chimes in, "You guys know he went back to work this week, full time plus more hours." I knew that but apparently Brianna didn't.

"He did! That's great!" Brianna smiles at me.

"Yes, it has definitely been a good week for him. I've been checking in with Notso on a daily basis – on the down low, you know, because I was afraid that Traxx may feel overwhelmed with so many of us checking up on him and I didn't want him to suffer a setback. As far as any one of us knows, he has not had any panic attacks or episodes. The nightmares, however, they haven't gone away. Notso hears him yell and talk in his sleep every night. He's most definitely still haunted by the events of the incident." Keagan adds to our conversation.

"Poor thing." Brianna lowers her head and crunches her nose like she does when she's trying to think of something. "I wish there was something we could do."

"Well," I confess, "I prefer that he continues to have nightmares than taking it upon himself to procure God knows what kind of drugs to help him block everything out, or to be in so much pain that hurting himself can be considered as an option." Brianna's eyes get really large and Keagan comes out of the kitchen, staring at me.

"What the hell was he taking?" Keagan asks.

"Oooh, don't say it. I don't think I wanna know!" Brianna covers her ears with her hands.

"Guys, don't get the wrong idea! I don't know what he was taking because he never told me. And I'm still trying to figure out how he hurt his arm – earlier that day he was fine and then later, there was a huge Band-Aid covering 'a scratch.' But if he's working, I don't think he would be taking anything while he works, because whatever he *was* taking, it used to put him to sleep. I'm sorry, I didn't mean to worry you guys. I will try to find out more information before I make assumptions."

The girls both take a breath and reluctantly move away from the topic. "So, what's your plan? Where are you taking him today?" Brianna asks quietly, as if I'm going to tell her anything when I know she tells Colton *everything*. Ha!

"Nah, ah... I'm not telling! You will have to ask him later when you see him *after* we do what we gotta do." I stick my tongue out to her. "You know that my number one goal is to make him appreciate life again – his life. He needs to believe that life's worth living."

"You are going to make us wait that long, no details?"

"Yep. It's only a few hours. But now I have to get ready, since we have to leave in less than one hour." Brianna looks at her watch and gets up from my bed, where she was sitting.

"Fine, okay, we'll catch up later. I think Colton should be almost finished, so I'm going to head on home. Have fun!" She looks over to the kitchen where Keagan is and yells, "Bye, Kay Kay."

I give her a kiss on her cheek and a hug. I really miss her and her sarcastic comments. After she turns to leave, I go to the closet and pull out what I need to wear today.

Traxx

My mood is not that great at the moment, but I'm sure as hell trying to work on it. My friends have been patient, giving, and most of all, caring towards me since the incident took me away from them. Some days are easier than others. If I'm lucky, work keeps me really busy. I'm working a shitload of accounts, more than I have ever managed before. I also volunteer for anything and everything. It makes the hours more manageable. Then I treat my body to gym workouts until I'm exhausted, until all I can do is get home, take a hot shower and collapse in bed. Those are the good days. I wish all days were more like that.

Other days like this one, I have to fake it. Like they say, fake it 'till you make it. Nobody wants a part of this hell I seem to be trapped in. The nightmares… God, the nightmares can be outright terrifying and very unsettling. Most times there's blood everywhere. All over me. On the floor. On the walls. On the furniture. It doesn't matter what I do or where I go, I can never escape the coldness that envelops me as the distinct smell of death captures me and invades my other senses as well. It's my own private and never ending hell and the sad thing – the one thing that keeps me nailed into this other realm - it's that I don't feel I belong anywhere else but here.

It's a quiet ride, but not difficult. It's comfortable between the two of us. I guess the familiarity comes from being around each other for years now. Being near her allows me to be calm. It reminds me of the carefree Traxx I used to be acquainted with. When she takes a glance at me, I can't help but notice the mischievous smile she charms me with. I follow the

GPS instructions and we pull into a parking lot. I look at the huge building structure right in front of us. As I turn off the truck, I admire the massive tower about six stories high or quite possibly even taller than that. The building is white and splashed with a bright shade of red color, brick red. It has a lot of glass on the front side of the building. The name "iFly" is plastered in huge red letters that cover the entire tower and I can't help the small twitch of a smile that I feel coming out on one side of my lips.

I *knew* what it was. I could not help the sudden burst of energy and excitement my body was feeling. I look at Ciara with as much amusement as a kid during Christmas morning and quietly ask her, "Is this really what I think it is?"

She gives me a nervous smile and then starts on her spiel. "Well, I had to come up with a plan to help you cope and ultimately move on with your life. This program – which I call BTB (Bring Traxx Back), is designed especially for you and will be revealed one step at a time. There is no rushing and most definitely, you can only work one step at a time.

Looking at her like she's lost her marbles, she smiles and continues.

"There will be no bribing, and most definitely, there is no room for negative connotations." She smiles brightly and as I sit inside the truck completely dumbfounded, she extends her hand and asks me. "Deal?"

I sit there, looking out of the truck and trying to come up with a palpable excuse so I can turn around and drive away. Unfortunately, I know Ciara will never let me off the hook. I was toast. With resignation in my voice, I grab her hand and we shake as if this is a common business deal of a daily occurrence.

"Excellent! Let's get started! Repeat after me: Step 1- Live your life in the moment."

"Step 1 - Live your life in the moment."

With a nod of her head, she swings open the door and jumps down from the truck then slaps the seat with her hand, the loud sound bringing me back to the here and now. My eyes grow wide, and I immediately start to get out of the truck, locking it and coming to stand next to Ciara. She positions herself in front of me and holds me by the arms. Her small hands don't even cover half of my biceps, but somehow it feels like she's using the 'jaws of life' on me, the gesture is as simple and as powerful as you can imagine.

Looking at me eye to eye, her smooth voice whispers just loud enough for me to hear her, "You are not alone anymore, Traxx. I've got you. Are you ready to feel free? Are you ready to fly and live in this moment – you, me, the wind beneath our feet?" Her eyes are full of hope. I feel a small squeeze inside my chest. Something so different, I have trouble identifying, something that takes my breath away – and it scares me. So I do what I do best: default to asshole mode. "Dang, girl! You sure can get sappy!" I laugh gently. "Where do you come up with this stuff?" I smile at her with a raised eyebrow.

"Too much Oprah, I guess."

She stops looking at my eyes, drops her hands and starts looking down, her smile gone. Suddenly I feel bad that I took this moment away from her, that I clouded the small ray of sunshine she was offering me. God, *I am* an asshole! I grab her hand, because in all honesty the warmth of the simple gesture provides me comfort and it calms the need for me to touch her in a more personal way.

"Come on, Nibblet, show me how to live in the moment, because that is certainly something I no longer find the ability to do." I wink at her, and noticed a small smile appearing on her beautiful face. She starts to walk ahead of me and I follow close behind.

Ciara

I was glad that Traxx was walking behind me so he could not see the major grin plastered on my face. When he took a hold of my hand, I had to grasp every ounce of self-control I possess to not look at our joined fingers. The heat radiating from his skin was strong enough to cause it to flow through my arm and disperse throughout my body, as if I was a chemical experiment with an unforeseen reaction and ready to explode.

Once we walked inside the building, the blasting air conditioning helped to control my temperature. Whew! It feels so much better here now that the coolness helps my mind clear away the naughty thoughts I was having about the sexy man behind me. I know, I know... He's hurting, how can I take advantage of him while he is like this, blah, blah, blah – I'm only human! How can I not, from time to time, acknowledge Mr. Sex on a stick? Just because I was thinking inappropriate things, it doesn't mean I was or would be acting on them. My inner thoughts come to a halt when I see Mav coming towards us. Maverick Penson is the owner of this indoor skydiving location and my personal trainer. I have been coming here for a couple of years now.

I used to crush on Mav from the first time I met him. He's tall, lean and strong. Olive skin, emerald green eyes, brown curly tussled hair with natural highlights, high cheekbones and a friendly smile that never quite reaches his eyes... Yes, he's almost perfect. Too bad he was not looking to engage with anyone. The boy has a ton of baggage and even though we were friendly with each other, he kept me at arm's length. Rumor has it he doesn't date and he never speaks of his past.

"Well, my favorite customer is here - what a treat to my sore eyes!" He gives me a side hug, and I feel Traxx holding my hand a lot tighter than before. He was not going to let it go anytime soon. I let out a quick, silent sigh and make the expected introductions. Now, I just don't get why Traxx feels so insecure towards any of my male acquaintances — they have nothing on him!

Traxx Maxwell is a very unique male specimen. A rare find: Tall with a broad back, he wears his black hair a little longer than most of the other guys. His skin is tanned and his muscles ripple with hardly any effort, but it's his presence that commands everyone's attention. He carries himself with a constant dangerous edge. If you don't know him well, it will make you feel uncomfortable. Sometimes when he looks at me with those warm honey-colored eyes, it feels like he's trying to read my soul. However, that look can switch on a whim and all of the sudden they can trap you in an inexplicable vice, and I was his silent victim. **Sigh**

I introduce them to each other, and Mav tells the girl at the front desk that he will be providing our instructions and lesson.

"Wow, I feel so special! Don't you have something more important to do?"

"Nah, I just finished my backlog so I'm caught up with everything. Besides, I have missed your smartass mouth. Also, Traxx will need the strongest instructor we have." Then he winks at me. When I look at Traxx, I catch him rolling his eyes to the back of his head, and I silently wonder if this will work out as planned.

"If we need the strongest instructor, then you better go get Ginger." I tell him with mock sarcasm.

"And, there it is. Didn't take long. Glad to have you back, Ciara."

Traxx pulls my hand to get my attention. "Ciara, how long have you been training here?"

"Couple of years. After so many years of gymnastics, this proved to be a great replacement. I've earned my certification, so I will be able to enter the chamber with you and Mav." Traxx nods just as we arrive in the training room.

"There are a few things we need to go over, some hand signals that you need to learn, and Ciara, I know you have watched the safety movie a million times, but Traxx needs to pay close attention, since it's his first time in the tunnel. Agreed?"

"Scouts' honor!" I cross my heart and look at Mav, smiling. He feels the need to point out the obvious, "Why do I have a strong feeling that you've never been a Girl Scout? You are more of the law-breaking type than the enforcer."

"He's got your number!" Traxx chimes in.

"Shut it, the both of you. Let's get this training over with 'cause I'm ready to fly and feel the high!"

Traxx

Mother fucker! Every time I turn around, we are finding some of these guys. Ciara's oblivious to the way they look at her. I can tell they want her and the Neanderthal in me wants to grab her, throw her over my shoulder and leave the premises immediately. I don't want to share her attention with anyone – friend or not. So far, she says they are just friends. I have met many of the guys who in the past tried to get in her pants. I think it's better for me not to know who she has been intimate with, because I can't promise I would react rationally. I know I was a manwhore before, but I have always known that I have feelings for this girl. I have shared that knowledge with Colton and Brianna, and they talked me out of pursuing her, because they didn't think I had what it takes to maintain a relationship. I thought they were right, but the more time I get to spend with Ciara, the more I realize it was the dumbest move of my life. And now…now I'm too broken and have nothing to offer her. The one thing I do have is desire to see this "BTB" plan through. I'm done being afraid – at least when I'm conscious. If I can get ahold and control my thoughts and feelings when I'm awake, perhaps it will also help me when I'm unconscious and in the dark. The guilt, however, I have no idea how I will be able to handle that. Guilt consumes me when I'm awake and also when I'm asleep. I truly have no idea how I will be able to move on from that.

We finish the video and went to a super large closet-like room to find appropriate sized gear. Nibblet found herself a wind suit really quick. I had to try on a couple before I found the one that fitted me best without making me feel that my nuts and butt crack were being carved by the tight seams. After all, I needed to be able to move a little, at least.

Maverick – who the fuck came up with that name? 80's much? At least we know what movie his parents were watching while getting down. Well, it didn't matter how hard I tried, I just could not stay pissed at this guy. He was inherently nice.

Once we were fully prepped and ready, Mav gave us a quick facility tour, where he explained how things worked and answered all our questions.

Come to find out this building is a converted warehouse. The tower houses a vertical wind tunnel and it's called the flight chamber. This chamber is 15 feet wide and 55 feet tall. The entire front is made of a special plexiglass. The back and upper levels of the tunnel are made of reinforced concrete, which keeps it quiet and reduces vibration. Its round shape helps with the air flow. The floor of the chamber is a trampoline floor of high quality stainless steel. Outside looking at all the action inside the tunnel, there's a tunnel operator controlling the wind. Starts slow and gets higher until you and the instructor are airborne.

The part that blew me away – no pun intended – was the one about the fans being on top and not on the bottom of the tunnel. The wind starts to generate from the top, and it's channeled and directed down the sides of the tunnel and then up the middle through the floor. Once the wind reaches the top, it recycles and repeats the flow.

Since the wind's controlled by the weight of the flyer and their skill level, I told Ciara she should go first and give me a demo.

"Nah, there are too many people watching. It really makes me nervous." She looks at me with wide, scared eyes.

Mav tries to reason with her, "You are a great and skilled flyer, Ciara, these people can benefit from watching you do some tricks. Plus it will encourage them to practice more so they can get better at it."

"You really think so?" She asks him with a hopeful tilt to her voice. I nudge her a bit, too.

"I would love to see you do some tricks, Nibblet. Live your life in the moment – remember?" And I give her my most dazzling smile. I catch Mav looking at me after I mention her nickname, first it was like a question and then the lightbulb went off inside his head. I gave him a grouchy frown in return. He better not get any ideas.

She starts to nod her head, "Mmmkay. I guess you are right to throw my words right back at me. Geez. I'll do it. But I need some good music, can you arrange it, Mav?"

"I'll take care of it. I think I have the perfect one. Fall Out Boy okay?" Mav asks her.

"Perfect!"

While we wait on the music to start, Ciara gives me her back and starts to stretch her legs and shoulders. Adapting a scene from the movie "Rocky," I start to massage her shoulders in an effort to help her out some.

Suddenly we hear Mav's voice on all the speakers. "May I have your attention, ladies and gentlemen, we have a very rare treat for you today. Last year's winner of the Solo Flyer Championship Division is going to grace us with a quick demo. Pay attention to the flow of her moves and her upper as well as lower body strength – it's flawless."

"Dear Lord! He needs to stop that shit." I hear Ciara talking to herself. Then the music starts and the trumpets of the opening chorus of "Irresistible" fill the entire building and suddenly all eyes are on Ciara.

She doesn't even hesitate. The second she steps inside the chamber, the wind carries her high up, where she starts her performance – it was like watching a contemporary dance with some ballet moves intertwined, her movements were not jerky but smooth, like a water dance. She was breathtaking. Everyone in this place was mesmerized – men and women, no discrimination. She was everywhere, upside down, up and down showing us movements and positions that would probably take the less practiced person years to perfect. She was a natural.

The demo was over and I had to wait for several people to finish talking to Ciara. When her time inside the wind tunnel ended, so many people were so impressed by her, they came around to talk, and others wanted to take selfies and get autographs. I have been friends with Ciara for a long time and I had no idea she had this experience hidden under her belt.

Now, it was my turn to try to learn how to fly. The idea was exciting and I could feel my adrenaline pumping. I catch Mav coming my way.

"Are you ready, Traxx?"

"I think so."

"Don't worry, since it is your first time, we will start the air flow really low and work our way up until you gain enough momentum."

"Oh, so it will not be like it happened to Ciara? It seemed she stepped right in and went up flying really high."

Mav chuckled. "Nope. That's because we already had the fans running at a really high power. And, no offense, Ciara's really tiny compared to you, plus she has a lot of experience." He taps my arm with his hand.

"Oh, yeah. That makes sense."

"Remember the hand signals we practiced while watching the video? It's really hard to hear inside there, so please make sure you use them. You and I will go in there first and then Ciara will join us, once I feel you are used to the wind."

"You got it!"

I'm so ready to try this out... Mav opens the door and goes in but stays on the inside ledge without touching the trampoline and he signals me to come in. Stepping on the ledge, he prompts me to move onto the trampoline. Feeling the air's increasing speed, Mav grabs the chest of my flight suit and as I lean forward, my legs rise up. He moves his hands to my back, so I don't fly out of reach. Then with the hand signals we practiced, he instructs me how to move, and as I perform the movements, I can feel how my positions change as the wind came by. It doesn't take me too long to figure out how to move inside the chamber and keep my body under control.

When Mav felt I was ready, the wind got stronger and we flew up high inside the chamber. I felt so light... I started to tuck my body and even though it was somehow awkward, I was doing cartwheels in the air – Me! Mav moved us down some, and tells Ciara to come in. Ciara steps in and shoots up in the air, passing us by and then descending to our level.

She makes a hand signal for me to watch her and as she was demonstrating several positions, I was trying my best to mimic her, but of course, I'm very clumsy and not graceful at all. We manage to do some splits, tucks and flips. I was able to do almost everything but for some reason, I could not do a summersault. I think my body is too long, too heavy and too big for the wind. I felt like a kid again, without any care in the world, *living in the moment*, and it felt so good.

CHAPTER 5

Ciara

Dancing and playing with Traxx inside the wind chamber was everything that I hoped for. The best moment was when we were doing tricks and he was able to keep up with me on a series of twists and turns… The look of wonder he gave me, once he completed the movements, followed by that flawless smile and laughing like a kid – it was priceless. The fact that I was the one who helped put the smile on his face because he trusted me to help him forget… That's what makes my heart happy. It makes everything else take a back seat.

I still wonder if I'm doing the right thing. We all know I'm not a doctor, but I have to trust my gut on this one. I knew Traxx pretty well before the incident. I can recognize the changes he's going through. When depression takes a hold of a person, it's so hard to overcome it. It helps to have someone to keep you pushing through. I want to be that someone for Traxx. I need to hold on to him because we are stronger together than he can be alone. And *I will* hold on to him. I won't let him fall apart again. He's going to learn that he can count on me and on our friends. Another kink in this chain, is the attraction I still feel for him which is not going away, unfortunately. *Or fortunately?* I wish I knew how to turn that off. I really need to turn it off, somehow, because any time my eyes land on him, sexy and carnal thoughts invade my mind and to tell you the truth, I like them. Maybe a little too much. *Sigh*

After flying, we drive back to the apartments to shower and get ready to go out to our favorite hangout. My shower? It's going to be a cold one, Lord, have mercy! Being near that much testosterone got me hot and bothered in the best kind of way – and no one to quench the thirst. For a moment, I wonder if I have enough time to play with one of my toys, and on a whim, I go and get BOB, my battery operated boyfriend, but as I reach for the drawer's handle, I hear my phone beep with a message, so I look at it instead.

Brianna: Where are you guys?

Ciara: Getting ready! Save me some food!

Brianna: You do realize who's all at this table, don't you?

Ciara: Tell Notso and Colton that if they eat all the food again, the wrath of hell's coming down on them – no mercy!

Brianna: They are laughing at you... and then when you get here, they'll be shittin' their pants. Hurry!

Ciara: K, c u in a bit

With a smile on my face, I decide to give up on BOB and hop in the shower, where I quickly believe this cold shower promise must be just for guys, because it's not doing shit for me. Frustrated, I hurry up and get finished.

Luckily, I had already picked out my outfit. It's a sexy little black dress. It has a silky top and skirt, but the long sleeves and midriff are made of fishnets – more erotic than tacky. I don't really like to show my butt cheeks to anyone, so the skirt actually goes to mid-thigh, and it's flowy, not tight. The dress is soft and racy, in a very feminine way… And I know it's going to turn some heads.

I blow dry my hair and give it some waves. Light makeup, dark mascara and bright glossy lips. Done! I put on the dress and slip on my favorite pair of strappy black sandals. I spritz my perfume in the air and walk through it, and I'm ready.

As I'm walking to the living room to get my purse and keys, I hear a knock on the door. When I open it, suddenly my world stops spinning, my music stops playing and my heart stops beating – all at once. I slowly smile. Traxx is standing in front of me oblivious to the fact that he looks like sex on a stick. A god of all that is male and raw sex. Realizing my mouth has started to produce an enormous amount of saliva, I swallow hard and take a last glance at the tall, dark and handsome male specimen in front of me. His normally messy hair is styled and brushed up and back, making his five o'clock shadow more pronounced. His clothes are simple: a black button-up with the long sleeves rolled up, dark wash jeans, and a large square belt buckle carved with a horse riding cowboy that makes me flush because of the idea that I can be a cowgirl and I could ride… well, never mind. We'll leave that thought for another time. His worn cowboy boots complete the outfit.

He's fixing his TAG Heuer leather watch and is looking down not paying me attention while I dissected him and his outfit in a matter of seconds.

"Are you ready? I'm starving!"

I keep quiet because I want him to notice me and I don't want to miss a beat of his face when he finally looks at me. Once he's done with his watch, I catch him moving his eyes to the floor from where he slowly licks every curve of my body with his eyes only, starting with my cute pedicured feet, all the way up until he finally reaches my eyes. Traxx blinks a couple of times, as if he feels he's dreaming and trying to wake up. His slightly open mouth shows a tiny smile that he tries to repress immediately.

I'm still waiting for him to say something… anything. So many emotions cross his face in a matter of seconds. Happy. Confused. Sadness. I don't know what to say. Perhaps I need not say anything at all. In the stillness, our eyes do all the silent talking. Our chests move with heavy breathing and desire pours out through our pores. It's unmistakable. The question is what are we going to do about it? The seconds feel like hours while we weigh each other's options.

Finally, Traxx mans-up to the situation, and he slowly takes a couple of steps until he invades all my senses. So close that I can feel his body heat, and the clean scent of his cologne becomes a part of the air I breathe. I look at him, my high heeled shoes giving me a closer look to his masculine face. His jaw is tense. His eyes intense. It's a lot more than I can take. He's everywhere and nowhere all at once. I want to grab a hold of him, and I want to turn around and walk away. Too many feelings…too much. I want it all. With shaky fingers I place a hand on his chest. I'm unsure if I should push or pull, so I leave it still instead. He is rock solid and soft at the same time, if that's even possible. His heat burns my hand, but I won't move it. It's the best burn I've ever had.

The heat moves through that hand and comes into me – inside of me, moving throughout my body and filling in my empty heart. One of his hands rises to cover the one I have on his chest, and as I turn my head to look at the Traxx sandwich my hand's caught in between, his other hand lifts up, and grabs my hair, moving it behind my shoulder. His hand caresses my shoulder, then my collarbone, never leaving my skin, until it finally wraps around the side of my neck and with his thumb, he gently rubs the outline of my jaw. Back and forth. And again – back and forth. It's a beautiful feeling. It's excruciating. I catch myself looking into his eyes and then my eyes move so I can stare at his lips.

"Ciara, you are breathtakingly beautiful."

I realize I can't talk and then something similar to a whimper escapes my lips. I recover quickly by clearing my throat and whispering, "Thank you." The time lingers on. I wish I could pull him inside my place and into my room. Keep him there, allowing myself to be selfish. There are so many things I want to do to this man that even eternity wouldn't be enough time. I also need to try and decipher these feelings I have for him. To show him someone cares and that he is worth it. His eyes say so much and nothing at all.

Raising my chin with his fingers, Traxx whispers, "It's time to go."

"Is it really... time?"

"Yes, it is. We may have to finish... *this*... another day. Don't you think?"

"Agreed. We really have to work on...*this*."

He kisses the top of my hand and steps away from me, back into the receiving hall, waiting for me to lock the door. I turn around and he smiles and extends his hand towards me. I hold on to it and follow him to the truck. The thought occurs to me that I would follow this man anywhere he needed me.

Traxx

I took advantage of Ciara locking her door so I could re-arrange my dick because *he* was starting to expand into a weapon of mass destruction. I know I'm exaggerating, but it was really getting into full attention, and then how was I to explain that one? How can I tell Ciara that I want to play connect the dots with all her freckles? That having her close to me incites feelings that I've never had? These *feelings* that I don't know how to handle or what to do with? How can I tell her that I want to taste all of her skin, that I want my kisses to define new paths throughout her body? That I want my lips to pour warmth on her skin to calm the goose bumps I could feel coming to life? That I look forward to the day I can have her completely – body and soul – and I could tend to her quivering body as she looks at me with passion? I can't… I won't. She deserves better than me. I have to hold on to all of these overwhelming things that are happening inside of me – I have to hold them at bay. I have to keep them chained.

Besides, I need to start thinking about how I'm going to stay out of jail and not kill whatever guy comes by trying to get her attention tonight. 'Cause they will come by, and I'm not sure how I'm going to contain the caveman in me. Man, she's fucking hot in a simple, understated way. And that little dress she's wearing. Shit – there he goes again! I shift on my seat, and start thinking of sharks, huge, hungry sharks. Shark week, sharks on TV. Okay, there it goes, back to normal. I chance a side glance at Ciara, but she seems to be looking for music. Good. Now, if I could just keep it that way all night…

We drive in a comfortable silence until we get in the parking lot of "Twisted," our favorite hangout. I come around the truck to open her door and help her out. We walk side by side and I want to go in hand-in-hand, with one arm around her, laying a claim and letting everyone know she is with me, and daring anyone who looks her way into a pissing contest. All of this it's swirling through my mind and I do nothing. *Nothing.* I let her walk in front of me and as if it was a movie queue, the moment she walks in, the spotlight that was going around and around the dance floor, stops briefly on her, and it follows as she walks confidently to our usual high table.

We love this place – all of us. It's your typical sports bar on one side, a dance floor/concert area in the other. We enjoy coming here for karaoke nights since Colton and Brianna can actually sing. The rest of us make a full time job of keeping Ciara away from the mic. She loves to sing but just… can't… Cats all around the neighborhood start meowing and dogs howl when she sings. Thinking back to the few times she did make it on the stage brings a smile to my face, she's just that cute.

I go around and give each of the guys a cool guy handshake, and a brief hug to the girls. Ciara hugs everybody, and then pops a piece of boneless wing in her mouth. I tell her that I'm going to the bar to get her a drink, she nods and then she sits with the girls and starts talking. I order a Corona for me, and a Michelob Ultra and some potato skins – her favorites - and while waiting, I casually look around. One, two… three guys are steadily checking Nibblet out. I knew it.

The worst part is that I have no right to lay claim to the prize she is. I need to leave it alone. So I grab the beers and the number for the table so they can bring the skins out to us. Once I get to the table, I casually stand next to her and place her beer in front of her. She smiles at me, mouthing a "thank you." I give her a wink and mentally prepare myself for the torture that's about to come.

Colton looks at me and asks, "How was your date?"

"Bro, you *know* it was *not* a date."

"She asked you to go do some stuff with her, so why is it not a date?"

"Because we are not that way with one another."

Notso butts in. "I remember at one time you wanted to be. Why is it different now?"

"Because if I remember correctly, you assholes told me not to pursue that girl. To leave her alone." I whisper-talk to them giving them a mean look.

"Yeah, well…" says Notso, "perhaps we were wrong about that. Don't you think so, Colton?"

Colton is steadily peeling the label on his beer bottle, without looking at me, he responds, "Yeah. Perhaps. Do you still like her?"

"Yes, I like her. I'm just not sure that I'm good enough for her. She's a top shelf drink, and I'm a house-poured shot, you know? Besides, I'm not all there yet."

"It *is* because you are not all there, indeed, that we think you need to give this thing with Ciara some thought. You are not a manwhore anymore, Traxx. Like it or not, the incident has changed you. We want to see your dumbass happy, and we think you and Ciara are right for each other now." Notso eggs me on.

Do I want to pursue something with Ciara? I give it a minute and imagine Ciara and me together as a couple. It gives me the – what do girls call it? – Oh! The warm fuzzies. Well, truly, what I mean is that when I'm with her, I forget about everything and the pain that is constantly residing within me goes away... But is it fair for her to have this part man, part broken soul person after her? No. Not yet. But one day, hopefully sooner rather than later, my vision will become a reality.

Looking at her, I watch her having an intense conversation with Brianna and Keagan. I try to tune in, but the loud music covers their whispering and somehow I feel like I'm missing something important. At that moment, some girl comes between Ciara and me, and throws herself at me – literally. I move fast to try to prevent her from falling face first on the floor. The girl is wasted.

"Hey there handsome, remember me?" Using her index finger, she touches my nose and although at one point in my life I would have loved it, today just makes me recoil in disgust. I don't want her touching me, so I put some space in between us.

"Uh, no. I don't."

"What? Look at me! Look at this face, my lips – you loved them wrapped around your d-i-c-k, remember?"

I groan in exasperation. "No. I don't – I said. Why should I?" I notice Ciara and the girls throwing daggers my way. I've got to get rid of this drunk. Suddenly it's really important to me that Ciara knows there's nothing going on here but I don't even get a chance to get rid of the girl, as Ciara jumps off the barstool, grabs Notso's hand and heads to the dance floor. Even though I know they are best friends, and that Notso would never take advantage of Ciara, I still feel something boiling inside of me and not in a good way.

Turning to look at the drunk girl, and practically growling I say, "Well, go find another dick to entertain you. I'm not up for the job now or ever." Her smile drops and she shrugs her shoulders, turns around and leaves.

All the eyes around the table are on me and I can't take the pressure of their stares, especially when no one is saying anything at all. It's like they are in shock.

"What?" I ask them. Silence. "I've got to go get another beer. Anyone want anything?" Nothing. So I move along, all the while watching Ciara and Notso dancing. They are laughing and joking around, having a good time. I know I need to keep heading toward the bar, that's the command my brain is sending down to my feet, but I find my feet have a mind of their own, when I find myself diverting towards them – towards her.

Notso sees me first, and he looks surprised, probably because it's a rare thing when I decide to dance. Just because I choose not to do it, doesn't mean that I don't know how. He tells Ciara something and she turns to look at me. I expected her to be somewhat upset, but she smiles and turns my way while Notso moves away from us.

"Traxx on the dance floor! Wow! What do I owe this honor?" She says into my ear.

"You guys look like you were having too much fun, so I wanted to join in…" I shrug my shoulders and grab a hold of her waist to bring her closer – not too close - I don't want her to know how obviously bad I want her. This movement surprises her, but she likes it, her smile and happy eyes tells me so.

"Tell me, Nibblet, when is our next lesson on the BTB plan?"

"Wouldn't you like to know? Still hate surprises, I see."

"Yep. Very much so. Come on, fess up!" I playfully tell her.

"I won't make you wait that long. Perhaps we can do it tomorrow. Are you free?"

"I'm always available for you, sweetheart."

Her smile grows bigger and she comes forward, kisses my cheek, and whispers, "Tomorrow it is, then. Be ready at noon, and I expect lunch before we get started." Moving back she winks and grabs my hand as we head back to the table.

The rest of the night passes in a blur, with me looking forward to what Ciara has in store for me tomorrow. I'm diggin' this BTB plan of hers. I realize that I'm actually looking forward to tomorrow. Crazy, right? Is this what "normal" feels like? I like it. I hope the feeling never ends.

Creepers

From afar, the creepers are watching every moment of Traxx's life. They sit at a booth on the opposite side of the bar. Although they could not hear one word of the conversations going on at Traxx's table, they were keeping tabs on everything everyone was doing.

"How late do you think they are going to stay?" One creeper asks the others.

"It doesn't matter. We are not leaving until he does."

"I hate to see him with the others. It was better when he sat at the bar and drank himself into oblivion." Another one says angrily.

"Do you think he's happy?"

"Not yet, but I think he's starting to want to be happy. You need to remember that our goal is to ruin his life. No matter how much he looks for it, I promise you, he will never find peace, because we will take it all away as soon as it seems he's found it."

"What about that girl, the blond one?"

"She's been a part of that group since the beginning. There seems to be additional interest, but for now we keep doing what we're doing until it's time to execute our plan."

All the others look at their leader and nod in agreement as they continue their vigil in complete and absolute silence.

CHAPTER 6

Traxx

Ciara's text came in mid-morning, right before my alarm went off. I was already awake, thanks to the recurring bad dreams. I never get a full night of sleep anymore. Might as well get up, because I need to make my way to the gym before we go out. That sentence feels so foreign to me, "going out" is not a true statement. I don't need to become delusional into thinking that Ciara and I are dating. I've never dated anyone and I have no idea what that's like. However, there's something there between the two of us. I feel it and I know she does too. I remove the bed covers, and make my way into the bathroom. I take off my briefs and place them in the laundry basket. After using the facilities, I think to myself that morning wood really sucks sometimes. Opening the hot water, I walk to the counter and look at myself in the mirror. I've always taken care of myself physically, and my body shows the results. After I put some toothpaste on my toothbrush and start my daily routine, I start flexing my muscles. I haven't been working out as much as I used to, but my body does show dedication and a lot of time spent on it. My six-pack ripples easily, and if I put my arm up, I can see my external oblique muscles rippling as well. As I finish brushing my teeth,

I come to the conclusion that the one set of muscles that need my immediate care are the ones sitting at attention in between my legs.

Entering the shower, I let the hot water and steam envelop me. I grab the shower gel and put a hefty amount on my palm. Taking a deep breath, I palm my cock while in my head I imagine it's *her* in front of me doing the deed. I feel it come to life and twitch all on its own as my brain replays the images of the last few days, images filled with her beauty and grace. I let my imagination roam free. My hand squeezes harder, as Ciara is kissing my chest and then my lips, then as soon as I engage her, the kiss becomes frantic, needy, heady. With my eyelids closed, there's no actuality, only the dreams I want to wish into reality and the feel of heavy silk on my hand. I stroke it, slowly at first and imagine it's her hand urging me to come to the brink of satisfaction.

Grunting loudly, I bite my lip as I grip my dick harder, increasing the speed of the movements. I lean my free hand on the tiled wall to keep my balance, as the intensity overtakes me, making me realize the need for her is stronger than I thought it was. My eyes shut tight, my hand is pumping harder, faster. My mouth opens to grunt out her name while finally, my cum shoots out hard and fast for several seconds. I let my body lean on the shower wall, because the power of the moment makes my knees buckle to the point that I can hardly support my own weight. I force my eyes open only to see my shit going down the drain, and again I'm alone, and my chest feels as empty as my ball sack is at this moment. Perhaps now I can think more clearly or at least with the right head. Regardless, I still wish she was here with me.

Ciara

After texting Traxx and getting ready for today's adventure, I made a quick run to Starbucks to get myself a Grande Caffé Latte with an extra shot of espresso. For Traxx, I get a Tall Caffé Americano, black. I also order a croissant that I start to munch as soon as I pay the bill. The mounting sexual frustration only makes me want to eat everything in sight. I haven't had the time to properly take care of my needs, either.

When I get back to Traxx's place, he opens the door and as I walk through, he grabs a hold of the last piece of croissant as I was getting ready to eat it and he pops it into his mouth.

"Hey! I was going to eat that!" He takes a large sip of his coffee.

He shrugs his shoulders "You snooze, you lose!" I give him a nasty look.

"This coffee is perfect, thank you."

He distracts me momentarily by licking his lips like only real men can, his tongue barely coming out of his mouth to slide over his bottom lip. I immediately imagine that tongue licking other lips and I feel the heat pooling between my legs. He catches me staring and smirks. I try to recover from the brief moment of weakness by turning around and sitting on the couch and quickly crossing my legs in an effort to stop the need in my southern parts. I look at him guiltily. "That's okay, 'cause now you're gonna buy me lunch."

Smiling knowingly he doesn't hesitate to answer me. "Okay. That's a deal, where do you want to go?"

"Well, we have to be at the place by 2:00 p.m., so let's go somewhere where we can eat fairly fast. How about sushi?"

"Ciara, seaweed does nothing for me. I'm a growing boy, remember?"

"Growing boy, my butt! You've already used up all your growth hormones, buddy. How much bigger do you think you can get?" I love to tease him and he seems to be in a great mood.

"Uh, I dunno, another 10 to 12 inches?" He looks at me and raises one eyebrow giving me a knowing look. At first I don't quite get it, so I look at him, puzzled. A couple of seconds later, I absolutely get it, my eyes get as big as the eyes of a lemur and I my face turns as red as a hot pepper. He starts to laugh.

"Sorry, sweetheart, you asked…"

"Ugh, really Traxx? Okay, nevermind. How about we go eat burgers or wings?"

"Ummm, yeah, that's more like it. Let me go put on my boots."

"Hey, where is Notso? Have you seen him today?"

"That lazy bum's still sleep."

"Lucky dog! Wish I could sleep late like that."

"We can always call this whole thing off and take a nap. I have a big bed."

"I know what size bed you have, I helped you pick it at the store – remember?"

"Ha! Yes, I remember. The sales people were losing their shit because we kept trying out the mattresses – all three of us: Notso, you and me. That was fun." I smile as he walks away and think back to those days, where he didn't have monsters peeking out of his nightmares, making his life difficult. But today seems like we are going to make progress.

The apartment is way too clean. What are these guys up to?

"Hey Traxx, how come your place is so clean? That's not your and Notso's M.O., you guys are super messy." I yell from the living room.

"Oh, we decided to hire a cleaning agency. A lady comes in a few times a week and takes care of everything. She's awesome."

"But, how does she gets in here, since you guys work every weekday?"

"She's got a key. It was part of the contract."

The place looks immaculate. "She's doing a great job."

After a few minutes, I'm finished with my coffee and move to the kitchen to throw away the cup in the trash. As I pass by the entrance to the hallway, I glance towards Traxx's bedroom and get a glimpse of his nice ass as he's bending over putting his boots on. I say a silent prayer so I don't jump his sexy ass while we are out and about.

I return to the living room just in time as he comes out of the bedroom.

"Ready? He asks me.

"Heck yeah! Let's go."

After he locks his door, as it has become our habit, he extends his hand and I reach for it. It's quite common among all of us to hold hands or embrace each other in a lot of hugs. We are a touchy feely kind of group. That's because we have always been more than friends. We are family. Although I must confess that before the incident, I used to get my share of hugs from Notso and Traxx not so much. I tried to stay away from him since I was so attracted to him but I knew it was not going to go anywhere. Nowadays, I feel he needs to know he is loved and cared for in order to help him put his life back together.

In his truck, I play the DJ role and find new songs by some of the alternative bands we enjoy listening to. He's tapping on the steering wheel and I'm humming. Both of us are moving our heads to the rhythm of the music.

We get to the restaurant and Traxx warns me he's getting the door and runs out of the truck to my side. I love it when guys remember their manners and make us feel special. We walk in and get a table. After we place our orders, we start chatting.

"So, Ciara, have you heard from your parents lately?" My dad is a prominent lawyer in Birmingham, Alabama. My mom spends most of her days donating her time and money to many charitable organizations. She has a heart of gold. So many of my friends had a less than wanted childhood, but I love my parents. I had it really good growing up.

"Yes. I talk to them every week. They want me to go visit soon, but between my work hours and all the graduate workload, it's impossible." Traxx frowns and looks down at the table. Impulsively, I reach for his hand and cover it with mine. "Hey, what's going on up there?"

"Nah. It's nothing really. I feel bad that all of you – specially you – are putting so much time and effort trying to help me get back to the way I was before... you know?"

I look at him straight into his eyes when I tell him, "Traxx, by now you've got to know that we do it because we love you, and because you are worth our time and effort. We wouldn't want it any other way."

His voice gets really serious and it's barely a whisper. "Ciara, I don't even know if I'm worth it. Most of the time I feel like I'm going crazy. I hear and see things and I can't trust myself to know if they are real or not."

"Traxx, you were witness to a terrible thing. Everything you are telling me is normal for people that have witnessed trauma like you have. At least you aren't alone. You have me, you have all of us." He turns his palm up and now he's holding my hand and his thumb is rubbing my fingers. Even unconsciously, he offers me comfort, when he's the one in need of it.

"I have a confession to make. I've come to realize that I don't like the person I used to be. I want to be better. I want to do better... But I'm scared you guys are not going to like the person I want to be. I'm not ready for all of you to leave me behind." He looks at me with decision and purpose in his eyes. "I'm still trying to figure everything out, Ciara, but I need all of you. I don't think I can make it by myself. Do you think you can all let go of the Traxx you know and love? Let go of the person I used to be and come to terms with the fact that I'm not *him* anymore?"

The waitress comes by to bring our drinks. We thank her and continue our conversation.

"Traxx, regardless of how you used to behave, we know the person you really are because it's all right here." I scoot closer and put my free hand on his heart. "The real you has always been defined by the goodness of your heart, regardless of your crazy behavior. Someone who's inherently good always comes out a victor in anything they pursue as long as they make all their decisions with their heart. When you put your heart in it, everything else naturally falls into place." I give him a sly smile. "And if it doesn't, you have me to kick you around until you get where you need to be. I'm not going to let you stray. We are in this together. Yes, your life is in pieces, all over the place, but I'm the best damned assembler you're ever going to meet." I grab him gently by the back of his neck and get a hold of his hair. Looking at him eye to eye, I speak with conviction. "We've got this! Okay?" He nods. "Say it with me."

"We've got this." He repeats. His lips part to the most sincere smile I've seen from him in a very long time. "Thank you, Nibblet, I needed that." He tells me.

"If you don't quit calling me Nibblet, I'm going to have to start the kicking part sooner rather than later." He laughs at me.

The waitress comes back with our orders. "Traxx, look at me. I need you to remember what I'm about to say. The tragedies of our past are stepping stones for us to reach the happy endings of our tomorrows. Please remember that. Guilt is not going to help you become a better person. Acceptance will."

"I never thought about it that way."

I smile and grab a piece of my honey barbeque boneless wing. "Don't you forget it! Now, hurry up and eat because we have to make a stop prior to getting where we are going."

"You and your mysteries! I must confess that after all the fun we had last time, I'm ready to see what we are doing today."

I wink at him and then we chat a lot about nothing in general: music, movies, work… All I could think about is how happy I was that he wanted to change and become a better person. My heart was full of pride. Now, all I have to do is plan how and lay out the groundwork, and he will follow.

Traxx

"Where is it we need to go, now" I ask Ciara as she's telling me which way to go.

"You will see. I just need to pick up a few supplies." She smiles coyly.

"You know what, Ciara? I've started to realize that even though I've known you for years, there's a lot more to you than I ever thought."

"Oh, Traxx, we are barely scratching the top layer… You really have no idea what you've gotten yourself into after agreeing to let me help you get over… well, you know."

"Yeah… I haven't forgotten. I'm not sure that I ever will."

She reaches over and holds my hand, at first she holds it in a tight grip, and then her fingers are weaved against mine. The sweet gesture makes me feel safe and comforted. I found myself staring at our entwined hands and when I raise my eyes to look at her, I realize she's looking at me. Our eyes flicker for a moment with something simultaneously powerful and peaceful making my heartbeat sprint with forgotten enthusiasm. Crazy traffic and the fact that I'm driving forces me to break our connection, but it's an unmistakable moment that I'm not going to forget anytime soon.

"Turn left at the light," she instructs me and after a few blocks we reach a climate controlled set of storage buildings. "Go on, approach the gate and enter this code on the security pad." She gives me a long ass number and the gates start to open.

"Which way?" I ask her.

"All the way towards the back. Storage number 68."

"Wow. You missed the best one by one number." I chuckle.

"Seriously?" She smiles. "Get your mind out of the gutter, just pull next to it. I'll be back in a few minutes."

"Oh, I'm coming in with you."

"Ummm, I don't think that's a good idea."

"Why not?"

"I'm pretty sure there are spiders here."

Crap. I *hate* spiders. They freak me out. I need to play this out. "So?" She looks at me annoyed.

"So we don't have time for me to play 'annihilate the spider'?"

I get out and follow her. "I'll be okay. Promise." Ciara rolls her eyes. She unlocks the storage and rolls the door all the way up. Reaching to the side she flips the light switch and it reveals several metal lockers against the walls.

"I need to warn you ahead of time because I really don't want you to freak the fuck out like Colton did when he came here with Brianna the first time." Ciara starts to unlock the lockers.

"Colton's been here? I wonder why he never said anything."

"You'll see. Brianna and I have a very uncommon collection – for girls, at least."

She opens the first locker to reveal an arsenal of guns. The second locker has rifles, the third one has knives and blades of all kinds, and the surprises keep coming. I'm sure my eyes are not playing tricks on me but I fail to understand what's going on. My vision immediately betrays me, because all I can think about is Marcy and what she did with her gun.

"Uh, Ciara, why are you gathering weapons and ammo in a duffle bag?" I managed to ask with my voice barely above a whisper.

She stops what she is doing and gently walks toward me. "Traxx, I wanted to surprise you, but you are terrible at following directions." She's trying to lighten the somber mood I'm currently sporting. "Bring Traxx Back plan: **Step 2 - Live your life without fear**."

"Ciara, I don't know if I'm cool with this."

"I understand you may not be cool with it, but you are going to do it."

"I don't think I can."

"Fear is an evil bitch when you let it take over your life. The only way you have a chance to get over it, is by facing it and for now you need to become very familiar and used to weapons, the sound of a firing gun, and the power behind it. You have to be the one in control, not the other way around."

"Ugh! Not cool, Ciara, not cool at all."

"No excuses. We need to get going to the firing range."

"What all are you are packing in the duffel bag?" I managed to move my hand enough to point at the bag on the floor.

"It's just a couple of pistols, a couple of rifles and ammo. Is there something else you want to do for fun? Like archery? I have a sweet compound bow with these new Helix broadhead arrows…"

"Nah, that's okay. We can try those another day. It's been a long time since I went hunting and I'm probably going to be a little rusty."

"Awww, don't worry! Brianna and I always clean all the guns after we use them, and they are all calibrated. You're not going to have any trouble."

I don't think that she is going to let me off the hook. All I can do is deal with it, because she's right, if it's left up to me, I'm never going to be ready. Although… I wonder if I can fake her into believing that I've seen a huge spider… she might let me freak the fuck out on that one.

"Traxx, stop thinking so hard. You're making *my* brain hurt!" She winks while locking up everything, then grabbing the duffle bag she starts to walk towards the truck. When she passes me, she pulls me by the shirt. "Come on, Braveheart. We have an appointment time to meet. Do I need to drive the truck while you defrost your fear?"

"Ha, ha! Real funny. You know nobody drives my truck but me." We walk out and she locks up the storage unit. I take a moment to be grateful she's on my side, because if she was my enemy, I would be terrified. Who knew the little Nibblet had so many secrets? I'm actually feeling somewhat excited to uncover her layer by layer. Oh, and Colton is not going to get away with this shit. He knew? What's up with being best friends? Well, I guess girlfriend trumps best friend. After all, it's not like I put out for him or anything. And now I'm rambling inside my head.

Ciara walks around the truck and opens the back door, where she sets the bag. Hearing the door slam makes me snap back to reality.

"Hold on, I'll get that door for you."

"Okay, thanks."

I lead her into the passenger side. When she is like this, seated on my high truck and I'm standing next to her, we are eye to eye. I like it. I look at her and smile, placing my hand on her knee and squeezing it. She looks at me, and I feel her leg flinch under my touch which immediately put my little head into motion and I feel it come alive inside my jeans. Bad timing.

"Thank you." I tell her softly.

"My pleasure." She smiles and I remove my hand before I embarrass myself in front of her. After I close the door, I walk around the back of the truck and take advantage that she cannot see me so I can re-adjust my now semi-hard cock inside my pants. I sigh in exasperation. Well done, cock. Well done.

CHAPTER 7

Traxx

We get to the shooting range and I'm expecting some guy to come and try to talk to her, like it happened at the gym and then again at the indoor skydiving place. However, I was pleasantly surprised that behind the counter was a much older guy. I'm sure he's not going to flirt with her, so I relax.

"Hey, Sam! How is it going? Is our range ready?"

The old man sees Ciara and immediately smiles and comes around the counter to give her a bear hug.

"Hey, beautiful! So good to see you! You are still as pretty as ever." He gives her a once over, but it's more like a grandpa admiring his grandbabies than anything else. That helps me keep my shit under control.

"I'm okay, Sam… I've been so busy between work and grad school and every day drama… I've missed you!"

Okay, the everyday drama must be about me…

The old man continues, "Anything I can help you with? Where is Brianna? Is she not with you?"

"Nah, she's working. Being a cop comes with some crazy hours, you know? I brought a friend with me." She turns to me and motions me to come closer. "This is Traxx, he's extremely out of practice, so make sure you give him an extra-large target and move it a little closer." She winks at him and then looks at me.

The old man laughs heartily. "What a sharp young man you seem to be!" Sam gives me a strong handshake and then turns to Ciara. "Child, his target can be 10 yards away and yours 300 meters and you will beat him every time – with the right gun, of course." Ciara's face turns a gentle crimson and I make a note to self to remember Ciara is not used to compliments.

"Did you bring your own stuff?"

"Yeah, we've got ammo too."

"Okay, come follow me then."

I'm nervous because I don't like the sound of gunfire since the night with Marcy. I steel myself to what I'm about to go into, and start breathing slowly. Ciara comes next to me and wraps her arm around my waist.

The old man starts walking towards the back of the building. We walk under an awning and there is an annex building. The entry building was well kept and clean, but obviously looks like a mom 'n pop shop. This annex is state of the art. Sleek and modern, with at least twelve shooting bays, the distance seems to be somewhere between 25-30 yards. It seems to have an automated retrieval system, too, as I can hear the motorized sounds in between shooting sessions. There is a half glass wall separating this receiving entry area and the shooting ranges.

Sam moves to the wall by the door and grabs some supplies. "Here, you're going to need these before you go in there." We each get a pair of foamy earplugs and earmuffs.

"The sound is not that bad because our walls are sound absorbent, but you can never be too careful."

Ciara is attentively observing me and my actions. After we sign some release forms, we proceed to move to the shooting bay. Looking for our number, we locate them towards the end of the range. There is a built in shelf alongside the wall opposite the shooting range and Ciara places the duffel bag there.

"So, what type of gun did you bring for me?"

"Well, I've got different ones. I figured we could trade guns after a while, so I brought two different ones. To get you started, I'm letting you practice with the Beretta 92FS, and I'm going to start with the Sig Sauer P229."

I nod in understanding and start to feel somewhat inadequate because to me a gun is a gun and there is not much difference other than size and ammo, but the way Ciara speaks about each gun, it has this tone I never heard before... almost like reverence.

We do the mandatory safety checks and load the magazines with the ammo we brought in. When I finish, Ciara sets her gun on the counter and she comes over to look at mine. She points at the safety and reminds me to disengage before I start shooting.

"Are you ready?"

I take a deep breath before answering. "Yes. I'm ready for **Step 2 - Live your life without fear.**"

She smiles. "Okay, perhaps the step by step program sounds very corny... BUT nevertheless, we are going to continue because if we don't, your next step is going to be group counseling."

"Ugh! Keep those nasty words to yourself! Stop stalling, I'm rusty on this shooting shit but I'm ready to kick some blonde girl's ass."

"We'll see about that." She moves back to the wall and presses an intercom button that until then, I hadn't noticed. "Sam! I'm ready."

"Gotcha, girlie! How far do you want it?"

"Let's go halfway. I want to give Traxx a fair chance." She winks at me. Ha! She has no idea who is she messing with. I nod so she knows I agree to that distance.

The clips for the retrieval system hanging from the ceiling move towards us. Ciara picks two human shaped targets from a box under the shelf and hands me one. I watch her set hers on the line, and repeat the same steps with mine. When we are finished, she does a "thumbs up" sign and I realize there's a camera behind us. The targets start to move back and stop at the midway point.

We readjust the foamy ear plugs and cover our ears with the earmuffs. I spread my legs and place my hands in the correct position for shooting and then, out of nervous habit I twist my neck until it pops. Then I line up the target in my sight and hold my breath as I slowly press the trigger. I was not quite prepared for the power of the shot, and the gun surprised me with a strong kickback but I was able to maintain it in position. The loud noise and the smell of gun powder residue hit my skin and that's the emotional trigger I was hoping to avoid.

Her image covered my vision all at once with vacant eyes and blood spatter. The one thing that surprised me was that she was not really dead. She was pacing around looking at me with disappointment. I feel hot and my head starts to spin. Slowly, I take a deep breath and right before I close my eyes to clear my mind, I move my hand and flip her the bird.

"Traxx! Hey! Look at me!" I feel Ciara grabbing me by the elbow. "Are you okay?" She removes my earmuffs and let them fall against my neck and shoulders. "The first shot is going to be the hardest for you."

"Working on it." I give her a faint smile because when I open my eyes, Marcy's gone. I'm sweating like a pig, my heart is racing like it's the lead car in the Indy 500, but I smile bigger, because I got rid of Marcy all on my own. I'm not saying that she's gone forever, but now I know that I can make her go away when she pops in my mind uninvited, and that by itself just makes me fucking happy.

Ciara's looking at me like I'm crazy. It's pretty obvious that she will recognize the symptoms of my stress-induced vision, but it's her caring demeanor that makes all the difference to me.

"I was waiting for you to get started and to make sure you didn't run into any problems, when I only heard one shot and then nothing… so I figured I needed to check on you."

I nod. "Go on, sweetheart. I'm fine now. Let's see how we do. I believe that I have another 16 rounds on this magazine and my trigger finger is itching to release them."

Nodding she agrees, "You got it!"

A few minutes later we are finished and we engage the safety, remove the magazine and check the chamber. I press a button on the wall and my target starts to move towards me. I grab it eagerly, like a kid getting ready to unwrap a birthday present, and my inspection and count reveals thirteen rounds hit the target and they are all in the chest area.

"It seems you've got this down pat, Traxx."

"Hell, yeah! On the chest – thirteen shots out of the full magazine that carries seventeen. So I only missed four. Let me see yours." She hesitates for a moment, turning around and stepping back to her shooting bay at the last minute.

"Okay, here is mine." She hands it to me. I look at her paper eagerly, only to realize all her shots hit her diagram on the chest as well, but instead of random shots, she used all the ammo holes to create the shape of a heart. I look back at her, handing her the target she 'decorated.'

"Show off." I tell her as she heads back, all the while shrugging her shoulders.

"Don't be a sore loser, Braveheart. Dignity is hard to come by and you are wasting all yours on some petty shit." She starts to load her magazine while looking at me with one raised brow.

"I was just warming up." I tell her trying to sound convinced. "You've got to remember that it's been quite a long time since I have competed against someone else in a shootout. You have the advantage in all these activities you are dragging me to because you have recently been practicing. First, with the indoor skydiving, now with this. Not an even playing field I'd say and most definitely not cool."

"Dude," she smiles moving her neck from side to side to show some fake attitude. "I suggest ya' quit your bitchin' and get on with it! 'Cause I'm 'bout to show you how it's really done 'round here." I laugh and then she kisses her fingertips and blows me a kiss. "Are you ready? Let's go for the head – the one above the shoulders, mmkay?"

I finish loading my magazine and slide it in place. "Oh! It's on! The real question is - are YOU ready? 'Cause I'm bringing it!" I hit the button on the wall after replacing the paper target retrieval system with a new one. Turning around, I assume my shooting stance, take aim at the target and let it rip.

The magazine was empty. I set my gun down and call the target back to me. I was very anxious to see the results. I grab the paper and start counting the holes. All seventeen rounds were decorating its head. "Ha! Look here! All shots are in the head!"

"That's awesome! You did really well!"

"How did you do, Ciara?" I can't help it. Yes, I know I'm being pretty arrogant, but come on! This is good!

Ciara brings her target to the window, and lifts it up so we both can see the results, and there's only *one* hole. What happened?

"Wait, you only hit it one time?" I don't give her a chance to talk when I start to laugh at her. "Is that all you've got?" I need to come with you next time and bet some money, honey, because I'm gonna be rich!" I look at her and she's pouting and frowning.

Right then, Sam comes inside the range and yells, "I've got it all on video – this is the best I've seen in a long time!" He's coming our way and seems very excited. My chest swells up with pride. I must be a natural at this. Then with my peripheral vision, I see Ciara making a 'cut it out' hand gesture towards Sam, and all my spidey senses are at full attention. Sam stops and gives her a questioning look.

"Hey, Sam!" Ciara says. "That's awesome! I'm so glad you've got it on video because this man right here did sooo good! He deserves the recognition."

Sam looks confused now, and I need to know what the hell is going on. I cross my arms in front of my chest and stare at her *hard*. She gives me one of those 'I didn't mean it' looks. I turn and ask Sam, "Hey man, do you care to elaborate what *exactly* you have on video?" Ciara lowers the paper, drops her shoulders and turns around to avoid looking at me.

Sam looks at me then looks at her. "You didn't tell him?"

"Tell me what" I ask finally getting frustrated. Ciara looks at Sam and moves her head from side to side.

"Son," Sam says in a more serious note, grabbing the target from Ciara's hand and shoving it on my chest, "the reason that there's only one hole is because all her shots went through the same hole. See? That's why the hole is a bit bigger and wider than one of yours, because all those rounds went through the same spot!" Then he boasts out laughing. Ciara looks at me with her eyebrows raised and duck lips.

"Damn! I should have known." I start laughing, my frustration giving way to amusement and grab her in a bear hug. "That was fucking awesome! Sam, can we see that video?"

Ciara

We spent another hour or so shooting more rounds, after Sam finished bragging about me and telling my stories to everyone who would listen. Truth is, I'm really good at a lot of things. I do try to be the best I can at everything I decide to pursue. There's no miracle formula, just a lot of hard work and dedication and absolutely no whining. And well, sometimes, I do get lucky.

When I was a member of the US Army Military Police, I earned the Expert Level of the Army Marksmanship Qualification for rifles and pistols. Let's just say that I know my way around firearms. It's just that I'm not a bragger and I'd rather keep these things to myself. So when Sam decided to talk about it, I was ready to go and hide. Since I wanted to practice a little more, I excused myself and went back to the range to gather my things.

Traxx walked back in with me. "You could stay with the guys, you know." I tell him while I busy myself loading everything in the duffle bag.

"Nah, what kind of gentleman would I be if I let you carry everything?"

"Traxx, I carried the duffle bag inside the building."

"Well, that was BEFORE."

"Before what?"

"Before I realized you are full of awesomeness and surprises all jammed into a cute, tiny package." He gives me his best panty-dropping smile.

"Ha-ha! Real funny."

He turns and steps over to me, invading my personal space and taking me by surprise. My heart races and my temperature rises. I'm not sure how much more I can tolerate keeping away from him, because to tell you the truth, the Traxx that's emerging from this terrible situation, has an appeal that is proving hard to resist.

I look him in the eyes – they are not sad this time, but they spark with *something* else that is hard for me to pinpoint – and I stay silent not wanting to betray the spell of this moment. He reaches his hand and cups my cheek. I'm afraid to move. My breath hitches a little and in that moment, all I can breathe is him. All I can smell is him. All I can sense is him. All I can feel is him. He's consuming me from the outside in and my body's giving up a battle that hasn't even started. His callous thumb moves across my cheek, and each raspy touch brings me back from my sinful thoughts into this moment.

"Nibblet," He says my name quietly, soothingly.

All I can do is whimper. "Uh huh…"

"Don't you know that some of the best things in life come in small packages?" He lowers his head and his lips are coming straight for mine. At the last moment, Traxx stops, like he thinks better of it, and veers his lips to my other cheek. Feeling his five o'clock shadow on my smooth skin makes me really happy. I think our friendship may be moving in a different direction and I have to think about this because I'm not sure we are ready.

Creepers

Parked across the street from the shooting range, the creepers are watching. Waiting patiently for a sighting of their target.

"How much can they shoot in two hours? I thought all the time slots were for one hour at a time." Asked a creeper.

"You know, some say patience it's a virtue. I get it. I'm tired of sittin' my ass in this car and waiting until something worthy of our attention happens." Creeper two speaks, quietly, with frustrated words.

"Can we go get a coffee?"

"I don't think we should step out of the vehicle under any circumstances. All it takes is one glance and we will be busted. If that happens who's going to call the boss?"

The creeper rolls his eyes and leans back on the seat. "Fine, then I'm taking a nap. Wake me up in thirty minutes."

"You are never going to get better at this if you go to sleep every time you get a chance."

"Whatever…"

One asleep, one awake, they continue their watch.

CHAPTER 8

Ciara

"And that's what happened." It's been a couple of days and I have crisscrossed paths with my friends one too many times, never having a chance to catch up. Today after work, I wasn't going to let it go again. I setup a video chat so I can update Keagan and Brianna, on the situation with Traxx. "What do think?"

Keagan is first. "Well, it sounds promising. The hand on the cheek it's definitely a sign that he's feeling something. And I know my cousin, 'feelings' have never been part of him."

"You know I'm not his biggest fan, I mean I love the guy, I just don't love him with you. He doesn't know what he's doing, *obviously*." Said Brianna. "It sounds like he's unsure of what to do. Anyway, we seem to have forgotten that he has *always* been attracted to you. Always. It's been hard for him to keep from crossing the line. I know it for a fact because I have heard him talk to Colton about it. Colton and Notso have talked him out of pursuing something with you many times in the past few years. I may have promised to rip his balls out of his body if he tried anything with you, too."

"Why?"

"Because if it didn't work out, it would have messed with our group dynamic. They were scared that if he tried a conventional relationship and it didn't work it would have affected all of us. I also agreed."

"So, whatever my opinion was on the subject, didn't matter?" I asked Brianna. "You've known for a long time that I have feelings for him."

"It did, but we thought you were not thinking clearly and I just wanted to protect you. Who loves a manwhore?" Brianna answered and I nod because I truly understand the whys. Traxx was a different person back then.

"Who loves a manwhore?" I repeat. "Someone who knows the real person behind the mask. He has always been different when it was just him and I. But it's all irrelevant right now. Guys, going back to the current events, am I reading too much into it?" I asked.

"Ciara, he just doesn't flirt anymore. We have not seen him give anyone his attention since before that night…" That was Keagan.

"Maybe he's just missing being able to flirt with girls in general and you are readily available." Brianna adds.

"My question to you, Ciara, is do you think he's ready to move on from what happened and start something completely foreign and different from what he's done in the past."

"Keagan, that's something that only he can answer. I refuse to think that my senses are so far off.

Besides, you girls are no help." I tell them and all they can do is shrug.

"Ciara, some things are for you to figure out on your own. And regardless what you decide and how it goes, we will be here for you and love you always." Brianna says and Keagan agrees.

"Okay, let's just leave it at that for now. Chat with you guys later?"

Frustrated, I close down the laptop and swiftly move to the fridge to get a beer and a koozie from the drawer. I go to the balcony and sit down on the shaded side. The sun is setting and the unforgivable heat is cooling off a little. I'm thinking about the last few months and everything that we all have gone through. Yes, Traxx was the original victim, but the rest of us were also victims and felt every ripple of this situation. Being close with someone means to experience their problems as if they were your own - and we are all close. We don't ignore. We don't brush off. When Traxx suffers, we do too. At the same time, when he experiences small victories, we do that as well. It's a blessing and a curse, but it makes life more meaningful. I can't imagine any of us going through life – day in, day out – without meaning, the only purpose being to blandly exist. Hell, no.

I finish the beer and go get another one. At times, I see him speak to me with his hands, his smiles. I don't want to sound cheesy and talk about a current moving through us, but what does exist, at least for me, is an unmistakable attraction. When he's looking at me – really looking – my heartbeat starts having a race with itself, my stomach drops, my temperature rises and lust takes over my brain and also my vagina. My reaction is that I want to get closer, to really establish a connection based on knowledge of the things that we love, the things that we fear. The things that make us laugh and those that make us sad. All the things that make us… well, us.

I get up to get my doodle notebook and while I'm at it, grab a third beer. I start to think about the things that make Traxx special to me, my hand moves as my thoughts get deep, putting all these feelings through the pencil and letting the lead show the results. After a couple of hours, I admire the filled pages and come to the realization that the good has always outweighed the bad, and in my book, that is the golden rule of love. We all possess qualities that we may not be too proud of and we work hard to hide them and only let the good ones surface. I knew these things about Traxx, but putting them down on paper reaffirm my hidden knowledge of what I really need to do.

Getting up from the chair, I take a deep breath and hope that I'm making the right decision.

Traxx

I leave the office early and no one says anything because I normally immerse myself in work, but today other things are taking place. For the past few weeks I have been in a state of pure tension, but not because of what happened months ago, it's what is happening right in front of my very own eyes. This situation is completely foreign to someone like me, a person that was unable to form a bond with girls because I was too scared to trust. I'm frustrated and confused.

I mean, Ciara is a knockout. She's not only beautiful, but she's also smart, brave and fearless. I feel like I have been missing out. Like all these years I have only been given a tiny glimpse of what she is really about. Who am I kidding? I was scared to know. I was scared to go against what my friends wanted because I didn't want to disappoint anyone. I was afraid to love and let others love me because what if they didn't like the real me? What was it she taught me about fear?... Oh, yeah, fear is an evil bitch and I should never let it control my life.

Am I ready to take that step? Am I *really* ready? Ready to let go of old inhibitions? Ready to dispose of who I used to be and ready to let myself feel? God, even the thought is scary and intimidating. Am I ready to take all my broken pieces, put them in place and confront the person that I've become, the real me? I think that it would be liberating. I had chained myself to what I believed I should be like instead of being the real me. I closed all the doors. If others care and love me, why can't I do the same?

Sometimes I think that life has punished me enough. I was a jerk and have learned my lesson. I live with regret for some things that I have done. All I need to do is figure out a way to make a difference. To help others the way my friends are helping me. *The way Ciara is helping me.*

I grab a beer from the fridge and head to the balcony. I hear music from below and I smile. Looking at the parking lot I spot her car. Ciara is home. I feel so emotionally vulnerable at the moment, I want to jump and run to her door, assault her lips and kiss her senseless. So many things I want to tell her. What I feel when we are hanging out, how I admire her on so many levels, and how grateful I am that she is opening my eyes to what really matters. Life, me, her, *us*. Fuck!

I want to be near her. I know she feels something for me. No one would give so much of themselves to help another human being if they didn't care. If you asked me this question a year ago, I would have laughed. I didn't know what it meant to be broken back then, but now, now that pieces of me are all over the place, I've experienced broken. I'm completely *dismantled*. But I'm luckier than most, because when I needed her most, she was there for me. She managed to step in, to unknowingly enter my thoughts, my life, and is trying like hell to push the right pieces towards me, so I can pull myself together and be the man I've wanted to be but hid away because I was too chicken shit to let him move outward.

I take the beer bottle to the trashcan, and as I'm getting ready to drop the bottle, I think that in the bigger picture, I'm actually throwing life away because I'm not living in the moment. I should know better. I'm aware of the importance to live in the moment and without fear, I'm still not doing the things that I really want to do, holding my own self back. A smile spreads on my face because the picture is finally clear. I know what I have to do and the knowledge is liberating.

Ciara

I have everything I need ready and I'm so nervous. I look outside to the parking lot from the balcony and find his truck without problems. *He's home.* Before I can talk myself out of it, I turn around and race walk to the front door, I don't bother locking my door because I'm hoping we will be right back here.

As I start up the stairs, I see someone is coming down. Instinctively, I move to the right side but I hear an unmistaken voice say my name.

"Ciara, hey! I was just coming to see you."

"Oh? Wow, this is a coincidence, because I was just coming to get you." There is something different in his eyes tonight. Something happy?

"Cool! What are you up to?" His smile is making his gruff face look irresistible. I make my hand stay in place when what I really want is to reach out and touch him.

"I've been baking. There is a bake sale going on at work to benefit Meals on Wheels and I have baked two different types of brownies and I was hoping you could come for a taste test." I smile coyly.

"I can't think of anything better than chocolate and great company. Let's go." He uses his hand to point the way to my place and I go ahead of him. I need to stop with the nervousness, because I will say something completely stupid. Taking a deep breath, we walk inside my place.

"Hmmm, it smells heavenly over here!" Traxx rubs his stomach, which makes me wonder…

"Have you eaten? I can make us some snacks while we wait for the brownies to cool off some."

"I was going to call in for pizza, but if you have something more appealing I will take it."

I smile and go to the kitchen. Opening the freezer, I pull out a box of loaded potato skins and another of fried green beans. "I think these will work."

"Heck, yeah! Perfect!" Traxx sits on the other side of the bar, while I pre-heat the oven and take out some flat baking pans, getting everything situated.

"What do you feel like doing in the meantime?" He asks me. If he only knew. Could I jump to the part where I get to touch all of him? I've never felt so devious in my entire life. God, it feels great!

"Well, I was thinking we could start with taking a shot of tequila? I have some cold Tres Agaves Anejo." I move towards the freezer to get the bottle out.

"Nice!" He gives me a questioning look. "Everything okay?"

"Yes. It hasn't been this good in a long time." I place the two shot glasses on the counter between us and pour the cold courage serum in each. This is not cheap tequila and there is no need to cover up the taste with lime and salt. We each reach out for our glasses and do a quick toast.

"To us." He says looking at me right into my eyes. I frown slightly because I start to wonder if he knows what I'm up to.

"To us." I repeat, we clink and throwback the warm liquid.

The oven beeps indicating it's preheated and I put our snacks in, setting up the timer so I don't forget to take them out or overcook them.

"I had a tough day." He offers. I immediately give him my full attention.

"What happened?"

I was reflecting on my past, present and future. I'm so ready to make some positive changes."

This is good.

"What changes would you like to make?" I put both of my fists under my chin and listen intently.

"Well, that's part of my problem. I'm not sure yet. I know I don't want to be selfish and take the important people in my life for granted."

Really? I nod and wait.

"Yes. I've decided that you are right and I need to live in the moment and without fear."

Oh, my!

"That's great news, Traxx. There is nothing worse than going through life, going through the motions, without living every day as if it is your last while enjoying all the experiences that life has to offer."

"So, are you willing to help me figure out the next step? I mean, I know that's not your job, but I must confess that when we hang out and create new experiences together, I'm able to put some distance from what happened with Marcy. I don't find myself thinking about it – about her - all day and most importantly having nightmares about her every night. I don't think about me, either. I find myself thinking about a person who's a hell of a lot more important to me than anyone else has ever been."

His eyes zero in on mine, and I'm trapped under his stare. I feel my insides melting and all that wetness is currently taking residence between my thighs. This man! He has such control of my body and doesn't even know it. My phone starts to chime – it's my message alert. I move to answer it, and Traxx grabs my hand to get my attention. I twist my shoulders to reach for the phone.

"I'm not finished. There are other things I want to say."

Nodding once to show my agreement, it pains me to pull my hand from under his, but I move towards the phone because emergencies happen all day, every day. I have an emergency right now. I'm burning from the inside out into invisible ashes because Traxx's smoldering gaze is proving to be more than I can handle.

Keagan: Hey! What are you doing?

Ciara: I was baking for work. Traxx's here. He's going to do a taste test.

Keagan: Is he now? ;) Oh, I wonder how that will end... Anywho, I was checking to see if you want to go to dinner with dad. He misses you.

Ciara: Awww, tell him I will catch up with him next time.

Keagan: I might stay at home tonight. There's no telling what kind of shenanigans will be going on at my apartment. LOL

Ciara: Stop it!

Keagan: I want a full report tomorrow!

Ciara: OK!

Well that was that. I guess I'm now all by myself in resisting temptation. The things that I get stuck with! I turn towards Traxx and smile. I move deliberately towards him. My fingers are crossed behind my back.

"Who was that?" He asks me.

"That was Keagan. She was asking me out to dinner with her dad." Traxx looks disappointed.

"Uh, okay, I guess I will see you later?"

I shook my head lightly from side to side. "No, you don't have to leave. I don't want to go to dinner."

"Why not? You know my uncle will be going to a fancy place and he pays for everything."

"Well, I hate to throw food away and we are already cooking a bunch of stuff." I said nonchalantly.

Traxx smiles deviously. "I can stay here until everything's ready and I will pack it up and put it away for you." He gives me a suspicious look.

"N-Nah, it's okay. I can catch up with them another time."

"Ciara, why does it feel like you are not being honest with me?"

I bring my hands around and since I have no pockets, I end up crossing my arms in front of my chest. How do I expect Traxx to be honest with me if I'm not honest with him?

"Well, that's only part of it." I take a couple more steps to be closer to him. "Would it be so bad if I say I'm enjoying myself right here, with you?" This takes him by surprise and I'm not sure that he knows what to do with the information.

"That wouldn't be bad at all. It would actually be really awesome for me."

"Okay, then." Nodding, I turn to walk towards the coffee table and pick up the pack of cards I had set there earlier.

Traxx comes to me with another shot and hands it over. "I think we both need one more of this 'truth serum' extraordinaire."

I grab the offering and lift my hand for a toast. This time, I'm the first one that says it. "To us." And a warm smile spreads on my face.

"To *us*." We clink and drink up.

After handing him my empty shot glass, I show him the pack of cards and ask the question. "How would you like to play Uno?"

He laughs. "It's been years since I played that game. Are you out of regular cards or what?"

"Oh, dear Traxx, where is your sense of adventure? Besides I can guarantee you that you will love this version of the game."

"Which version?"

I smile and wink at him when I answer his question, "We are playing *strip* Uno."

He gives me a double take. "What do you mean strip Uno?"

"It's just like strip poker, but we will use Uno cards instead. There's really not that much to it." I was trying to keep calm. This is the moment to sink or swim. If he says no, then I will know for sure that it's time to move on, because I'm obviously wrong about his feelings for me. And if he says yes... well... I know what I'm hoping for.

He's awfully quiet, and he's pinching his bottom lip between his thumb and index finger. It's a sure sign that he's nervous. I keep quiet because I don't want to influence his choice, but I'm dying! I do know that I don't need to resort to these games. I could talk to him and find out what's on his mind, but where is the fun in that? Besides, there's a method to my madness, a reason for all of this. I need to make an impact because he needs to understand that some decisions need to be made in trust, and this is one of them.

"Okay, BUT..." His voice lowers to a whisper, "strip to underwear only. I'm not responsible of the things that may happen if we go further than that." He gives me a smile and a wink and just like that, Step 3 of the "Bring Traxx Back" plan is on!

The buzz of the oven gets my attention and I hand him the pack of cards. "Shuffle these, please? I will get the food."

When I come back with our snacks and a couple of beers, he has the game setup. I place the tray on the other side of the coffee table, and sit across from him.

"Are you ready to lose your clothes and be my bitch?" I ask him trying to keep it fun.

"Bring it!"

The game is on.

CHAPTER 9

Traxx

This ought to be interesting... What is Ciara up to? I'd be a fool not to take the bait. She's so adorable... Strip Uno, for real.

"You know, I could go get regular cards and we can play strip poker." I give her a wink just to see the pink color move up her sexy neck until it reaches her cheeks.

"Red reverse. My turn again. Red skip. Uno! Are you scared that you may lose? I'd rather keep playing this game."

"I don't have a red card."

"Dude, help yourself and grab a card from the pack until you get a red one or a skip." She's so proud of herself that I'm sitting here barefoot, no tie, no shirt, no belt. Only have my pants and undershirt left. She has on her tank top and yoga pants. We're pretty even so far.

I grab a card from the deck. "Draw four!"

"Ugh! I don't know how you do it! You are the luckiest Uno player I've ever seen!" We laugh.

"I know! Here, look blue reverse, wild card, Uno! I call yellow." She puts down a yellow nine and looks at me expectantly.

"Boom! I win!" I jump up and do a happy dance.

"Crap, crap, crap!" She is laughing hard. "Okay, there goes my tank top." I swallow hard. Frozen in place, I'm hypnotized by what's happening as Ciara gets up from the chair and starts to shimmy out of the tank by grabbing the bottom seam and working it up slowly over her head while dancing to the music and moving her hips rhythmically. The girl has some enticing curves. I swallow dry and try to pay attention – I don't want to miss a thing. I have seen her in a bikini before, but there's this unspoken intimacy about seeing someone in their underwear. The delicate fabric is enticing in addition to the beauty of what it's hiding. Will it spill its secrets for you to admire?

With the tank top now gone, Ciara spins it with her finger, throwing it straight to my chest, breaking the spell I was under.

"You like what you see? Huh?" With her hands on her hip, she's spinning slowly from side to side.

"It's been a while since I've seen you in a bikini. I forgot about your tattoos." I come closer and take a chance by lightly touching her skin. I know I'm playing with fire here, and boy do I feel it – right on contact. The heat and sensation that happened the moment we connected, is something I've never felt before. It's scorching and unexpected. I put my fingers on her right ribcage and trace the nautical star with wings. "For your grandmother, right?" Her grandmother passed away when she was still a little girl, due to cancer. It was a hard time for her and her family as they were very close.

A nod. She inhales sharply through her teeth. Opening her eyes, I watch her face while my hand moves to her side and I look to see the next tattoo's writing is in Latin. It is a vertical line covering her right side.

"What does it say?"

"It says: 'Every breath I take is a memory of how much you were loved.' Also in honor of my grandmother."

It was my turn to nod and take a deep breath. I was forgetting to breathe because her wholesome beauty took my breath away. I was getting lost looking at her perfectly laid out freckles, waiting for me to trace them and reveal a hidden message. I find myself only a step away from covering her body with mine, and I'll be dammed but I refuse to walk back. This here is warm, feels comfortable... easy... feels like something I've been missing.

Raising my hand, I move her hair away from the left side of her neck, and she bends her head slightly to give me the access that I seek. Her hands are no longer on her sides - she has moved them to either side of my waist. My lips get as close as possible to her ear without touching her. I'm afraid if I get to feel her soft skin on my lips, it will be my undoing.

"I thought I remembered this one." I whisper next to her ear. "It's a beautiful cross hidden behind your ear." I blow on it and I feel Ciara shiver. That's when I realize that I want to wrap her in my arms without letting go.

Why do I feel so emotional? This isn't me – or is it? I have hidden away my feelings for so many years I don't know what's going on with me anymore, but it feels... it feels really good, and it scares me. The fear of the unknown acts like a bucket of cold water that has been thrown at me. What the fuck am I doing? I can't go there with Ciara unless I'm absolutely sure that it's what she wants and what I want. I let go of her hair and take a step back. As I put some distance between us, I lose the warmth and security that I felt just mere moments ago.

"I thought this may happen." She states matter of fact as she straightens herself and fixes her hair. "You are wrong from wanting to run away from it. This is your **Step 3 – Live your life with no regrets.**

I'm dumbfounded. Ciara moves towards the side table I was sitting next to, grabs my phone and hands it to me.

"Wait for it." It's all she says.

As she walks away, I let myself fall into a chair holding my head with both of my hands. The things that are happening around my head and my heart are foreign to me, but when I let go, they feel so good. It's an internal satisfaction that I've never experience. Not long after, I hear the familiar beep of my phone indicating I have a message. Only this time it's a video. A video that Ciara sent me just now.

I look around, stretching my neck, trying to get a glimpse of Ciara. Nothing. She must be in the bedroom.

I stare at the video screen. My heart's racing and I feel very nervous. What if she's tired of my inability to make a decision about her? Maybe she's decided I'm not worth saving, after all. Maybe she's tired of trying to put me back together. Can I make it without her? *No!* I don't want to. I need to know what's on this video and I'm scared as hell to press "Play."

I force my thumb to slide over the fateful triangle on the center of the screen. Ciara is smiling. She has a stack of paper in front of her. She grabs the piece on top and shows it to the camera:

Traxx

She lays the paper down and grabs the next one. This is going to be one of those message videos like the ones I've seen on YouTube.

You think it's your fault
but it's not
stop blaming yourself
I want you
to see what I see
when I look at you
I see a man who's
honest
kind
giving
strong

loyal
bold
thoughtful
GOOD
you need to see yourself
the way I see you
I'm your mirror
Look at me
and see yourself
love yourself
the way I love you
you <u>are</u> worth it
Live your life
with no regrets

The video ends. I have no words. I have never seen myself the way she sees me, what she sees *in* me. I lift my head in time to watch her walk from the hallway entrance towards me. No words are said. No words are needed. Our eyes are each other's slaves, captured and kept away from anything else. She's all I see. She's everything I've ever wanted. I want to feel her love. I've never been with anyone who loved me and cared, really cared about me. Something inside is stirring and making an appearance. I feel need, but I also feel something else I can't quite pinpoint.

At that moment, Ciara is in front of me. Although I'm already looking at her, her hands run through either side of my hair and as she makes a fist with my hair tangled around her fingers, and pulls down hard enough I can't look away.

Putting the phone on the seat next to me I take a moment to inhale everything about her. She's still wearing the cute pink bra with black polka dots she had earlier. She smells like fruit and sin all mixed into one beautiful package. We look into each other's eyes and before anything can be said, I try to store away this moment of pure perfection.

With her hands still in my hair, Ciara starts to move closer… She straddles me and sits on my lap, but not quite on top of *it*. My male instincts want to grab her and move her so close to me that we cannot know whose heartbeat is the one we hear. So close, that the air fails to circulate in between us, and no one would know where her skin begins and mine ends, in a seamless body full of passion, heat and desire.

I force my hands to land on her tights, and I squeeze gently. Still looking at her eyes, I ask her, "Ciara, what are you doing?"

"I thought I was being pretty obvious." A small side-smile appears on her glossy lips.

"This may not be a good idea." I found myself saying in a painful show of resistance.

"Traxx…" She whispers. "I'm here for you. Not part-time, not sometimes, not when I feel like it or when you want to be distracted. I'm here for you always. *Always*. Whatever happens, there will be no regrets on my part, as it shouldn't be on your part. Who knows? You may like it."

"Ciara..." I swallow hard. "Your eyes... The way your eyes are looking at me... You are seeing the real me and you want me, still. Your eyes are like a summer's midnight sky, a pair of jewels that make me the luckiest bastard in the fucking world."

Smiling, she takes a deep breath. She scoots closer, *hell yeah*, a lot closer than before. I feel her weight fully unload on top of me. Wrapping her arms around the back of my neck we are so close that, when I breathe, my chest's raising up and down cause her to move as well. I find that I like having her close like this on top of me. I fucking love it.

"Traxx... We can't keep denying us from each other." She lands a gentle kiss on my left cheek. "We deserve to know what this could be like." Another one on the right cheek. "I'm not going to say that it will be easy, but I know for sure that it will be worth it." Her succulent lips are now barely a breath away from mine. Anguish makes its presence known inside my head, as I struggle to decide what the right thing to do is. She carefully looks at me, and I tighten up the grip I have on her thighs. They are my anchor and if I let go of them there will be no other options, I will not only take this woman - I will brand her. I will possess her. I will ruin her the same way she's ruining me for anyone else. Her lips move and I try to make my brain clear the lust fog and listen coherently.

"Marcy doesn't define you, Traxx. *You define you.* Be yourself. Stop the self-bashing and self-hate. If you don't want to be the Traxx of your past, you don't have to be. Leave that Traxx behind you. Take all the goodness you have to offer and move forward. Make a new trail and lead the way so that when you look back, you can feel proud of who you've become.

"I'm not asking for a lifetime, Traxx. Only one night. Tonight. Let's make it memorable. Not like those one night stands from your past, but a special night where we give *us* to each other one hundred percent. I want you to experience something beautiful. I want to give that to you."

She kisses me gently on the side of my mouth.

Fuck!

I tried! Hell, I tried so hard but I'm only fucking human. This girl… She makes me feel things deep inside my chest. Things I've never felt before but they are so good, I don't want to ever stop.

My hands finally let go of their self-imposed prison. One goes directly to her waist and the other to the back of her neck. Now they have the control they've been wanting. My palms fill with her skin, my thoughts of restraint and proper behavior float away, leaving me in completely and utterly raw form. As I pull her slowly, closer to me until our mouths are perfectly aligned, I finally let go, crushing her lips with mine, fast and furious. This kiss is powerful, strong, sensual and freeing. That's the moment when I allow myself to feel unbound and happy, to let this *thing* between us consume me all the way to my bones.

Ciara

His brown eyes have gotten darker, filled with desire and lust. I'm so close, *so close* to him that in every breath I take, I inhale his masculine scent, and *I want it*, I want him to mark me, brand me, fuse me to him. Do with me as he pleases. I want to lose control and find myself in a world where there's only him and me. I speak from the heart. We will never find out what this thing is, unless we explore it, and I'm sitting here ready to let go of everything I feel. I'm ready to let him have me. Yes, I'm willingly giving myself to him because I don't think I could walk away even if I wanted to. And just for the sake of clarification, I want to be right where I am. There is no better place than on top of this beautiful man who I have grown to care so much for.

Finally after what seemed like forever, his lips crashed with mine. Tender and wanton, soft and firm, expert and curious all at the same time. An explosion of longing, a union of cravings that finally starts to diffuse the edge we were threading before now.

My hands tangled in his hair, his fists pulling mine to get me closer still. We fill each other with touch, leaving words out of this equation of parallel desire and passion. When the temporary assault on my lips slows, he moves to my jawline, following the defined edge of bone and skin and leaving an angry trail caused by his unshaven face. I'm enjoying every second of this. When his purposeful lips find a particular spot on my neck, the kissing starts all anew. I feel his tongue marking me right below my ear, where I his hot breath collides with my wet skin causing me to shiver. His deep voice interrupts his actions and all I can think is that I need more of him.

"Shhh, baby, it's okay, I will keep you warm… I need to taste *you*."

Gently, he bites and runs the edge of his teeth down my neck, ending by kissing me first on my shoulder, then lower and lower still, until he reaches the upper curve of my breast.

"Are you sure this is what you want? I can't promise tomorrow, Ciara, all I have is right now. Is that going to be enough? If not just tell me to stop, baby, and as much as it would fucking kill me, I would do it for you."

The sincerity in his eyes gives me pause for a millisecond. I know what I want, who I want. Even if it's only for tonight, I had come to terms with that possibility. I'm unable to answer in any other way but looking at him trying to emulate everything I've felt for him all these years, words escape me so I do the next best thing and capture his lips with mine once again. I can't get enough of him. I'm living in the moment, without fear or regret. A whimper surfaces between the two of us.

"Fuck, Ciara, it's not fair for you to make those sexy sounds. When I hear you do that, it makes me want to do bad things to you, bad things that you'd enjoy so much you'll beg me to do them again."

"Traxx, I need you." While I kiss him, my hand moves between our bodies and glides against his pants until it finds the one thing between us standing up. I grab it confidently and stroke it from bottom to top, enjoying its length and thickness against my hand.

Hissing, his hands move to cup my breasts and pinch my nipples while licking and gently biting them. "Are you trying to get ahead, baby? You are not playing fair, girl. You are forcing me to be naughty in order to even out the game."

His hands take the cups of my bra and simultaneously pull down on them, exposing my bare breasts to him.

"Fuck! Look at these perky tits." He sucks on one of my nipples. "They are so hard for me." He moves on to the other one. "I think they are trying to compete with my dick to see who gets harder." I feel the heat move up to my cheeks. "There it is! I love it when you blush."

"Traxx," I grab his face and make him look at me. "I *need* you."

"Baby, tell me what you need? I want to give you anything, anything at all, but I can't read your mind, so you need to talk and tell me."

I growl on desperation, because he wants to make me talk dirty and I'm not good at it. So I decide that I need to show him. Covering his hand with mine, I move it south. We encounter a bit of resistance on the waist due to my yoga pants, but driving on, I get him to the area that's drenched with want.

"Shit baby, you are so ready. I have bad news and good news. Which one do you want first?" I take my hand out of my pants and leave his there, letting him to gently touch around my needy parts but not putting pressure on anything specific, causing me to move around some, to see if I can persuade him to get to the goods faster.

"Tell me the good one." I whisper-talk to his ear.

"The good news is that I know exactly what to do in this situation."

I smile. That's fucking great news. Like I had any doubts. "And the bad one?"

"I can't let our first time take place on this tiny couch. There are plenty of things I'm about to do to you, and I need space and comfort." He gets a hold of my ass and swiftly lifts me with him, which causes me to giggle. "Hold onNibblet, we are moving thisto your bed."

Tightening my legs which are now wrapped around his waist and once again I cross my arms behind his neck. We are now forehead to forehead and nose to nose. "You are so hot, Ciara, I need you. I want you so badly. It feels different. Being with you is special in ways I cannot yet say."

"I know. I feel it too." I try to convey the sincerity of this truth. He smells so good, clean and masculine. I place my face on the crook of his neck and inhale deeply. When we get to the bedroom, he's gentle as he releases me on the edge of the bed, and kneels in front of me.

After another hot kiss, Traxx places his thumb on my lips and traces the lines around them. I can see the concern on his face, when he softly looks into my eyes and asks, "Are you sure?"

I nod with certainty, and start to remove my yoga pants when he interrupts me. "Oh, hell no, I'm doing it. You have no idea how many times I imagined this moment happening and I'm going to enjoy every fucking second of it. You are mine, Ciara, to do as I please, and I promise, you will love it." He gives me his panty dropping smile and I smile back at him. He grabs my hair and guides my mouth to his again, his tongue moving in and out, touching mine. With it and his expert lips, he tastes everything, my tongue, my lips, the roof of my mouth, the inside of my lips where they meet the gums. I didn't expect that to feel sexy, but it does.

"Scoot up, baby, I'm getting ready to see your entire sweet body, and planning to taste every fucking inch of it."

I do as requested. His dirty talk has me soaked between my legs. The anticipation is killing me and it's the best, sweetest torture I've ever been under. As I move up in the bed, he's removing the rest of his clothes, leaving on a pair of red boxer briefs with black band and trim. I can see a small wet spot at the tip of his large dick and I want to taste it so I reach out for it.

"Nope, not yet... Lean back down. Good, just like that. If you touch me right now I may lose my shit, we gotta do this in a proper way, baby."

Leaning on top of me, he supports his weight with his hands so that his body is not touching mine, and it feels so cold. I need his touch to set me on fire. Wanting something, any kind of connection, I reach for his uppers arms and hold on to him.

"I'm going to taste you now. Be a good girl and tell me when it feels good and when you want more, mmmkay?" He lowers his body and I feel like I'm way overdressed, but let him do his thing.

He starts to kiss my chest and then entertains my breasts taking care of my hard nipples by sucking hard and after releasing them, his teeth gently go around each one with the perfect amount of pressure earning him a runaway whimper. He's such a biter – I would have never pictured that! Feeling like I'm falling behind, my hands rub all over his back, his shoulders, his hair...

"Traxx, I need *more*..."

"Mmm... I know... My little minx is getting desperate, huh?" I shake my head up and down. He leans down and reached for my bra's hooks and swiftly disposes of it.

"Now we are getting there, I love your tits. They are the perfect handful. I'm gonna love to see them jiggle and can't wait to hold on to them when I take your pussy from behind."

I feel the heat rushing to my face.

"There it is. I'm going to live the rest of my life just looking forward to every moment I get to put that on your beautiful face." I smile and look away because I'm embarrassed with the dirty talk.

I feel a hand cupping me between my legs. "There is no looking away in this game, sweetheart." That gets my attention. He moves his fingers to the seam of my pants and slides them painfully slow to each one of my sides, then he starts to pull my yoga pants down. When my pink thong with black lace ribbon is revealed, I see his dick twitching.

"Well, hello there, Mr. Twitch."

He smiles and continues. "I'm not sure if I want to take it off or just move it around out of the way." He pulls my thong string up and to the side. "Let's play it by ear, shall we begin?"

I nod frantically. *Finally*.

"If I remember correctly, I think someone was saying something about needing more? Is that still the case?"

Another nod.

He holds the string to the side with one hand and then with the other, uses one of his skilled fingers to enter me as deep as possible, the anticipation makes me jump a little, until his finger is all the way in and I can feel him circling around, looking for my sweet spot.

"Hell, yeah, baby you are so ready for me, I love it."

He pulls out his finger, way too soon, but when he brings it to his mouth and sucks hard on it, I feel a new wave of heat flood between my legs.

"Mmm, salty and sweet. It's fucking perfect. I need some more of that." His head lowers between my legs and I let the man begin his work.

Traxx places my legs over his shoulders and his arms go around them to keep me secure in place. *Oh, my!* He starts by licking me from bottom to top, and then he goes around a couple of times, ending with firm flicks on my clit. The pleasure is more than I can take so my hands leave the strangling hold I had on the blanket and replace it with his hair. My hips start to move into a game of finders keepers, where I want to be the victor.

"Hell yeah, baby, you like that?"

I mumble something unintelligible but it resembles a yes, so he keeps going, adding humming and a little chin action where his five o'clock shadow causes havoc on my pussy. "Fingers! Please?"

He chuckles and I feel his lock on one of my thighs give away so that he can bring his hand around and penetrate me with his fingers. The other hand continues to open up full access to the bundle of nerves being attacked by his mouth and tongue. He's alternating from sucking to licking. On the inside, his fingers have found the right spot and it's all too much… Too much… Everything's tightening up and then… I break apart into beautiful stars flying all over the place invading the darkness of my closed eyes. I ride the waves and shake until I can't take it anymore, then I gently release his hair, which until now, I hadn't realized I was pulling.

Traxx's kissing my abdomen, building a line of kisses that divides the left side of my body from the right one, slowly moving up my chest, neck, until he reaches my lips. When he kisses me, I taste the remains of myself all over his mouth and it's sexy as hell.

"You are very vocal when in the throes of 'pleasure.'"

"I'm not vocal. You have me confused with someone else."

"Baby, that's impossible. I heard you loud and clear and I enjoyed every single little sound you made while I was taking care of you. But we are barely getting started. That was only the opening act. Are you ready for the headliner? I heard he's a hardass and gives as good as he takes." He winks at me.

"Seriously? Conceited much?" I place my hands on his chest where I can feel the beating of his heart and it just makes everything a lot more real. "I like it that you have not lost your confidence in the sack, 'cause I can benefit a lot out of it."

He gets off the bed and a few seconds later comes back without underwear and with a golden pouch on his hand. I sit up and try to get my lips around his cock before he wraps it up. Traxx grabs my chin and pulls my face up so he can look at me.

"You can't do that right now... I'm way too needy and I, well... I will not last five seconds if your lips touch me *there*." He points to a very hard dick that's waiting for his reward. I lick my lips when I see a droplet of cum on his tip, and gently reach out my hand and with my index finger I wipe it clean. The loaded finger comes back towards my mouth, where I finally get a taste of him.

"*Fuuuck!*" He growls at me while I smile back. It's fair game. Using his teeth, he rips open the foil and has the condom on before I can blink. "C'mere baby." He gives me a burning kiss as I slowly fall back with him on top. He pulls the side strings of my thong and rips them up, pulling to one side in order to remove the very wet pink thong I still managed to somehow keep on until now.

"I hope you didn't like them too much. I needed to get to you fast."

My nails rake his hard back starting on his shoulders and ending on his ass. Using his knee, he opens me up and lines himself perfectly on my opening. His hands go to either side of my head when he starts going in slow and steady.

"Oooh, fuck, Ciara, you feel so fucking good!" As he stretched me, his mouth got busy with mine and his kisses grew intense and hungry to distract me from his final push to the hilt that showed me how good this was about to be.

His mouth moved to my nipple, while his pelvis was doing a dance of its own. After the first push, he never again entered me on a straight line. He was moving in what felt like a small circle, pulling out while moving from top to bottom and pushing in while moving from bottom to top. These actions were causing his cock to hit my g-spot every time, and as the pleasure was making us climb higher, the friction was promising an unbelievable release.

His mouth moved from my breasts to my neck, his grunting got louder and his drilling got harder. Then he lifted up my ass, never leaving me empty, and twisted me around so I was on my hands and knees. Then, one of his arms crossed in front of my chest pulling me up to a semi-seated position. His hand was squeezing and massaging my breast holding me in place, the other hand took a fistful of my hair, pulling me hard so that my exposed skin was in front of his mouth. After that, his mouth was on my shoulder, neck and ear – I was so drenched at this point… and his dick was exactly where it needed to be, deep as hell inside of me. With his legs on the outside of mine, he had much better balance and was able to move fast and hard. It was heaven.

I was holding on for dear life to a pillow on one side and one of his arms on the other, loving every second of his grunting next to my ear, as his skilled hips worked me back up into a frenzy and after a few minutes of glorious pounding, with the sound or rawness all around us, he muttered, "I'm coming!"

Almost there myself, I'd already started to feel the tightening of my walls, and when he went from licking my neck and ear to biting me on my shoulder, we finally climbed that peak, screaming each other's names and reaching a high that made us feel like we could float away from reality and leave our problems behind.

I felt needed. I felt cared for. I felt loved.

I wondered how it was for him.

Creepers

From the apartments' parking lot, one creeper writes on their notebook the time they started watch and what they have been able to observe.

"Where is he?"

"Not sure. He has not been at the apartment all night. I saw the other guy, the blond one, but not him."

"You don't think he's back at it again, do you?"

Putting the binoculars on its face, the creeper takes another look around.

"He ain't there, but his truck is here. He's either in the blonde girls place, or somehow we missed him leaving with someone else."

"We didn't miss him. We've been looking at everyone coming and going all night and he wasn't one of them."

"I believe it's time."

The other creeper nods in agreement.

"Let's go to the house for a few hours and then we'll come back and go inside. Maybe we can find something to benefit our plan."

With that said, the creeper on the driver side starts the vehicle, puts the car in gear and drives away for now.

CHAPTER 10

Traxx

It was the best night of my life. I can't believe that I finally had her. All those nights I spent jacking myself to images of her, were a drop of water compared to the ocean of the real thing. It felt so fucking good. We played the game of give and take until we were sated and tired as hell. I ended up waking her up twice and she woke me up once in between. If I could have her again, I would, but she's finally in a deep sleep and the sun is peaking through the blinds, which means my time with her is about to end.

Reality can be a bitch sometimes. I finally found a girl that I can trust. She's beautiful, sexy and smart. Loyal and the best friend anyone could have. She has been giving everything to try to help me work on my issues. And I'm still scared. I'm scared that I don't measure up. I've always said she's too good for me. But yet, here we lay in each other's arms. Exhausted because she felt I *was* good enough. This night…I can't call it fucking because it meant something to me. It's a whole lot more than that. It's so different from all those one night stands I used to have. She has my heart right now. She's been pulling me together and she has the power to break me apart. Should I take a chance? I can feel my insecurities taking over and I'm disgusted with myself.

Does she know she has my heart?

Is she capable of breaking the one person she claims to care for?

If I cannot give her one hundred and ten percent, then I need to walk away.

Walk away, man. Walk away.

You've been doing it your whole life. It shouldn't be hard.

Don't let her get more invested.

She will hate me.

She will hate me more if I don't measure up to her expectations.

What if I never heal?

What if I stay dismantled?

Sigh. The pressure and stress are taking over and I just can't…I don't want to deal. I slowly remove myself from her embrace. She stirs around a little but doesn't wake up.

Marcy is back in my ear. "You are back to your old antics, Traxx. I knew it wouldn't last."

"Shut up!" I blink and realize I've spoken out loud.

"Huh?"

I curse silently and notice that Ciara's wiping her face with her hands. She's waking up. I panic and start to put on my pants. I can carry everything else in my hands.

"Traxx?"

"Yeah?"

"Where are you going?"

Her question is less of a question and more like concern. My lack of an answer makes her more aware of the situation and she sits up on the bed, covering with the sheets.

"I see. Were you going to leave me without saying goodbye?"

I can't even look at her when I nod my head to let her know she is correct.

"Why?"

I take a deep breath. "I can't answer your questions right now. I'm suffocating at the moment and I need to leave."

"Traxx," she says calmly, "this is in no way a threat, but if you leave right now without telling me what's going on, I'm going to assume that everything that has happened between us was a mistake and… if you leave right now, I'm going to believe that you are giving up on us. I will move on. I can't keep waiting for you to be ready. It hurts too much."

My heart's racing fast and I'm afraid I'm going to have a breakdown in front of her. I can't have her see me like that again. I need to leave and get my shit together and talk to her when I figure it all out. "I can't Ciara, I just can't deal with all of this right now. I'm so sorry."

All the prevention I was trying to put in place for protection fails me, because the moment I see a tear running down her cheek, the few parts of my heart that we worked so hard to put together fall completely apart, pain and shame fill the hollows inside my chest and even then, I still turn around towards the door and walk away, leaving behind the only person that has ever truly wanted me.

Ciara

Stupid. I'm so fucking stupid. I can't believe that I thought if I showed him what true love was, that he would realize it was the one thing missing from his life.

Wiping the tears running down my face, I grab a tissue from my nightstand to take care of my runny nose. I can't continue to wait for him. He needs to figure out what he wants, what he needs. Oh God please let it be me!

I take a minute to think clearly. What the fuck am I doing? I have *never* cried over a man, and I'm really not about to continue doing this. It's been a couple of hours since he walked out of this apartment and away from me and I'm done crying my eyes out. It doesn't mean that I will not miss him, because I most definitely will, but I can't live my life like this.

I made a promise to myself: To live in the moment, without fear or regret. I wanted last night to happen. I enjoyed it immensely and now that it's over,

I will move on. No more crying. If he doesn't think that I'm worth it to sit down and talk to like grown-ups, then fuck him. He doesn't get to have one more minute of my time. I just wish I didn't feel like my heart just shattered in a hundred million pieces.

When I was a little girl, my mom always taught me that when we feel sad, or down, I need to make sure I wear something that makes me feel beautiful, do my hair and makeup as if I was going to a pageant, because if I look good, I will feel good. It's not a remedy, but a temporary solution to be able to put one foot in front of the other and keep on keeping on.

I hear my phone ring. It's Notso. Taking a deep breath, I mentally prepare myself to not break down while talking to him. We're really close friends. He knows me really well. I slide the green button and answer.

"Hey Notso, what's up?"

"Why don't you tell me?"

Shit.

"I'm not sure what are you talking about."

"I'm talking about Traxx, Ciara. Please don't play dumb with me."

"What happened?"

"He came in half naked talking on the phone with Wyatt, and next thing I know, he's getting a bag ready because he's flying to Texas to help his brother pack and drive down here. Traxx and Wyatt have never been close like that. Why now? Last I heard, he was going to stop by your place last night. By the looks of him this morning, he not only stopped, but he spent the night with you, although he would not tell me. Did he hurt you? 'Cause I'd kill him! I would go to the airport and bash his pretty face right in. Just say so, sug, and I will do it."

My eyes produce yet more tears that threaten to spill. Notso is so sweet. He's always been like my big brother and he has looked after me for years. Even though I want to bash Traxx's face myself, I'm not going to sell him out. I knew what I was getting into.

"It's all good, Notso. No worries."

He laughs sarcastically on the phone. "Are you sure?"

"Yes, I'm sure… Notso, let's keep this between us for now, please?"

"Of course, sweetheart. Whatever you want, but please, call me if you need anything or if you just want to talk. Okay?"

"Okay."

I hang up and get back with the plan – pick nice clothes, hair and makeup. Oh, and awesome shoes – how did I ever forget that? Also, I need to make an amendment to my mom's teaching: Getting drunk.

Alcohol is calling me. I must get drunk tonight, then I will have the liquid courage to finally let go.

Creepers

They sat in the now familiar parking lot waiting for Notso to leave for the day. They already saw Traxx drive away with a large bag. Now they want to find out what's going on with him.

As soon as Notso pulls out of the parking lot, they are on the move. Grabbing their supplies from the back of their vehicle they set out to do what they came here for.

After opening the door, they set the supplies to the side and start snooping. They go through the mail, the kitchen, the trash, the laundry. In Traxx's bedroom, they find a notepad with an airline's flight information. A picture is taken of said note.

"The boss won't be happy about this."

"It's not our fault." The creeper shrugs its shoulders. "I'm getting tired of the following and the snooping. I'm ready to take our plan to the next level."

"Yeah, yeah. We need to find out where he's going and when he's supposed to come back."

"Let's finish up this job and go back to our place to do some research on flights and destinations."

After the other creeper nods in agreement, they set out to do as agreed and continue with their plan.

CHAPTER 11

Traxx

It's a long fucking drive from Texas to Florida. Ass face over here hates driving long distance, so I'm doing it. I've never been too close to my brother – or should I say half-brother, mainly because our mothers couldn't stand each other. But our dad tried to make sure we saw each other at least once each year. We would take a flight and go to Dallas, Texas to pick up Wyatt and then we would go away for two weeks, just us boys. Damn, I miss those simple days. Some years we would go fishing, other times we would get lost visiting a city we've never been before, but we were always happy and had fun. I glance at him and we are almost identical. He's buff like me but about one inch taller. We both have dark hair and olive skin. Our lips and jaws are identical. He has green eyes and I have brown eyes – that's the main difference, that and our personalities. He was blessed with the easy going kind and I'm the brooding kind.

Now Dad has convinced Wyatt to move over to the Florida office and created a position just for him. Wyatt is a nice guy but ruthless when it comes to business. If I was a customer, I would want him handling all my accounts.

The first few days I was away, I spent my time working hard trying to forget about Ciara. I haven't been successful. She is always inside my head and in my heart. I can't believe I left the way I did. I know she believes we should go through life without regrets, but there's no fucking way I don't regret walking away from her the way I did. I'm such a fucking asshole. I've picked up my phone to call her at least a hundred times, but never make the call. The groveling I'm going to have to do, will have to be done in person.

I've been wondering what she is up to. Torturing myself thinking that maybe she hooked up with some random dude. The thought alone that someone may be kissing and touching her soft skin... No! I refuse to believe she has moved on. No fucking way. Our time together may have had a rough start but it was special. I'm ready to make amends. I've been so consumed by thoughts of what I let go of, that I haven't had any visions of Marcy since I went to Texas.

"There's that look again. The one that makes you look constipated but you're really just pissed off."

"Fuck off, Wyatt." He aggravates the shit out of me.

"Tell me, bro, what's got your panties in a wad? Or should I say who's got you like this"

"I sure hope that's not the way you talk to the investors."

"Hell no! Dad would have a conniption. But really, what's got you thinking so hard? I'm a good listener."

"I don't want to talk about it."

"It's a long ride, we still have hours to kill."

I say nothing.

"I bet it's about a girl. I was the same way a few weeks back when Sarah broke up with me. *So I know.* That's another reason why I agreed to move."

Silence.

"Okay, suit yourself." His hand reaches for the radio, set it on Bluetooth and the sad guitar strings of country music come thru the speakers. Fucking great.

Traxx

We finally get to the apartment and I quickly scan the parking lot for her car. I don't see it. She's normally off work by this time. I try not to let my mind wonder too much. I *obviously* have a wild ass imagination given that I can see dead people interacting with me, so no, I try not to think too much about it.

I help Wyatt carry his bags upstairs, and leave his furniture in the locked trailer so we can take it to the storage unit later. He's planning to buy a condo anyway and will be making an appointment with a realtor in the next couple of weeks, as soon as he knows where he wants to go.

"I bet you are wore out, Traxx, after all that driving. Thanks for doing this."

"Don't thank me yet. Payback is gonna be a bitch for you."

"Shit, it ain't my fault that I fall asleep when I drive long distance!"

Putting the bags down, I search inside one pocket for the key and then the other pocket. I can't find it. Maybe it's in my bag. I bend down to start looking for it when I hear a familiar set of steps coming up. *Fuck!*

Of course, she lives on the second floor, so she shouldn't be coming this way. I hear her unlock her door and then music floats through the stairs. I smile because she always has music on. She said she had the system installed for Brianna, because Brianna hated silence but I think she got used to it, too, so after Brianna moved out, she still played music 24/7. The knowledge that she's so close makes me smile. The fact that I have to beg her for forgiveness takes the smile away. I hear her door close and then her steps seem to be getting closer. Yep, she is right here on our landing, looking like an angel.

Ciara's still wearing her work clothes. She had a tight black skirt that hit right above her knees, with a pale blue shirt. Her long blond hair is sporting a loose braid to the side, and she's got some fuck me heels on. My dick just got hard.

She looks at me with a frown on her face then takes a glance at all the bags on the floor. When her eyes get to Wyatt, a fucking smile shows out of nowhere. *What the fuck?*

"Hello there, you must be Wyatt." She moves towards him and extends her hand.

"I'm afraid that I don't know who you are and that's a real shame." He gives her his hand and sultry smile.

"Let's fix that. My name is Ciara, Ciara Collins, a *friend* of your brother's and Notso's. I stopped by to drop off some things that Notso asked me to get from the store. I think he's planning on grilling this evening. Here, can you put these groceries in the kitchen for me?"

Another fucking smile. Bastard. "I can take those." I say hoping she looks at me, but she doesn't.

"Nah, brother. You're busy looking for the keys. Carry on, I've got this." And then he winks at her and she blushes FOR HIM. Motherfucker. I'm pissed. If he thinks he's gonna take her away from me, he's got another thing coming.

I hear Wyatt explaining that I've misplaced the keys and how unreliable I can be. I literally bite my tongue because I'm about to kick his ass.

"Traxx, here, use my key." Ciara comes towards me, but refuses to look at me in the eyes.

Aggravated, I try not to snatch the key from her, but after I unlock the door and disable the alarm, I hand the keys back to her. While passing the key to her with one hand, I grab her wrist with my other one.

"Can we talk? I really need to talk to you, Ciara."

Her angry eyes finally look at me. "The talking time has passed, Traxx. We've got nothing to say to each other except for polite comings and goings."

The coldness of her words freezes me in place. I'm shocked. I've never seen her like this. If I was worried before, I'm stressing the fuck out now. I've got to fix this. When Notso gets home, I will grill him for some answers.

She pulls her hand with the keys away from me, and turns around to walk back downstairs. When she passes Wyatt, she smiles like nothing's going on and says goodbye and see you around. Oh, hell no!

We hear her heels step on the wood at a leisure pace, until she reaches her door and all sounds disappear inside her walls.

Wyatt grabs some bags and as he passes by me he shoulder checks me, causing me to stumble a couple of steps.

"What was that for?" I ask him, aggravated.

"For being doggone stupid, that's why. It took me less than a second of your little exchange with Ciara to figure out what was going on between the two of you!"

I invade his personal space and lower my voice to a growl. "Stay out of it."

"The hell I am! You have been acting like a zombie since the incident and I see your reaction in front of this girl, it's obvious. You've got to fix this."

"I can't! Like I always do, I fuck everything up. She warned me and now she's following through with her promise. I can't fix it."

"Okay, then. Since you give up so easily, I guess Ciara's fair game." He gives me a mischievous smile that sends chills all over my skin.

"Fuck, no! Stay away from her!"

"Nah, the girl is a looker! What? Traxx, are you afraid to lose something that you just said you ain't got? Newsflash, you can't have it both ways."

I have to leave or I'm going to bust his ass. I walk to my room to get my spare set of keys. When I open the front door to leave, Notso was getting ready to come in.

"Hey, man! What's going on?" He looks at me and then looks at Wyatt. "Hey, Wyatt! Welcome. What's going on?"

I start to walk away. "I need fresh air. I'll be back later."

As I passed the second floor, I hesitate in front of her door. I put my palm on it and try to decide if I should knock or not. I don't even know what to say. At the last minute I walk away. I'm always walking away. She was clear she didn't want anything else from me. I don't blame her. I've always known I'm not good enough.

Ciara

I can't believe the pull I felt when I saw Traxx earlier today. All I wanted to do was to throw myself at him and forget about all the stupid things he did. It was so hard not to look at him. Although, Wyatt could be his twin. My goodness, they look so much alike, it's uncanny. Ultimately, I was strong. I did what I was supposed to do. But, wait, if I did what I was supposed to do, why do I feel so rotten inside?

Keagan comes in as happy as usual. I've been so sad these past few days, everyone has been walking on eggshells around me.

"Hey sweet pea! Whatcha doin'?"

"I'm sitting here, feeling sorry for myself."

"Wanna talk 'bout it?"

I take a deep breath. I haven't told anyone. They think Traxx and I had a fight and that's it. I'm not ready for all of them to feel sorry for me and be mad at him.

"Nah. Maybe later. What are you doing for supper?"

"Notso is grillin'. He wants *us* to come and eat with him and Wyatt. I can't wait to see my cousin! I've missed him!"

"Just him and Wyatt? Where's Traxx?"

They don't know for sure. They think probably at Colton's. If not, he's probably drowning his problems at a bar, visiting with Jack Daniel's. Don't you worry about him. He's a big boy and he can take care of himself."

Feeling like the entire world is on top of my shoulders, I get up off my couch slowly. I've changed into jeans and a comfy shirt. "Let me go put on some shoes and I'll come up with you." Keagan nods, and even though I don't feel like it, I have to face my friends and face the world. We'll see if those acting classes I took in High School were worth it.

Ciara

Wyatt opens the door and Keagan jumps on him into a big embrace. They look so sweet and happy, I feel a small twinge of jealousy inside. I want to be happy too, but first I need to figure out a way to resolve my feelings for Traxx.

Wyatt sets Keagan down and she leaves for the balcony to see Notso, and Wyatt turns towards me with an assuring smile. "Welcome back, Ciara." He extends his hand, and I politely put my hand on his. He takes it and brings it to his lips, placing a gentle kiss on top of it. It makes me smile.

He looks down and sees my cowboy boots. Smiling he asks, "You own cowboy boots?"

"Heck, yeah! Boy, I'm originally from Alabama, of course I'm going to have some. I put them on to show you support since you come from Texas and all."

"Awesome!"

"I hear you guys are grillin'? I'm starved. Is the food ready?"

"Almost, come on, let's go outside. It's a beautiful night. Would you like a beer?"

"Yes, please."

As the night went on, I learned a lot about Traxx's childhood. I kept staring at Wyatt and inside my head I imagined that he was Traxx and that everything was perfect between us. Don't ask. I have no idea why I continue to trick myself into thinking that we can be something great together. He doesn't want me.

At the end of the night, Keagan and Notso headed to the stair and then something unexpected happened.

"Ciara, before you leave, I wanted to ask you if you have some time, would you like to go out to dinner tomorrow? As friends, of course. It's been a while since I had the company of a beautiful girl, so yes, I'm taking advantage. What do you say? It will really be great for my ego, and I will let you pick the place."

I think about it for a minute. "As friends, without other expectations, correct?"

"Yes, ma'am, that would be great."

"Okay, yes, why not? That sounds lovely. I really want to hear some more stories of your life in Texas."

"Okay, awesome! Let me put my number on your phone..." I reach into my back pocket and pull out my phone, I unlock the screen and pass it to him. He enters his number first and sends a text after. "Now we can be in touch."

I nod and start to walk to the front door. Ever the gentleman, Wyatt ensures that he gets to the door first and opens it for me. I smile politely and say goodbye. For now.

CHAPTER 12

Traxx

I drive around the block five times before I pull into Colton's driveway. I have no idea how I'm going to talk about this shit with Brianna there. I really don't think Ciara has told anyone all the gritty details of what a coward I am, because Brianna would have been looking for my ass in order to skin me alive. I better get prepared for my ass whopping.

Obviously, I waited too long to apologize. Especially since I left town, I should have called her the second I realized I'd made a mistake, which was as soon as I landed in Texas. There were too many days in between for her to soothe her wounds and start to move on. Me? I'm still in turmoil. In retrospect, if I hadn't panicked that morning and freaked the hell out, she wouldn't be so mad at me. I should have sat down with her and told her all the crazy shit that was going through my mind. I'm such an idiot.

I'm sitting on his driveway and I decide to text him first. A few minutes later he opens the door and has two beers in his hands. He motions for me to come by and sit on the porch.

"Hey man, want a beer?" He greets by passing me the beer and we sit down on the porch chairs. Before he can start an inquisition, I ask him about Brianna.

"Brianna is taking a shower, so you can go ahead and talk."

"You and Notso can be such girls when it comes to gossip. I may need to do an equipment check on you, 'cause I'm afraid you've lost your manhood."

"Dude, are you going to talk or what?"

"Well, I don't even know where to start." I say truthfully. "It seems I've created a clusterfuck and I have no idea how to get out of it." I take a deep breath and go on. "You know I have always had a thing for Ciara, right? Well, we have been doing a lot of talking and she's been helping me get over the anxiety and PTSD from the incident. I mean, she's absolutely awesome, she's helped me sort out a lot of the guilt and negative thinking."

"Yeah, I'm with you." Traxx takes a drink and keeps looking at Colton really intensely.

"So, I was convinced that I was getting better, that I could move on with my life. So what happens when two people who are attracted to each other spend a lot of time together?"

Colton looks at me with a blank stare on his face. I stare back at him. Then the lightbulb goes off, he flies off of the chair and starts pacing from one end of the porch to the other. "No, Traxx, you didn't! Fuck! Please tell me you did NOT bone Ciara"

"Dude, it wasn't like that. Don't be so fucking crude. That's the problem, I have serious feelings for her." That statement makes him pause.

"And? Why are you here talking this shit out with me, when you should be with her." He's whisper-yelling now. Shit.

"Because, after well…you know, I freaked out and she asked me not to leave, but I felt like I was suffocating, because I thought I was never going to be good enough for her, plus when I realized that I have deep feelings for her, I was scared shitless of what she could do to me! The pain she could put me through… So I left before she could hurt me. I left her there on her bed, crying… I fucked up so bad!"

"It seems to me she had already made a choice and she wanted you, asshole!"

"You did *what?*" Oh fuck, that was not Colton's voice, that was Brianna's and she's coming straight for me, and luckily Colton blocks her.

"Brianna, calm down, I'm sure we can all talk about this calmly."

"Colton, don't make me hurt you!" She looks at me. "You fucker, I need to get my hands on you! I told you not to fuck with her! She's the only family I have and you hurt her?" She's is coming at me like a spooked horse without a jockey. I would be lying if I said I was not a bit concerned. I've seen her kickass! I've even seen her take on many guys at one time. The girl is an expert in Jiu Jitsu and Krav Maga, and I don't want to be at the receiving end of what she can dish out.

"Brianna, I'm really sorry, I didn't mean it... I'm so messed up inside and she was so perfect, when she's near me I just feel... complete, fulfilled, loved."

"Motherfucker!" She turns around and goes back inside.

Colton stares at her trying to figure out her next move. Suddenly, his eyes get really big and he yells at me, "The gun, bro! She's gone to get her gun! Get the fuck out of here!" And sure enough, Brianna was coming with her gun drawn out.

I hear her yell, "You are a fucking coward! I should take your balls, because you sure don't need them!"

Fuck! I jumped the porch's railing and start running. I reach my truck while I'm trying to calm her down. "I'll fix it, Brianna! I promise." Colton is back in front of her trying to hold her gun down, and I got lucky because she will not hurt Colton. If she wanted to hurt him, he would have been flat on his back in the middle of the yard next to me. This girl don't play.

Burning my tires on the driveway as I back out in a hurry, the entire time yelling promises to Brianna that I would have everything under control in a couple of days.

As if I know what the fuck I'm gonna do.

Ciara

It's been a couple of days since I last saw Traxx. That night I also had a visit from a very upset Brianna. She was really pissed. She said that Traxx had gone to her place to talk to Colton, and she overheard most of the conversation. Then all the 'how could you?' and 'why didn't you' comments started. I told her I was hoping to get it all worked out before she had a chance to find out and she made me promise not to hide things from her again. Then she plain and simply said I better find me another guy because she was going to neuter Traxx. I laughed. Gotta love her!

Tonight I'm going to hang out with his brother. I have to keep telling myself that it's okay for girls to be friends with guys. I'm not over Traxx, as a matter of fact I don't think I will ever be. He's pierced my soul with all the pieces of his broken heart. I'm still not sure why I said yes to Wyatt. It's probably because I'm tired of sitting around here, spending all my time off wallowing in my sadness. Or, it could be his easy going personality, although his looks and Texas accent helped a lot. Well, I have eyes, dammit, and I'm human. Looking is not a sin.

I look in the mirror. The image reflected back doesn't look like someone who's been crying for days on end. Thank goodness. My heart feels like it has been drained and has no purpose beating because there's nothing there for it to keep pumping. It's pointless. But I make myself get up and keep going. I have to live. There are no regrets. That one special night with Traxx is one that I will remember and cherish until my last days. The emotional ties that were released that night between the two of us were crafted with the most special ribbons: love and rapture. I don't care how hard Traxx tries to fight it. It was all there in between the two of us, it was real and we both felt it. I have to have faith that in the end, he will make the right choices.

A knock on my door brings me back to the here and now. "Come in."

"Hey, Ciara – Wow! You look great! What are you up to?" Keagan looks at me with a mischievous smile.

"I'm going to the movies with Wyatt. Want to come with?" I ask her.

"Oh, nooo, I already have plans."

I look at her with a raised eyebrow, because it seems like she's up to something, so I ask. "What are you up to?"

"Meee? Nothing. What makes you say that?"

"It seems strange that you'd be so happy for me to be going out with the wrong cousin."

"It matters not which one you choose as long as you are happy." There goes the smile again.

The doorbell rings.

Keagan turns and goes to open the door. As I give myself a final look in the mirror, for some crazy reason, I start to reconsider all of this. Suddenly I'm nervous and I wonder what would be Traxx's reaction. Well, it doesn't matter because he was very clear he didn't want to have anything to do with me. So if he sees me going out, it shouldn't bother him – right? We'll see.

As I walk to the living room, my eyes feast on the handsome man in front of me. Wyatt is very sexy in his cowboy boots, jeans, rolled-up long sleeved shirt and eyes that seem to say "sin with me." Kegan and Wyatt look to be having a somewhat serious conversation, but they stop as I approach them.

"Howdy, there, looker!" Wyatt grabs my hand and twirls me around.

"Ha! Don't you try to use your Texas charm on me, Mr. Maxwell!

"Hmm… I'm pretty sure I'm the luckiest one out of all the Mr. Maxwell's. You've got everything that you need?"

I grab my purse from the receiving table. "Now I do." I smile at Wyatt.

"Oh, wait a second! I promised my momma that I was going to send her lots of pictures from my life here. So… Keagan, can you take our picture? I want my momma to see the pretty girls I'm making friends with." Handing the camera to Keagan, we pose side by side, because all I'm thinking is that I wish I had a good picture with Traxx, we have tons of group pictures and silly pictures, but not a real good one of him and I, but then again, maybe it's better that way.

Keagan snaps the picture, then her phone dings with a text message and all of a sudden she says, "Uh, you guys are going to be late. You need to go." I didn't know she knew what time the movie was, but maybe that's what she was talking to Wyatt about when he got here. She's literally ushering us out the door.

As we step into the hall and turn around to take the stairs, we hear steps coming up. My heart recognizes who it is before I can see his face. From the second his eyes sees us, his expression goes from sad, to serious, to worried, to angry. On the outside, I'm shocked. I wasn't sure if he would care or not. On the inside, I'm shaking. All I want to do is to walk into his arms and stay safely there, forever. Life hands you a lot of things, but it doesn't give you directions. You have to figure out what to do all on your own. And this scene? The one going down right now? I was not expecting it, at all.

"Hello, *brother*." The anger's just dripping off of Traxx. Surprisingly, Wyatt is very calm. How…?

"Hey, Traxx. How was work today?"

"Don't you fucking stand there like nothing's going on." He's keeping his voice low, as if he wants to keep himself in check and not lose control."

"I don't understand. Ciara and I are going to the movies and then hang out for a little bit. Am I missing something?" Wyatt's tone it's just so casual. Traxx's eyes look to me and there's so much pain in them, I start hurting, too.

I look at the brothers, now standing in front of each other. Something's going on here. I feel like I'm missing something. They are having some kind of silent standoff.

"You can't!" Is all that Traxx says.

Wyatt, squares his shoulders and with a daring smile on his face, he answers. "Oh, but I am." Then he reaches for my hand and since I'm frozen in place, he grabs a strong hold and starts moving us towards the stairs. As we move away, all I can do is watch Traxx. Traxx turns to see us go. Nothing else is said between the two brothers.

As we reach the last step at the bottom, I can hear Traxx's voice talking to Keagan.

"And you, why are you letting this happen?"

"What am I supposed to do about it? She deserves to be happy. *Somebody* broke her heart. You wouldn't happen to know who did it, do you, Traxx?

At that moment, Wyatt gets my attention.

"Ciara, don't worry. He'll get over it. We know it's not a date, so stop thinking about it. Let's have fun."

I think about it for a few moments. "Yes, you're right, Wyatt. I'm tired of feeling sad. Having fun sounds really good."

He opens the passenger door of his truck and supports my hand while I get in. As he's closing the door, I could not help but think that I need to close the chapter of my life that belongs to Traxx, but his attitude just now, tells me there is more there than I thought and I need to know what that is. So I decide to leave that door open for a little while longer.

Traxx

I'm going to kill that fucker. My own brother is trying to take her away from me. As I run upstairs taking two steps at one time, I'm trying to come up with a plan to bury his face in the fucking dirt. Asshole!

As soon as I enter my place, I see Notso standing in the living room, with a grin on his face. He's putting his phone in his pocket.

"Hey Traxx, you're looking a little rough. What's up?" He tries to hide the fucking smirk and I just give him a dirty look.

"Maybe I should be asking all of you what the hell is up!? Why don't you tell me, Notso. We've been friends for a long time, so choose your loyalties wisely."

"I'm not sure what you're talking about, dude. Tell me what's got you in this brooding mood."

"I don't have time for this shit. I've got to be somewhere."

"You do? Where are you going?"

I don't bother to answer. Out there in a movie theater, there's a truck with Texas plates that I need to find.

Ciara

"Thanks for letting me pick the movie, Wyatt! Did you enjoy it?"

"Yeah, I did. I like actions movies, especially when there are a bunch of super power beings dressed in costumes trying to save the world. It was fun! Are you hungry?"

"A little… I can munch on something. What do you have in mind?"

"How about some beers and hot wings?"

"That sounds good." I smile at him. I really appreciate him trying to keep my mind away from Traxx. On the way here, he tried to convince me that Traxx just needs time. I've given him so much time already, how much longer could I wait? My head tells me not much longer, but my heart tells me forever. He reassured me that his brother is stubborn and sometimes he just needs a push in the right direction.

We get to his truck and immediately notice that there's something wrong with it as it's leaning to one side.

"What the fuck!" Wyatt, goes around to the driver side to see what's going on. "It seems we'll be here for a little while."

I come around to his side and my eyes show surprise when I see that not one, but both of his driver side tires are completely flat. What the hell?

"Well, I have one spare. But that will get us nowhere. And at this hour, there's nowhere I can take it to replace them."

"We can call Uber, the car company, and they can pick us up and take us back to the apartments."

"I really don't want to leave my truck here overnight, though. That would be asking for trouble. Luckily I do know someone who has a truck just like mine and can probably let me borrow his spare."

He's talking about Traxx.

"Where are you? I *know* you are not too far." Wyatt is talking on his phone.

"What happened?"

"Like you don't know. Some *asshole* flattened two of my tires. Yeah…" He grabs the bridge of his nose with his index finger and thumb.

"Can you let me borrow your spare? We have the same type truck and tires." Yeah, okay." He puts his phone on his pocket.

"Traxx will be here in a few minutes. Sorry, Ciara. Here I am trying to help you forget about him and end up bringing him front and center. This was very… unexpected."

I nod in agreement and prepare myself for what was coming. I don't fear him, it's just that my body and soul respond to his presence in a different way than when it pertains to anyone else. Wyatt jumps on the back of his truck, unlocks the toolbox and takes out his jack, a wrench and a flashlight. He then gets to work replacing one of his tires.

I sit on the driver seat, waiting it out. "So, Wyatt, what's your story? I ask in order to kill time.

"What do you mean? You know my story."

"I meant the part that really made you decide to move away from Texas. That's the story I want to know."

He takes his time. Then he turns to face me, his shoulders drop and he gives me a defeated look. "The short story is that I was engaged to this girl, a couple of weeks before the wedding, she decided she was not ready to get married and broke off the engagement. Texas has too many memories. Every place I went, I had something to remember from our time together. That's pretty much it. Let's keep the long story for another time, okay?" I nod and he continues to change the tire.

"What about you? What's your story with Traxx?"

I contemplate the question for a few seconds. "I sometimes think we never got a fair chance. Although we always got along really well, he had trust issues before the incident. Then, everyone meddled and it never went anywhere. I was dating around, nothing serious, mind you, because I didn't want to commit full term with anyone. It was like my feelings for the guys I was dating would completely halt after a couple of months. My heart was always silently waiting for Traxx to be ready. Then the incident happened and he was messed up for many other reasons. He had made so much progress with his PTSD. We were spending a lot of time together, getting along so well, it seemed we were finally on the same level, but I was wrong. He was not ready. I misread him, I guess." Just then we hear a vehicle approaching us. It's Traxx.

Wyatt looks as the vehicle approaching and quickly says, "I don't think you misread him." Then he gives me a wink. I wanted to ask him about that, but couldn't because Traxx pulled up like he was driving a race car approaching the pit.

Traxx gets out of the truck with a suspicious look on his face. "Damn, Wyatt, you must've really pissed off somebody, 'cause they did a number on your tires!"

I roll my eyes to the back of my head on that one.

Just like Wyatt did a little while ago, he jumps to the back of his truck and pulls out some tools. Then he goes to the rear of the truck to dismount the spare tire.

I decide to chime in. "Save it Traxx, I have a feeling that whoever got pissed at Wyatt was just trying to start something. Wyatt didn't deserve this."

He pops his head out from underneath the truck and gives me a look that said he was incredulous I'd said that.

"Are you serious?"

I decide to dish out some attitude. Living with Brianna for years has taught me a lot. "As a fucking heart attack."

"Unbelievable." He goes back to loosen up the tire lug nuts. Then drops and pulls the tire from under the truck and rolls it to Wyatt. Looking at me, he takes a deep breath. "Ciara, can you please ride with me back to the apartments."

"Ummm, no. I don't think that would be a good idea. Besides, I'm not about to leave Wyatt hanging." I hear a giggle from Wyatt, who's now replacing the second tire. Traxx starts pacing around and runs his hands through his hair several times, like he's thinking hard about something.

"Fine! I will catch up with you later, Ciara. I will see you at home, Wyatt."

I nod in agreement and then he gets in his truck and speeds towards the exit. He needs time to decide what he really wants. A little beggin' never hurt anyone.

Traxx

I'm sitting here nursing a beer. No one is home at the moment, which is good because I have to talk to Wyatt once he gets here. I need to know what his plans are. I need to talk to Ciara but I don't want to force her to talk to me. She needs to *want* to talk to me. Maybe in a few more days she will be calmer and she can be more open to this conversation we *have to* have.

I stand up to look over the balcony's railing. How can I make so many mistakes and expect her to still want me. The more I think about it, the more I know she is the right person for me. Still, there are some other issues that I have to work out. The nightmares, for one, keep happening. Marcy won't leave me alone. I have read many articles that explain that my mind is trying to work through the remaining guilt I have.

Every day I remind myself that I can do better than the day before. I can be a better person. I didn't pull the trigger. Then, I also remember the things that Ciara taught me: Guilt is not going to help me become a better person. Acceptance will. I'm living in the moment, working on my fear and trying to have no regrets, all because of her efforts in trying to make me better. I know that even though after our night together I felt regret, I no longer feel that way, because it made me realize how much, how deeply I care for her. I'm ready for the next step with her – whatever that may be, and I'm ready to fight against anything or anyone to make it happen. Nothing else will do.

I hear the door opening and Wyatt is coming through the door. I walk back into the living room.

"Hello, *brother*."

"Hey Traxx, what's up?" He steps in the kitchen and grabs a beer from the refrigerator.

"You, asshat, that's what's up. You are up to no good with *my* girl."

"Your girl? Who is that?"

I take a menacing step towards him. "I'm not in the mood to play games. You know damn well that

I'm talking about Ciara. And you, my own flesh and blood, are trying to put the moves on her."

He dares smirk at me. "Nope, the Ciara I know is a free agent. She doesn't belong to anyone, because if she did, I'm sure that person would grab on to her and never let go – come hell or high water. Yeah, she is that kind of girl. One in a million. Don't you agree? So, since she is not seeing anyone – oh, wait, she did go out with me today, perhaps she is ready to change teams. Cowboys are in, you know?"

Oh… I'm going to fuck him up. I put the beer bottle down, just in case. "You need to stop putting a claim on her, because as soon as I can get her to talk to me, you'll hardly exist. You will be a speck of dust in her life. Better yet, a fucking fly trying to get her attention but becoming nothing but a pain in the ass bug that needs to be smashed and I would love nothing more than to take care of that."

He smiles as if he has won. "We'll see about that. As of right now, I'm cooking her dinner tomorrow night. You see, our night got interrupted before we made it to the restaurant, so I owe her. You know what they say… 'Cooking is love.' She may enjoy my cooking a bit more than expected."

That's it! "Fuck you!" I take one giant step and grab him by the collar of his shirt. By the look in his eyes, he was not expecting that. He recovers quickly and puts his arms inside of mine and pushes out, breaking my hold. I almost go back at him again, if not for the front door swinging open, and Notso busting in.

"What the fuck is going on here?" Says Notso.

I take a couple of steps back. "Nothing. I was just going to my room." Wyatt looks at Notso and then looks back at me for a split second. It seems he may give a damn about my situation after all.

CHAPTER 13

Traxx

I spent the night in bed tossing and turning. I don't know what the fuck I'm going to do today. Cooking her dinner! Damn it! Unbelievable. All day long at the office, I haven't been able to think about anything else but Ciara spending time with him! My own fucking brother's breaking the guys' cardinal rule number one. I had to close my door and asked the office assistant to please take messages for me.

I hit the steering wheel with my palm because I'm so frustrated, I don't know how to release these feelings. Should I go talk to her? Nope, I'm too worked up and I would probably say the wrong thing. Can I ask Wyatt to cancel? Nope, the asshole's probably still pissed at me for last night.

On a whim, I stop by the gym to work out this anger. I always carry a bag with some workout clothes because I try to squeeze time there whenever possible. After I change, I immediately stretch and go for the elliptical. Yes, I like torturing myself.

I spend thirty minutes on the machine and decide to see if anyone is up for a game of racquetball. As I'm walking to the courts, I see Ciara's friend, Blaze. He looks up, recognizes me, and start coming my way.

"Hey, man. Traxx, right? Is Ciara with you today?"

"Hi Blaze, unfortunately no, not today." I answered.

"Uh… That doesn't sound good. Sorry, man, you look like something's bothering you."

I've never had verbal diarrhea, but for some unknown reason, I fucking do today. "Yeah, I'm trying to work out some shit."

"Does it involve Ciara?"

I give him a small nod. "It also involves my brother. It seems he's trying to put the moves on her."

"Fuck, man, that's bad. Is she into him?"

"I'm not sure, but I hope not. We were getting along really well, then, we had a fight, you see…"

"Oh, I get it. He's the distraction. You know? He's taking her mind away from the situation, probably because she's still pissed at you… Don't you see? She's not really into him. She's just waiting it out, probably checking to see what you're going to do about it all."

"Ciara is not like most girls." I tell him in a more serious tone.

"Yeah, you're right, but I would bet money on it that this is what she is doing."

"Well, either way, I don't know what to do about it."

He laughs. "Man, step off of the soap box for a moment. The answer is clear and it's right in front of you."

I look at him puzzled.

He takes a deep breath and tells me the secret solution to my problem. "Dude, you need to boycott the situation. Don't let it be successful. Cheat if you have to, and let me just add that Ciara *hates* spicy food."

Then, it all becomes quite clear. A long lost smile appears on my face and I can't believe that I didn't think about it myself.

"Shit! You're right! I know exactly what I need to do. Gotta go! – and thanks for the help!"

"You'd better not tell her that I gave you the idea, she would kick my ass for butting in!"

I turn to show him a thumbs up and then run to the locker room to get my shit. I've got shopping to do.

Traxx

When I get home, as expected I find Wyatt in the kitchen cooking. I say a curt hello. I have to figure out a way to "touch up" his food before they start to eat.

"What time is Ciara coming, because I much rather not be here when that happened."

He looks at me with suspicion. "She will be here around seven."

"What are you making?"

"Chicken Alfredo with garlic toast and salad." *Perfect.* I feel so evil. But all is fair in love and war — isn't that what people say?

"She'd like that. That girl loves Italian food."

He smiles at me and for a brief moment I feel a sliver of guilt. It was very brief.

"Hmm. It's good." Says Wyatt after testing his sauce. "It needs to simmer for a little while. I'm going to hit the shower. Do you mind keeping an eye on this, and stir every few minutes?"

Ding!!! We have a winner. "Nope. Not at all."

He sets the cooking spoon on the counter after rinsing it, and heads to his room. I go into the living room and wait for the shower to start, before I do some damage to that awesome meal. When it's time, I head quietly into the receiving area, where I left my keys and a small bag with white pepper, sriracha sauce, and wasabi powder.

I go in the kitchen and doctor his sauce with white pepper and wasabi powder. I don't think I can put the red sriracha sauce on anything, because the color will not blend with this particular meal. I also put a hefty dose of white pepper on the salad and on top of the garlic toast. I do a quick finger test on the sauce, and after coughing for a few seconds, I decide that should do it.

I hear the shower stop. I walk to the hall and tell Wyatt that since he's finished, I was going to head out, at which he agreed that it may be a good idea. *Asshole.*

Ciara

Last night I stayed up thinking about all of *this*. Maybe I should not get my hopes up, but yesterday when Traxx came by to drop off the spare tire, I think I recognized a person who was not giving up. I think he still has a little fight in him. Not sure what he's planning, but he's planning something, which makes me hopeful and… *excited*.

As I go upstairs to have dinner with Wyatt, I'm hopeful that I get to see Traxx again. He's acting a little passive-aggressive, and that's not his regular type of behavior. I ring the bell and after a few seconds, a good looking Wyatt opens the door.

"Howdy, girl! Come on in! I hope you are hungry, because I slaved in front of the stove making one of my more famous dishes: Chicken Alfredo." His smile is contagious.

"Hmmm, smells great! I'm so hungry!"

"I was waiting on you to get here so I can stick the garlic bread in the oven, it will be ready in a few minutes. Would you like some wine?"

"Sure." Disappointment fills me, because the wine offer shows how little Wyatt knows about me… Traxx would have known that my favorite alcoholic beverage is beer, Michelob Ultra to be exact, even if it doesn't go with the meal.

I smile politely when he brings it to me, and take a small sip. Wine gives me a headache. So I will not be drinking a lot of it.

"So Ciara, how was your day?"

"Long but never boring. I updated a lot of patient records. I truly enjoy listening to the recorded sessions. You know, there are a lot of people out there with major issues. It really helps to put my life into perspective. It helps me appreciate my life a lot more. What about yours?"

"Well, I don't have to report to work for another ten days. I'm hoping that I'm able to find a place soon. There's only so much brooding I can put up with around here. I don't know how Notso does it." He smiles right as the timer goes off.

"It takes a special person. Traxx used to be so lighthearted and fun to be around. He was getting to be that way again, although he had some setbacks here and there. It was wonderful to be able to see him carefree and happy, even if just for a little while. So worth it." I smile thinking back to all our outings and conversations. Even thinking about it gives me a gooey feeling inside my heart. *Sigh* I wonder what is he up to right now. "Need help?"

"Naw, I think I have everything setup already, come on, please, sit down." Wyatt pulls out a chair for me. I smile and sit down as he pushes the chair in and moves to take the seat across from me. Everything's already plated and ready to be eaten. "A toast to new friends." Wyatt raises his wine glass, so I meet him with mine.

"Yes, to new friends." I smile and take another sip of the wine. I set the cup down and grab my fork. "Looks really great, Wyatt." He smiles at me and we start to eat. The pasta is cooked to perfection and the chicken is sliced rather than diced, which is my favorite. Wait. Something's wrong. At first I thought that it was just really hot and needed to cool off, but the heat! Oh shit! The heat is burning my mouth and I feel hot from head to toe. My eyes start to water... I look at Wyatt and he's having a similar reaction. The shock on his face tells me this is not meant to happen. I want to spit it out because my throat is on shutdown mode and it won't allow me to swallow. I take the napkin and spit the mouthful on it, grabbing the wine glass and gulping that mother fucker all the way, but after a few seconds it comes back hotter, if that's even possible. I see Wyatt reaching for his glass and I force him to put it down, while we are both coughing and crying like crazy.

This is a disaster. Wyatt is having trouble breathing and tears are falling down both of his cheeks. I'm crying in agony as well... Then I get an idea and run to the kitchen. Milk, milk, where is it? Spotting a jug of milk, I grab a hold of it and a couple of glasses from the cupboard. The milk is supposed to neutralize the heat – I think I read it somewhere, God I hope so. With two glasses full of milk, I run back to the dining area and hand Wyatt one of them. We chug them down, leaving the last sip on our mouths for a few seconds longer before swallowing.

I sit back down on the chair, and after a few minutes, I am able to start breathing again. I look at Wyatt, who's still wiping his eyes, and ask him point blank, "What the fuck was that?"

"I swear, Ciara, I have no idea what happened. I tasted the sauce right before I went to take a shower. I even asked Traxx... *Mother Fucker!*"

"What?"

"Traxx! He did this. He fucked up our dinner. Everything was fine until I asked him to keep an eye on the food. You know, I thought that was weird that he didn't say anything about you coming over for dinner... It's all so clear now..."

The whole thing is so crazy I start to giggle. Traxx *does* care. Shit. My tongue feels heavy and still burns. The heat may have skinned it... I can't taste anything, that's for sure. I giggled louder, and Wyatt looks at me at first like I'm crazy, then understanding flashes on his face and he joins me. Soon after it becomes full belly laughing. We are crying again, but for a whole bunch of different reasons. Fucking Traxx.

"I don't think I can taste anything right now, but I'm still hungry. I don't feel like taking a chance on the rest of this food. Let me throw it away and how about we go eat a bucket of ice cream?"

"That sounds like a great idea. Here let me help you." I get up and start carrying things to the kitchen. I rinse the dishes and put them in the dishwasher.

After drying my hands, I'm ready. We are heading downstairs and I notice Wyatt furiously texting on his phone.

"I think I know who you are texting." I look back and wait for his answer.

"Payback is a bitch and my brother has it coming." He gives me the most devilish smile I have seen on him yet.

Traxx

I've been sitting at the office, waiting to hear from Wyatt and Ciara.

Ding.

There goes my text message alert. Let's see what my dear brother has to say.

Wyatt: Good one, asshole

Traxx: What are you talking about?

Wyatt: I'm not gonna play games with you. Dinner's ruined. We are going out instead. Ice cream. We both like to play with whipped cream. Perhaps kissing her sweet lips tonight will be the cherry on top. Full report to come later

Fuck. Now all I can think of is licking ice cream off of her sweet lips.

Traxx: I'm going to kick your ass

Wyatt: You're gonna have to catch me first
Traxx: Stay away from her
Wyatt: Last I checked she was a free agent. Thanks for putting her right on my lap, brother. She's fantastic

Motherfucker.

CHAPTER 14

Ciara

The other day, after Wyatt had texted Traxx, I thought Traxx was going to come and find us at the ice cream shop, but he didn't. This is the reason why I'm so confused. Sometimes he acts like he's jealous and sometimes he acts like he is not. I realize that it takes two, and I can easily go find him and clear the air, but it's hard.

When he turned his back on us and left me alone, that moment, that pain was bottomless. Not because it was a rejection, but because it was Traxx's rejection. He's the one man that I've always wanted. I love him and all his imperfections. I'm not about to lay my heart down for him to stomp on it once again. I don't know if I could withstand that kind of agony again. I want him to come to me when he is completely sure that I'm what he wants, but in the meantime I need to keep living. I cannot put my life on hold because of him.

Wyatt and I talked about us and where are we in our lives. He's on the rebound and I'm obviously very much in love with his brother. We are good friends and during our conversations we agreed that there is no attraction between us. It was good to get it out in the air, because that helped me understand that he's just trying to get his mind away from the past and I'm trying to look out for my future.

Today we are hanging out with Notso and Keagan at the ballpark. Its baseball season and I'm ready to admire players in their uniforms, drink beer, eat hot dogs, peanuts and cotton candy. Bring it on.

"They are ready and coming down!" Keagan yells from her room.

"Okay, I'm ready!"

The doorbell rings and Keagan and I step out of our rooms simultaneously. She opens the door and I make a stop in the kitchen to get a couple of bottled waters for the road.

As we come out into the hallway, Traxx gets our attention from the top floor, so when we get to the stairs, we look up.

"Y'all be careful driving and take your time even though you are itching to get there."

When I look up, my eyes lock with his. He looks sad and disappointed. I almost asked him if he wanted to come along, but didn't. I could not take my eyes away from his. I could just sit there and stared at him all damn day.

"Ciara, are you coming?" Keagan is calling me.

"Yeah, on my way." Nothing is said between Traxx and me. It was not necessary, because the silence carried the sadness and dejection of our situation.

The guys sat in the front seat and us girls in the back. I was lost in thought and looking out the window. The guys and Keagan were having a discussion on players and stats. The car line to parking took a while, but we finally made it to the ball field and found our seats. The guys went to get us beers, and as they were walking away, I noticed that Wyatt kept scratching his shoulders. How strange.

Keagan and I are just looking at the fields, some players are warming up, there is great music on the speakers and the cameras are zooming in and out looking for people – especially kids – doing funny stuff. Although the weather feels great, once you are sitting down without a breeze coming through, makes it kind of warm.

"Hey, Keagan, have you spoken to Traxx lately?"

"Not really. I see him around in passing, but we have not carried a conversation. I think all the progress you had made with him is slipping away. He hardly ever smiles and is obviously immersing himself in work."

I nod to let her know I heard her. Perhaps Traxx and I need to come to a truce so that we can continue his "treatment." But can I withstand being near him and not touching him? Can I keep all contact on a professional level? Impossible. It would be more than I could handle. Our time together was pure perfection. I felt him give himself to me the same way I gave myself to him. We spent that time doing a love dance of our own, where the music branded our hearts and now that we are apart, the music has died and there is no rhythm to our existence. Neither one of us can find our way back to the other.

I look back at Keagan. "I was wondering if he was making progress. I'm having a hard time moving on, and I was hoping he was not having a hard time, since he was the one who wanted to stay away. Well, you know…"

"Yes, I do. I also know he is stubborn and an idiot when it comes to the real thing because he has never had it. I believe that he realized the truth. You'll see."

I give her a sad smile and then take out my ChapStick and I apply some of it. When I lower my mirror, I noticed this good looking guy staring at me while he was trying to locate his seat. He smiles and I smile back. At that moment, Wyatt and Notso come around, and after the guy notices they are with us, his smile fades and he quickly looks away. Perhaps I need to re-evaluate hanging out with these boys. They are really cramping my style.

By the time the game starts, I've eaten my hot dog and I'm already tearing into the cotton candy.

"Hey Ciara, can you please scratch my back?" Wyatt asks me.

"Sure thing, where, exactly? I ask him.

"Everywhere. I don't know what's going on. The hotter I get, the more it itches."

I start to scratch him, but as I do, I start to feel these tiny bumps.

"Hmmm, Wyatt, I'm not trying to get 'fresh' with you or step over the line, but I'm feeling some bumps and I need to look at your back... Can you raise your shirt a bit?"

He looks at me and gives me a dirty look. I stare back at him with a questioning look.

"Can we at least go to the corridor? I don't want to flash these people."

"Wyatt, I'm not asking you to take it off, I'm just saying let me take a peek."

He nods and leans forward a bit. I lift a little, and I don't need to see anymore. I know exactly what's going on.

"Guys, I hate to break it to you, but we need to go, like, right now."

Wyatt looks at me with major concern on his features. "What's going on?"

Now I'm the one who's leaning forward and try to tell them as quietly as possible. "Wyatt has a Poison Ivy breakout all over his back. We need to go, he needs to get treated or will end up with a back full of huge blisters and a lot of pain. So we are leaving, right now."

I grab my phone and start to locate a nearby pharmacy. The connection is a bit slower than I would like, but at least it's working. As we get closer to the car, a flashback hits me:

"Y'all be careful driving and take your time even though you are itching to get there." Shit!

We are in the truck and I'm giving Notso directions how to get to the pharmacy. As soon as we get there, I go to the allergy section, get some

Benadryl, calamine lotion and Cetaphil wipes. After I pay for them, I grab Wyatt's hand and take him to the family restroom.

"Take your shirt off." I ask him.

"I'd rather not." He tells me with a stubborn voice.

"Wyatt, there is a good chance that the shirt is what's full of poison Ivy and giving you the hives. I will text Keagan to buy you a t-shirt from this store and we just need to throw this one away.

"Fine, okay!"

He takes his shirt off and I can see all the hives. They are still small, so I think we are treating this right on time.

"I'm going to use these wipes first all over your back, arms and shoulders. They are like soapy water, but for very sensitive skin. They should clean up the oil that the plant releases, which is what causes the irritation. Then the calamine lotion will dry out the allergy blisters and will help with the itching."

Keagan knocks on the door and I open it. She brings in the new shirt for Wyatt to use.

"Ouch!" She says to him.

"It feels better now. It was getting pretty bad. I didn't know what the hell was happening. I thought I was bitten by some type of bug."

Keagan and I are blowing on his back so that the medicine dries out and when he puts on his shirt, it won't come off. After a couple of minutes Wyatt starts thinking this situation out loud.

"How in the hell I got near a poison ivy plant, I have no idea... I have not been outside, my shirt was washed and put away right after it came out of the dryer..."

Oh, crap... I look at Keagan on a silent plea that maybe she can change the subject... She looks at me like I'm going crazy...

And the lightbulb goes off... Wyatt has figured it out.

"Motherfucker! I'm going to kick his ass, for real this time!"

I close my eyes, because I don't really know what to say. Keagan is alarmed. "What are you talking about, Wyatt?"

"I'm going to kill Traxx! It had to be him. No! As a matter of fact I know he did it! Especially after that little comment he made as we were going downstairs. Fuck! That's it. I'm done trying to help his ass out. He's officially going to get his ass kicked."

Oh boy! This it ain't going to be pretty.

"Where's Notso? We've got to go."

I take a deep breath and I'm actually laughing on the inside at all of Traxx's shenanigans. This is the third time he's tried to sabotage my outings with Wyatt, and he really has nothing to worry about. There is not even one drop of attraction between Wyatt and me. This is about to get interesting. I'm almost tempted to text Traxx and let him know what's coming... Well, almost.

Traxx

Standing on the balcony, my body is shaking with adrenaline and anticipation. I know by now Wyatt has figured out that he didn't get bitten by a bug... Somebody in that group should be smart enough to know the hives and rash are not normal.

I know I'm being childish by going through all this effort instead of going to talk to Ciara... I just could not pass up on picking on my brother. After all, he was the one to have the *audacity* to start going out with my girl. I know that we are not in a relationship – yet. I'm going to fix this because I know she owns me starting with the smallest piece of my dismantled heart and she's the only one who can help me pull it back together. When we are apart, I feel restless and all I do is relive the moments we spent together reflecting on how happy I was. She calms my busy mind. She strengthens me and gives me hope for a happy future. I was stupid to let her go. The thought of her moving away from me and towards someone else gives me unbearable pain. I really know what I want now. I'm ready.

I see Notso's truck pulling into the parking lot. I move away from the balcony and walk inside the apartment. This is not going to be easy, I hate fighting with my brother, but I know he will not be very rational after today's events. I'm standing up facing the door. I'm not going to wait for him sitting down, as if I was bait. This is going to be face to face.

I hear the keys on the door, and I still myself. Wyatt comes through it like a man who's possessed. The moment was very surreal, almost like a movie playing in slow motion. Wyatt takes giant steps to get to me, he looks intimidating, but I hold my ground.

"Why the fuck would you do this?" He shoves me on the chest with his hands. I take a tiny step back, but I don't really move. He's going to need more than that if he wants me to be afraid.

"You know why." I tell him in a very sarcastic tone. Two can play this game. Looking at him, I see so many questions passing through his eyes, that it makes me wonder if I've got it all wrong.

"No, Traxx, I don't. I need you to talk to me and tell me what's going on between you and Ciara."

The mention of her name gets me emotional again. "You are my blood, my only *brother*. You are not supposed to try to take her away from me. That was one fucked up move on your part. Ciara is mine! We belong to each other."

Wyatt is only a couple of inches away from me taking over all my personal space. "No she isn't. YOU left her before things even started. YOU gave her up. I'm helping her forget about your sorry ass. All because you are too chicken to tell her how you really feel."

"How would you know how I really feel? I don't advertise it. How I feel is my motherfucking business, not yours."

Notso finally gets here, comes inside the apartment and closes the door.

Wyatt is beyond irritated and continues talking. "ANYBODY with common sense would know. When you are around her it's all over your ugly ass face! Stop denying it!"

"No it isn't!" He shoves me again a little harder this time.

"Yes it is! You are so stubborn you will end up losing her. The next guy that comes on to her will have other things in his mind. He won't be doing it because he's trying to help his brother, like I did."

"I don't need your help!" I yell back at him. "Now leave her alone!"

"The hell I will." He turns around and starts to walk away, which pisses me off even more. I take a step forward and grab him by the shoulder making him turn around, and when he does, I throw my fist on his left chin.

He stumbles, but charges at me. "Motherfucker! Now you've done it!" He lands a punch on my left cheek.

Before either one of us knows it, we are down on the floor, wrestling like we used to do when we were kids. At first we are even, but after a few swings and lucky strikes, Wyatt has me pinned to the floor. *Shit.*

Notso is trying to talk to the two of us, pull us apart, to convince us to stop fighting.

"Say it!" Wyatt tells me. One of his hands is on my face, pushing it to the side, and the other one is holding one of my arms down.

"Fuck, no!" I say through my teeth.

"Tell me the truth that you are in love with Ciara."

I can't say it because when I confess it, when I finally make it a reality because I will say it out loud, I will say it to her and admit it to myself at the same time. Not to this fool who fights like a baby.

"I won't tell you!" Suddenly, I just quit fighting and Wyatt – who is now straddling me, falls forward due to the lack of resistance.

I take a deep breath and tell him what's on my mind. "Won't tell you, because I want to tell her and only her, how I really feel,"

"Thank God! I'm way too old for this shit. He gets up off me and extends a hand to help me up. "You better hurry because she thinks I'm killing you."

Notso finally can get a few words in. "Yeah, I told them to stay in their place until you two were finished. I didn't want them to get in the middle of this."

I look at Notso and suddenly feel grateful. "Good call. Thanks."

I look at my brother, and feel nothing but pride to have a brother like him. "Wyatt, I'm sorry about the poison ivy…"

He laughs. "It's all forgotten for today, but you never know what tomorrow may bring. I hear payback is a bitch. No, go on, brother. Go on and get your girl. She is dying for you to make amends..."

The bastard winks at me. Wait a minute... "Wait, why do you look so happy?" Wyatt looks at Notso, and they start chuckling. "Was this your plan all along?"

"Yes. I talked it over with Notso and Keagan, to make sure they knew. I thought I could find a way to push you back towards her... I almost gave up, you are so stubborn! Now, stop wasting your damn time with me and go find Ciara. Don't hold back, Traxx. She deserves to know how you really feel."

I nod, and literally run to the one person who holds my heart and soul: Ciara.

Ciara

"Keagan, I'm dying to know what's going on!"

Keagan is sitting on the couch reading a book. She's way too calm about all of this. "Why are you not worried?"

"Because they are my cousins. I have grown up watching them fight things out since we were babies." She smiles at me. "They always figure things out in the end. You'll see."

There's a knock on the door!

I'm shaking inside because I'm not sure how all of this is going to pan out. I look at Keagan. She gives me a small smile and nods to let me know it should be okay to open the door.

I move towards it and look at the peephole. It's Traxx. I turn around and look at Kegan with wild eyes and I mouth who it is without making a sound. She nods much more enthusiastically than before, so in a hurry, I reach for the doorknob and open the door.

Heat floods me immediately at the mere sight of him. Then I notice that he's not his usual flawless self. His face is swollen right below the left eye and near his lip. There are red marks on the other side of his face, too. He looks worried and tired. His clothes are a bit disheveled but there is no blood or cuts that I can see.

"We need to talk." Traxx speaks in a very soft voice that makes me melt but at the same time it's a vivid reminder of our situation.

"I don't think we have anything to talk about." I tell him while blocking the door. It would have worked out perfectly had it not been for Keagan in a huge hurry to get out.

"Where are you going?" I ask her as she passes by.

"Ciara, this is a two-way conversation. I have no business being here. Besides, this thing between the two of you is long overdue." She looks at Traxx. "You're welcome and you better not mess this one up. Get your shit together, already." He nods at her and moves out of the way so that Keagan can pass. I open the door all the way and let him in.

We are standing in the receiving area, doing a stare contest. He looks remorseful which makes me feel hopeful, but I don't want to give it away.

"Well?" I ask him.

"Ciara…" He pinches the bridge of his nose and closes his eyes as if he's thinking hard. "I need to start with an apology." I look at him unconvinced. Can we please sit down?"

I gesture towards the living room and he starts walking in that direction. I sit on my big reading chair and he sits on the ottoman, so we are again face to face but a lot closer than before.

Traxx grabs my hands and I tried to pull away, but he holds them tighter. "Please don't. I know I deserve this, but please, don't pull away from me." His voice is cracking and I can literally feel the pain on his voice. My eyes fill with tears, but I'm able to hold it together a bit longer. My heart aches for him.

"Ciara, I could say that I was sorry a million times, and that wouldn't be enough. I've never been very good at expressing myself, but I will give it a try, because you deserve so much more than an apology…"

It hurts me to see him like this. So I reach over my hand to touch his cheek. He leans towards it, rubs his cheek on my palm and wraps his fingers over mine. He then looks at me. "Go ahead. I'm listening."

CHAPTER 15

Traxx

She said she will listen. I'm a lucky bastard. I'm hurting, but I also don't fail in seeing the pain reflected in her eyes. This is going to be my only chance at redemption, so I will let everything go. I'm going to give her my heart because she owns it already. I've got nothing to lose.

"Out of all the moments in my life that I could rewind and get a do-over, you would think that I would want to go back to the night that Marcy ended her life, because perhaps I could do something different and maybe, just maybe I could stop her from making that mistake again. But I would be lying. My heart tells me that the one moment I really want to go back to is the night we spent together. That's the one I really want a do-over. I want it. I want *you*. It was the best night of my life. Can you blame me? Before you showed up with your BTB plan, I meandered through life never wanting to emotionally attach myself to a girl, because I was scared that they would rip my heart in two. I ended up doing the ripping all by myself when I decided to walk away from you.

"I've never felt anything for anyone until that night when we became one. You filled me when I was empty and barely existing. You gave me a new life when you gave yourself to me. That night you claimed me and I became yours. I never thought I would care for someone, but I care for you. You have made a difference in my life. Your love has put me back together." I kiss her hands and feel my eyes brimming with tears threatening to escape. "I don't want to continue barely existing. I want to be happy. I want my life to be meaningful. I want to be with you, now and always. When I try to think about my future without you, all I see is darkness. When I think of you and me, I see fireworks. I see a world full of possibilities, because you are my light and your love keeps me sane. I was a fool for trying to walk away. Please forgive me."

Our hands are now in between us, mine wrapped over hers. She lifts them up and places them on her lips, leaving a gentle kiss on my skin.

"Traxx… I'm here for you always. I know I promised this before you walked away from us. What I don't understand is why didn't you want to talk about what was bothering you? Why such a drastic decision? And how do I know it will not happen again? I need you to reassure me, because when you went away, it affected me deeply and I don't want to be in that situation ever again."

I drop to my knees and settle between her legs. We are eye to eye. I'm determined and serious. "Ciara, I'm getting ready to come clean with you. I'm going to tell you everything. Please hear me out." She nods and is attentive.

"I was bullied by girls in Middle School. The girls who bullied me used to be my friends in Elementary School. I felt betrayed and thought that all girls were going to be like them. They pretended to be my friends and then turned around and ridiculed me in order to become popular. I spent all my time trying to hide from them and keeping to myself. I was afraid to make friends. Later on, Colton became my ally and he protected me the best way he could, but the damage was done. Who would have thought that cute little girls can grow up to be so mean and vindictive?

"When I started High School, it was a different school from that of the girls. I was finally free, but again, I was damaged. In High School girls were seeking me out for other reasons, so I decided to date them on my own terms so that I could feel as if I was in control. I've since learned that I was lying to myself. By not building a connection to women, I became more and more cold and uncaring towards them. The only exception was my cousin Keagan, and then later on Brianna and you. You guys were so different to all the others, you were kind and giving and always trying to take care of everyone else, it made a difference in my mind. I was intrigued. I wanted to get to know you better back then, but that was when Brianna and Colton got in the way. I figured it was for the best.

Then, the incident with Marcy was a huge wakeup call that my behavior was affecting others in a negative way. I had become the one thing that I hated: A bully of sorts. To say that Marcy's death traumatized me, is to put it mildly. Since she spared me at the last minute, I feel obligated to change and use my life for something better – I just don't know how yet. In the meantime, Marcy is always in my ear, whispering hateful things which reminds me that I'm still stuck somewhere in between of who I used to be and who I want to become. I've had nightmares that made me wake up sweating and shaking. I see her from time to time and she's always cruel. She wants something out of me but I don't know what that is. Most recently I have been successful in turning her off and ignoring her, because I know she only exists in my mind. I am aware that she is not alive and I'm not crazy, although sometimes I think she would love that.

"Spending time with you, having all these conversations and learning to let myself fall for someone were new things for me. I was changing and feeling for the first time… it scared me. I was terrified and I absolutely had no clue what to do and how to heal. But I was so immersed in you already, that when I tried to do it without you, I felt as if I was dying. I hated myself. I didn't know how to stay afloat, so I ran. I ran away from the one person who was teaching me how to be alive and happy. That day when I arrived in Texas, I realized that I was dying instead, because you had my heart and I could not survive without it.

"Then came my brother and instead of letting me handle things, he pushed me around to let me know that if I didn't hurry up and do something about it, I could lose you forever. It scared the crap out of me. A life without you… wouldn't be worth it.

"There is something that I know for sure and I have to let you know before it's too late. All these feelings that I have when I'm near you and that I've only experienced with you… Now I know they mean *love*. I didn't know it before, but I understand now. I love you Ciara, with all my heart and all that I am, but the best thing is that all that I will become will be because of you and the love I feel for you. I want you to be proud of me, always. I love you, always"

The thought that I love her compressed my chest and there was a warmth that calmed and enveloped me. When I looked into her eyes, tears were free falling on her cheeks. I raised my hand and wiped them with my thumb. She was so emotional and it was hard for her to talk.

"Traxx… Always is a long damn time. It's longer than I've ever wanted to be there for someone. You are my always, Traxx. You are my beautifully flawed, a little off your rocker, a master skilled in certain 'special' things and I could not be happier to have found you. Perhaps I should say I could not be happier to have thrown myself at you when you needed me most. I love you, too. Always" Her smile lights up my life, and I can see everything a lot more clearly now.

"Ciara… I'm going to kiss you now. I'm going to kiss you until you have no doubts of how important you are to me. I'm going to touch you – all of you – until the moment comes that we can no longer stand the coldness of being even an inch away from one another. I'm going to please you, brand you and love you until you know without a doubt that I'm the only one for you and you are the only one for me... Are you ready?"

She gives me a happy smile that is infectious and so damn sweet. Her head is nodding frantically and while smiling she whispers in my ear, "Bring it!"

Challenge accepted.

Ciara

My world's finally set in its right place when I see Traxx's smile. There is no possible way I can still be upset with him after his explanation. I have no other options, because he already owns me and I don't want to be away from him anymore. My heart is beating fast and loud, leading a drumline inside my body, where everything's shaking in anticipation and looking forward to the pleasure of being in his arms again.

"Ciara... Thank you, baby I love you so much." He leans his forehead against mine then both hands take a gentle hold to my face as his lips hover over mine. He kisses me softly on each side of my mouth at first, and then his probing tongue captures the seam of my lips. Feeling greedy, I raise my hands to reach behind his neck. I pull him into me and kiss him with urgency and want. I don't want to waste another second, life's too short. I want him now and always, and I want our always to start right now.

Trying not to keep up with him, my tongue enters his warm mouth, and I taste grape and seduction mixed with love and need. His lips are full and gentle, leaving me to be the demanding one. I've got this.

"Traxx, this is **Step 4 – Let others love you, you are worth it.**"

I grab a hold of his bottom lip and bite gently, pulling it between my lips and sucking on them a little bit.

"Fuck!" He responds with a deep kiss that breathes a new life into me, where our tongues start dancing and appreciating the many things they can accomplish with each other. His mouth moves to my cheek, under my ear, seeking, searching the special spot that makes me cry out without shame and makes me ready with want. He bites my neck and I realize that I not only like it but I'd missed it more than I wanted to admit it to myself.

He's gets up and carries me from the chair to the couch, where he takes off my shirt before he lays me down and admires me for a few seconds.

"You are so beautiful."

I smile and ask, "Still breathtaking?"

He smiles, never taking his eyes off me. "Hell yeah, and totally mine." He lays down covering me with his body, kissing me senseless, until our chests are heaving hard, our skin is burning with the seduction trails made by our mouths and our minds are drunk with wanton thoughts of all the things we need to do to each other.

His untiring mouth moves to my breasts. After his hands remove the front clasp of my bra, he cuddles each one, pushing them against each other, allowing him to play with both pebbled nipples at the same time. I grab a hold of his hair and pull each time his tongue makes my nipples tingle, emitting a pulsating shock to the area between my legs. I am so ready for him.

When Traxx lifts his body off of mine so he can work my belt buckle and the zipper of my pants, I feel cold and lost because I'm already so used to him being near me. He immediately rips the bottom string of my thong and I look at him puzzled.

"I have plans for this string later, and yes, we will go shopping for more of these babies soon." He winks at me and moves his hand between my legs. I'm so primed that I know it won't take long for me to reach my peak.

His thumb rubs the small bundle of my body that holds thousands of nerve endings, putting gentle pressure at first and after one good lick, he's able to move his thumb around. It feels so good. I hum in pleasure. He inserts one finger inside of me and then another, causing me to cry out at first because it's tight, but after he starts to move them in and out, I adjust. He's working my 'G' spot that promises to give me trembling fireworks and I'm ready to welcome them all.

His big, strong body is trying to find a less awkward position. He gets off the couch and puts a cushion under my hips, pulling my legs over the couch's arm. On his knees, his mouth is perfectly aligned to where I want it the most. He spreads my legs wide and then invades me with everything he's got. I respond by moving rhythmically, but then I want more, so my hands reach out and pull his hair and as a result, he increases the pressure of his tongue and the speed of his fingers. I can feel my insides constricting, and I believe he does too, because with his other hand, he slaps me between my legs, right on my clit with just enough pressure to finish the job. I tense up as I shake the buildup and then crumble as I come down from the high.

"That was beautiful, baby. You are so fucking perfect." He leans over me and kisses me on my mouth, so I can taste myself and it's exciting. He moves away and licks his fingers, then wipes them on his jeans. Wait, why is he still in his jeans? I reach to undo his button and zipper, rubbing the length of his thick, long cock over the jeans. I stand up to have a better angle, and my hand pumps the soft skin. A drop of semen makes an appearance on the tip, and before he can say 'not now', I move my head down and swipe it with my mouth. I want to experience everything about him.

"Fuck!" His grunt tells me he liked it, so I get on my knees and start to play with him. I lick and put as much of him in my mouth as I can fit without choking. Then I nibble, suck and lick on the underside of his cock, while my hand plays with his balls, which earns me another grunt and a hiss.

"Shit! I'm not going to last. Com'ere and ride me." He grabs a condom from his wallet before sitting on the couch. I'm standing in front of him, so I take the condom foil from him and I rip it with my teeth, hand it back to him and he guides my hand while rolling it in place. "So hot!" Grabbing my hand, he pulls me toward him, kisses me deeply and positions me so that his cock's head is right at my entrance.

"Go for it, sexy. I'm yours. Ride me, possess me. Make me feel what I already know, that the best life I can have is the one I can share with you."

His lips crash on mine at the same time I push down with everything I have. He grabs my ass and is helping me move up and down. Our sweaty chests are rubbing together creating friction and heat. It's so fucking good!

Traxx moves one of his hands to my nipple, pinching it and torturing me very thoroughly. I have my hands on the back of the couch, holding myself in place. I lean back and move my hands behind my back, leaning them on his knees and I continue to ride him like this. The angle helps his dick rub inside of me, right on my 'G' spot again. One of his hands moves to play with my clit and the buildup is so high, I'm flying once more in mere seconds.

"Damn, baby. You're so tight!" He holds me in place for a minute until I come down from the high. Traxx kisses my face, eyelids, nose and ears. When my eyes finally flutter open, we shift positions so that my stomach is on the arm of the couch, my face down on the seat, my ass is up in the air and my feet on the floor.

"Baby, do you trust me?"

I nod. *Yes.*

"Okay, I'm going to secure your hands behind your back with the remaining elastic from your thong, okay? Then I'm going to hold on to your hands because this is going to be hard and fast. Ready?

Excitement courses through my body and I tremble in anticipation. I nod again. He secures my hands and pulls on my hip in order to line his cock against my pussy. Then in one swift motion he's all in.

"Fuck! You feel so good, baby…" As he promised, one hand is holding my hands behind my back and the other has gotten a hold of my long hair, which he's pulling on to keep himself steady.

"Harder, Traxx! Fuck me harder!" His speed increases and his moans and grunting sounds are doing something to me, it all feels so primal and raw, I'm surprised to find out how turned on I really am.

"You are so wet and tight, shit!" I'm all into this moment, so when he leans over my body, and starts to kiss me on my exposed neck, I whimper in pure pleasure and bliss. He bites my neck, right below my ear and I know he's close. His speed increases. The sound of skin against skin and the feeling of his balls hitting my pussy finally carry us through the pleasure threshold into pure, raw satisfaction.

CHAPTER 16

Creepers

They have been observing the blond girl's apartment since they spotted Traxx looking out the window hours ago.

"Make the call."

While one is on the phone finalizing their plans, the other goes to the back to make sure they have everything they need at hand.

After re-entering the vehicle, the one who was making a call speaks to the other. "It's time."

A nod passes from one to the other as they finish getting everything in place.

Traxx

I was tempted to call in sick today and stay in bed with Ciara all day, but I have an important meeting this morning, and she has to be at work today as well, so we make plans to spend the weekend together. I will make reservations at a nice hotel and we'll spend a couple of days enjoying each other.

I get up and kiss her good morning, promising to stop again on my way down. She gets up and gets going while I go to my apartment to get ready.

Thirty minutes later, I'm heading back out and have a plan to shuffle some afternoon appointments around so that I can get off early and surprise Ciara with a home cooked meal. I plan to cook it at her place, because Wyatt will pay me back big time for ruining his meal the other day.

I step out of the apartment and as promised I knock on Ciara's door on my way down. When she opens it, her beauty and radiance has me staring at her and making an adjustment to my crotch.

"Hi Nibblet." I wrap her in a hug and kiss her deeply.

"Hi baby." She says sweetly.

"Walk down with me?"

"I wish I could, but I have to finish making my lunch. Somebody kept me up all night and I was pretty sluggish this morning."

"Okay. I wish I could wait, but I need to be on time today for the appointment I was telling you about."

"No worries. Talk later?"

"Sounds good." Giving her one last peck on her lips, I leave. As soon as I step off the building, I notice this morning's weather is chillier than normal. Very odd. I reach my truck and start it turning on the heat immediately.

After a few minutes, the truck is ready. I buckle my seatbelt and pull out of the parking lot, hoping the day goes by quickly because I'm ready to see my Nibblet again.

Fuck. I'm so whipped.

I chuckled to myself and turn on the radio.

Creepers

He comes out of the apartment building and looks happy. It won't last. That's what we are here for. We're going to make sure he is never happy again.

It's early in the morning so there's not a lot of traffic on the street. Perfect.

We open the walkie talkie signal, and advise our partner that he's almost there. There will be a spike strip on the road in order to disable his truck.

Three, two, one... The truck veers to the left and then to the right. He's able to control the vehicle – barely – and the truck ends halfway on the emergency lane and the other half is going down in the ditch.

We got him.

We pull up next to him and move quickly out of the van.

The other one of us picks up the spike strip and takes off.

Traxx cracks the door open and we take advantage of his vulnerability. When he looks at me, seems like he recognizes who I am, but before he can say anything, I spray him with pepper spray and my partner injects him with the tranquilizer. The guy falls down on the grass two seconds later. We grab him by the arms and drag him to the van.

He's a big guy and we have a little trouble getting him inside. We hear a vehicle approaching, so we hurry. We lock the door and run to the front seats. The van is still running, so we are able to pull out and take off quickly.

It's done.

CHAPTER 17

Ciara

The cool air is very welcomed. I breathe it in to clear my lungs. As I walk into the parking lot, I see Traxx's truck pulling out, but he doesn't see me. I'm absolutely crazy about him. Remembering our time together last night, I feel my face blush. It was wonderful.

Walking to my car, I notice a creepy van driving away. Who the hell drives such a thing nowadays? A bad feeling comes over me, but I shake it off. I must be watching too many crime television shows.

I don't have to wait for my car to warm up, because I like the colder morning air. I use the windshield wipers to remove the built up moisture and take off.

Just a few miles down the road, I notice the creepy van parked to the side, and as I approach, there are two people closing the back doors. I get chill bumps all over me and quickly take a look at the license plate and memorize it. This is a habit I have from my Army days and something I also do for Amber alerts and things like that.

They pull out and as I pass the spot they were, I look to the side and notice a truck going down in the ditch. Oh, fuck no! It's Traxx's truck.

I immediately pull over and place my car in reverse. I reach for the glove compartment and take my gun out. One can never be too careful. I tuck the gun in the waist of my skirt and go check things out.

My heart is slamming on my chest, and a feeling of dread is now in the air. *Shit!*

I approach the truck and it's empty. All four tires are flat. I call for Traxx and look around but there is no damage to the truck. The only marks I see on the ground are the ones from the driver side. I study them and decide they are drag marks, so they must have incapacitated him somehow.

What the fuck is going on?

I run back to my car, and immediately place a call to Blaze. Thank goodness he answers right away.

"Hey, gorgeous! What a nice surprise…"

"Sorry Blaze, I don't mean to be rude, but this is an emergency." He must have heard the panic in my voice, because he immediately flips this into business mode.

"What's going on?"

"I need you to do a trace for Florida license plate CRP-3RS and text me the address it's registered under and who it belongs to. Traxx has been kidnapped. Please hurry." I hang up and make my second phone call.

"Brianna, Traxx has been kidnapped."

"*What?*"

I tell her what I saw.

"Text me the address as soon as you have it. I also need you to follow the proper channels and call 911 to report what you saw, but do not give them the address. This will allow us to get there and do a sweep of the place before the police get there. Motherfuckers, better not hurt him. I'm taking Colton with me. Do not engage alone, wait for us."

"Sounds good. See you in a few." I'm freaking out on the inside, but I'm thankful to my military training, my mind is clear and I can mentally prepare myself for this confrontation. They picked the wrong person to fuck with.

While I'm talking using the Bluetooth, my phone pings with the address. I forward it to Brianna and then copy and paste it on my phone's GPS app. Then I notice the name listed as property owners: Sam and Lilly Smith. *Who are they?* My memory has a flashback of Marcy's funeral and the cards from the funeral home. *No! Fuck!*

I call 911 and make the report as Brianna asked me to. Then I hung up. I don't have time to wait on the line.

It's so early, traffic's still light. I arrive at the property and do a quick drive by. I cannot do a slow one because it may attract people's attention. I end up parking around the corner, and I text Brianna to let her know where I am.

Brianna and Colton get there a couple of minutes after me. I'm halfway inside the trunk, looking for the weapons I have in there. I feel lucky because I didn't get to take my stuff back to storage after my last visit to the firing range.

Brianna and Colton are prepared. I take a second gun and stuff my pockets with a couple of loaded magazines. I break the news to them. "Guys, this house is registered to Marcy's parents."

Brianna talks first. "Marcy as in the girl from the incident?"

"Yes."

Colton brushes his hair with his hand and starts pacing. "No, no, no… If they took Traxx, then there is a big chance that they are disturbed like their daughter."

I nod in agreement

Brianna takes charge. "Let's do this."

We move casually and slow so it would seem we are doing a morning stroll. When we get to their driveway, I signal the others to let them know I was going to do a quick recon or walk around the building.

In addition to the front door, there are a side door and a back door. It looks like there may be a basement too. The house is two levels. The windows have blinds and they are all closed. I could not see inside. There is no indication that they have dogs, but we need to be prepared just in case.

I come back to my friends and give them a full report. Brianna nods, and says, "Let's go get our friend."

I follow her and Colton is behind me.

We go to the front door and we hear voices but quickly determine that it's a radio or a television. Colton moves forward and uses his lock picks to unlock the door. They radio is blasting, probably for it to drown any type of human noise. I know Traxx well, and he will not go down without a fight.

Quietly, we move in, clearing every room as we pass. Colton goes down to the basement, but we stay guarding the door, in case he needs help. He emerges from the stairs and makes a 'negative' signal with his hand.

As all the rooms downstairs are checked. Is time to move upstairs. I'm grateful that all the floors in here are carpeted, because otherwise, I would have had to take my high-heel shoes off. We are now in the hallway. We move to the left and clear the master bedroom and bath. We move to the opposite side of the hallway, and as soon as we pass by the banister, we hear loud voices coming from one of the rooms. As we go around the corner, one bedroom is dark and has the door open, the other bedroom door is closed, but there is light coming from the bottom.

Brianna takes one side of the door and I take the other. We are listening first, to give us an idea where the people inside are located.

"She was in love with you. She said you guys were going to get married." A male voice is talking.

"Sir, that's not true. I barely knew her. We only went out one time. I didn't know she was this serious about me until she came to my house that night." That was Traxx.

"Our daughter is gone because of you and you must pay." A female voice.

"Your daughter was not well. You guys are not well because you cannot just take people against their will. You need to let me go. LET.ME.GO!!!"

"That ain't gonna happen. We brought you here so you can see everything we found in her apartment that showed us you and her had a relationship." The man spoke again.

"There was no relationship, all those pictures are photoshopped! She has put her face in all of them. I have the real pictures and I can show you, but you have to let me go. I can prove it to you."

"Liar!" The woman yells and it sounds like she slapped him. "I've been at your apartment many times and there are no pictures there."

"That's because they are in storage. Hell, check out my phone. I'm sure there are at least a couple of these pictures in there as well."

"We don't need to check anything. You need to shut up and stop tainting our daughter's memory. Your time here is limited. Lilly, put the gag on him."

"No! Get away from me! Help! HELP!" After that his voice is muffled.

Brianna and I look at each other, but before we could break the door down, a second, younger guy comes up the stairs and charges at Colton.

Brianna and I get ready, because we know the door is about to be opened by the people inside in order to check out the commotion going on here.

Colton looks like he has the upper hand, and now I remember seeing him at the funeral. Must be Marcy's brother.

As expected the door swings open, and Brianna attacks the woman. They are fighting on one side of the room. I come in looking for the father. He has an evil smile on his face, and a knife on Traxx's throat. He's pressing really hard. A couple of blood drops are dripping under the blade, and he's using Traxx as a shield.

To my right, I can hear Brianna landing one good punch to the woman, who falls on the bed. Brianna turns her around and cuffs her. The woman is out cold. After Brianna finishes, she talks to the old man.

"Sir, you obviously don't have any idea of who we are and what we are capable of. I know you've got a knife, but this girl right here, will take you out before you can even use it. That's all the warning I'm going to give you. Good luck." She steps into the hallway to help Colton with the brother.

I look at Traxx and I'm hoping he understands what I need him to do. He barely nods and I reciprocate.

"Mr. Smith, this is your last chance. Let go of the knife. We can talk out this situation and come to an agreement. I'm sure of it."

"There is nothing to talk about. My daughter is gone... Gone. She was so young... and she was a good girl. Good grades, too. She had her entire life ahead of her and this piece of shit ruined her!"

As the old man is getting more and more upset, he's putting more pressure on Traxx's neck. I can't continue to let him hurt Traxx. I can't take a chance. If something happens to him, my heart will stop beating as well. I look at Traxx, he's been attentive and looking at me, waiting for my sign.

"Well, now you can tell your daughter we say goodbye."

The comment catches Mr. Smith by surprise and he looks at me in shock. Traxx takes advantage of his distraction, leans forward as much as he can and then slams the back of his head onto the guy's nose, causing him to lose the grip on the knife. When that happens, Traxx throws himself, chair and all, to the floor and I fire the gun. One round in his forehead is all it takes. He's dead on impact. I don't ever miss a shot.

Engaging the gun's safety, I move as fast as I can towards Traxx. I untie him, take the gag off, and help him up.

I'm taking a look at the cut on his throat, and even though it's bleeding some, it's still superficial. I take the rag that was gagging him and place it against the cut.

Brianna comes walking in. "Colton's okay. The guy hit him on the temple and Colton lost his balance, allowing the guy to land a few punches before I could get to him. We need to get comfortable. This is going to be a long night with a lot of explaining on our part. What are we going to say about how we found the address?"

"I think we need to tell them that I thought I lost the van, but I came up to it down the road and that I followed them here."

Brianna nods. "I'll tell Colton." She looks at Traxx. "You okay?"

He smiles at her. "Yeah, I'm fine now. Thanks for coming to my rescue."

"Don't get used to it, asswipe. I still want to kick your ass." She gives him a huge smile and walks back to the hall. Traxx laughs. It's a beautiful sound.

Traxx

We waited for the police to arrive. Oh, they were pissed. Poor Brianna had to take most of the heat. After the crime unit came and took pictures of everything, Detective Hall told us that we needed to go to the Police Station to give our statements and to be interrogated.

We spent hours at the station. More pictures were taken and they also collected DNA from all of us. We had to write down all the events of the night. We were all in separate rooms. After a while, we were finally released, but were warned not to leave the city. So much for my planned weekend getaway.

When we got back to the apartments, we updated Notso and Keagan on everything. Keagan fixed us something to eat, and after that, I was ready for a shower and to relax with my Nibblet.

After today, I value my life a lot more than I did yesterday. I finally know for sure that I am loved, not only by my friends, but also by this amazing woman who's resting on my chest. I adjust my arm around her and move her closer to me. I love being with her and I love *her*. My hand is rubbing up and down her arm and I can't get over at how happy I feel.

"Traxx?"

"Uh huh…"

"We need to talk about something." *What?* Isn't this soon for a "need to talk" speech?

"What's going on?"

She moves and rests her elbows on the mattress next to me so we can look at each other while we talk. I have come to learn this is important to her. "It's time to talk about Step 5."

"You mean to tell me we are not done with the BTB plan? Because it seems we are doing very well so far." I give her my best smile.

"Not done. The best is yet to come." She smiles back at me.

"And what is that?"

"Step 5 – Pay it forward."

I laugh. "I should've known. Go on, tell me about it."

As she described everything to me, it all made perfect sense. I was happy, loved and now I would finally be able to live my life with purpose. As Ciara continued to talk about what I needed to do, I felt a warmth radiate inside my chest and it was as if the rest of the dismantled pieces of my life slid back in place, and for the first time ever, I was at peace. I finally felt whole.

EPILOGUE

Ciara (Six months later)

It's another cold, misty day. This is important for Traxx, so it's important to me. We are at the cemetery, visiting Marcy one last time. I feel so bad for that family. Not only is Marcy gone, but her father too, at my hands, no less. Her mother and brother were convicted of kidnapping and attempted murder, and are now spending their days locked in a mental institution. After weeks of investigation, the police decided not to press charges against me for taking Mr. Smith's life. I feel bad to have done it, but I have no regrets.

I stand back to give him some space while he talks to her, but I can still hear him. He has brought her flowers and placed them on the little metal holder next to her headstone.

"Hi Marcy. It's been a long time since you last whispered things in my ear. No, I'm not here to give you a hard time. I'm here to update you on everything that has been going on with me.

"When we first met, we both were in a very dark place. The difference between us was that I was still trying to stay afloat, but unfortunately the darkness had already pulled you under. We were not that much different about the fact that we wanted to be loved for who we were but didn't know how to go about it the right way.

"After you were gone, the darkness claimed me. That's were our lives became apparently different. You drowned because you didn't have anyone to help you. I got lucky, because even though I wanted to go under, my friends and family wouldn't let me. They stuck around and it meant so much to me, although I didn't know it at the time. I'm sorry that you didn't have anyone. I'm sorry that I was so late in trying to take the gun away from you.

"A while back my girlfriend, Ciara, had an excellent idea. She talked me into volunteering with the local suicide crisis center. I spent months in training, to make sure I could communicate in a positive manner and that I would say the right things to whoever was on the other side of that call.

"Today was my graduation day and I needed to come and tell you about it, because everything good that has happened in my life in the past few months has been a direct result of your visit on the night you decided to come and confront me. I needed to stop by and say thank you, from the bottom of my heart.

"I know I didn't do right by you, but I cannot go back in time to fix it. All I can do is to look forward and hopefully make a difference in someone else's life. I will be saving lives, Marcy, and it's all thanks to you. I'm pretty sure that if you had not done what you did, I would still be the careless asshole I used to be. Now I have someone who loves me unconditionally and I can love her back. You would have liked her, I think. She's is full of spunk, greatness and goodness. She is a wonderful example to others, and I love her. She's the first person that I have given my heart to, and it has been worth it. Now I sit back and wonder why I was so afraid to do this in the first place."

He stays quiet for a little while, as if he was listening for her to say something. After a few minutes, he gets up and touches her headstone.

"Goodbye Marcy. Thank you."

Tears were rolling down my face and his, too. He reaches for my hand and I happily give it to him. I would happily give him anything. We walk back to the car in silence.

"I'm so glad that you are happy." I tell him.

"I'm only happy because you are a part of my life. You helped me become a better man, a better human being. Someone that we can all be proud of."

"You are awesome, Traxx. That's the bottom line."

He embraces me, and rubs my back soothingly. I wrap my arms around his waist. Traxx kisses my forehead first and then places a light kiss on my lips.

"Thank you for loving me, Nibblet."

"I will love you always, Traxx. Always."

The End

Thank You!

First, I want to thank you for reading my work. The fact that you bought my book and invested time in reading this story doesn't go unnoticed. **I appreciate you. I'm grateful.** I would not be able to create stories, if it wasn't for you, the readers.

If you enjoyed this book, I need to ask you for a huge favor: Please take a few minutes and leave a spoiler free review. It doesn't have to be long. You don't need to recount everything that happened inside the pages. Just a couple of sentences will do. As an Indie author, reviews are our most important marketing tool. It's the truth. A lot of people will not purchase books unless they take a look at the reviews.

Also, as Indies, we have to cover all expenses that go with releasing a book: cover design, promotions, book tours, prizes and giveaways, formatting, editing, the list goes on and on, but I hope you get the idea. We need to sell books so we can publish some more.

Please **help me** to be able continue writing and publishing books. Your words count.

Until next time,

Yara ♥

Acknowledgements

My family – My husband **Scott** and my son **Sean**, who patiently eat hot dogs more times than they care to, and get super excited on those nights I am able to pull away from writing in order to cook a decent meal. Thank you for cleaning the house and doing the laundry. Thank you for waiting on me to be ready so we can watch "Castle" together, even though sometimes may be two weeks after it aired. Thank you for not giving up on me and supporting me on this crazy dream. I love you guys so much! My oldest son, **Ricky** you may live far, but you are not forgotten. I hope you find your path soon. I love you. My niece **Ciara**, Thank you for allowing me to use your first name and likeness for one of my favorite characters, and although you two have different personalities, all her good attributes come from you. <3 **Cindy & Mike,** I could not have asked for a better extended family. Thanks for treating my kids like they were your own.

Janie Thornley – You saved me! This book would not have happen if it wasn't for you. You are an awesome friend. Thanks for having my back. Thank you for your great editing skills. I promise, next time I will follow the schedule! Love you bunches!

My Book Club – The Crazy Ass Book Bitches – Ashley, Jamie, Karina, Kelsey, Leighton, Natalie, Randi, Sarah, Shannon, and Vanessa – One of the best days of my life was when we decided to branch out on our own. Thank you for all the laughs, opinions, pictures and chats. Sometimes, the best part of my day is catching up with you every evening. I look forward to seeing y'all every month. Love you guys so hard! **Especial shout out to Karina and Jamie** for being my first guinea pigs when I started this story, for wanting to read pieces of it knowing that I was going to leave you hanging for a while… Thank you for being the best cheerleaders anyone can have.

Elexis Darden – Thanks for beta reading, all your input, for sharing my books with all the blogs posting teasers and links. I'm so touched that you love my work so much. Your help and ideas are always welcomed and appreciated! Most of all, thank you for listening all those times I just needed to vent and not necessarily about the book. I love and care for you and your family as if I've known you for years! Can't wait to meet you in person!

Paige Boggs – One of the best decisions I've made this year was to bring you into the fold. Your help has been invaluable. Thank you for creating all the forms, the teasers, for sharing my books with blogs and for being available to help me anytime I needed you. You are awesome!

My work family – Nick, Amy M., Stephany, Lindsay, Cleo, Henry, Norma – Thank you for listening to my crazy ideas, showing interest on my progress, telling people about my book and supporting me during this wild ride. It really means a lot… You guys rock!

Rebecca Berto (Berto Designs) – Thank you for creating my covers, making changes and taking the time to make sure I'm happy with the final product. I look forward to working with you more in the future and I can't wait to see what you come up with next!

Erin Dawson Photography – Can't thank you enough for the wonderful pictures! I hope we can work together again in the future!

To all the Book Bloggers – OMG! Thank you! You guys are a vital part of the Indie Book Community. Thank you from the bottom of my heart for the endless amount of support and enthusiasm you have shown for my stories. I can't believe how many of you I have interacted in the past year – you guys are amazing! I hope I get to meet you guys during some of the author events I will be attending. So PLEASE drop by my table and I promise I won't squeeze you too hard! I can't wait to hear what you think of "Dismantled." Get in touch with me, I'll be waiting!

Readers!!!! – You guys make my life a happier place. Even though I don't write on a full time basis (oh, but I want to!) It's because of all of you that I am able to chase my writing dreams and create these characters for you to enjoy. You make it possible and I'm delighted and humbled. A little over a year ago, the fact that I wanted to write a book was nothing but a dream. Thanks to you, I can make my dreams come true. I'm so excited about the future and all the stories floating through my mind… I hope you are too, because I cannot wait to share them with you, always!

About the Author

Yara Greathouse likes to write contemporary romance dashed with elements of suspense. She grew up in Dominican Republic, moved to the Unites States at the age of 17 and served in the US Army. Always an animated storyteller, she finally gave into her friends' requests for her to write. Her first series, "Girls On Top" is about strong female lead characters and the sexy alpha males who love them.

She currently resides in Texas, but calls Georgia her "home" state. She lives with her husband, has two boys, a little mutt named Hank and a cat who acts like a spoiled child. Her days are dedicated to a job she loves as a Business Analyst, and during her free time she writes, takes care of her family, and indulges on her love of reading, cooking and travel. She loves to hear from readers, bloggers and other authors. You can find her at:

Website: yaragreathouse.com
Amazon: http://www.amazon.com/Yara-Greathouse/e/B00KIT4OSC
Facebook: www.facebook.com/YaraWrites
Twitter: @yarawrites
Instagram: YaraWrites
Email: YaraWrites@hotmail.com

National Suicide Prevention Lifeline

http://www.suicidepreventionlifeline.org/
Call 24/7 - 1-800-273-8255

Some of us have passed through some dark times in our life. You are never alone. Talk to someone. I know it feels like the end and you don't want to face anyone, or you don't want to make it through the next day. The pain is real. Don't keep it all to yourself. Share it with someone. Anyone. There are a lot of people who care. I do. I've been there. Don't give up.

Unavoidable

By Yara Greathouse

(Excerpt)

Chapter 1

Brianna

(A little over three years ago)

Some people expect greatness out of life. My only expectation was survival. You can say someone has bad luck when they are able to crawl out of a fire pit after years of torture only to fall into a lion's den, but I am strong enough to survive both and scared enough to do something crazy in order to get away.

My heart is beating so loud and fast I think it may give away my location. There's not much time before they come looking for me. Luckily, it is late in the evening and the bus station is rather empty.

Get a grip, Brianna.

I cannot call attention to myself. Stepping casually into the restroom, the first thing that hits me is the nasty smell of urine. God knows when this restroom was last serviced. Then I notice the pale green walls and the pink sinks. This room has not been touched since the early 80's - literally. I notice my reflection in the mirror and quickly spring into action and start to remove all traces of my current life. Take the makeup off. The most masculine clothes I have will have to do - Baggy and saggy jeans and an extra-large sweatshirt. Pulling up my long brown hair around my head and fastening it with pins. Then, I put on the wig of short black hair which I took from a new girl before I left. I don't think she will miss it, after all she had like twenty of them. Putting on the baseball cap, I chance a look in the mirror. Almost done. The finishing touch: brown colored contact lenses I had gotten from the super store's vision center a while back in order to cover my blue-green eyes. Stepping away from the sink, I stared at the image in the mirror. I just might be able to get away with it.

Snap out of it.

I have to hurry. Opening the black trash bag I brought with me, I take the clothes I took off and placed them in the bag. Placing my trash bag at the bottom of the bin, I put the restroom's trash filled with discarded paper towels on top of mine. Hopefully if they look inside this trash bin they will only see the paper towels and not realize my clothes are underneath.

Calmly, I sling my back pack on my shoulder and walk out of the restroom making my way to the ticket window. Looking at the board, I see the next bus is headed to Miami, FL. There is an older lady inside the booth and it looks like she's reading a book. As casually as I can, I say: "Excuse me, ma'am, one ticket to Miami, please. When is the bus leaving?"

Without looking at me, she says "It leaves in 20 minutes." She rings up my ticket, I hand her the cash and she gives me my change. *Shit!* 20 minutes is 15 minutes too long. I have to find a hiding place *pronto*.

After I get the ticket, I turn around and scan the room. I decide to chance it and step outside. I look around and find the bus arrival/departure area. The bus was already waiting for passengers, but I am not stupid. Those goons will show up in a few minutes and the first place they will look will be on that bus. The second place will be the bathrooms. At the moment I am covered by the shadows in the parking lot. I have to find a hideout fast. My head starts hurting and my heart is thumping.

Breathe. Breathe.

A vehicle is coming. I hide around the corner of the building trying to figure out where to go. When the vehicle pulls up next to the bus, I realize it is a white van. On the side, there is a sign that says "Joy of Clean, Janitorial Services." The driver and another guy get out of the van and then they go to the back of the van to get their cleaning equipment out. They are talking about their weekend plans, joking and laughing. I find myself wishing I could joke and laugh about my current situation... Once they are in the building, I make my way to the van and try the handle – the door opens! While climbing inside the van I hear a loud engine approaching. I don't bother to look, my heart is telling me it's them. And I still have ten more minutes before the bus is ready to go. I quickly slam the door, lock it, and hide behind the driver seat, next to all the brooms and mops and cleaning solutions.

Just as I settle behind the seat, the vehicle pulls up near the van. I recognize the voices. It's Jesse and two of his body guards. I tried to stay calm, but my body is not paying attention to my brain at the moment. I am so scared I shiver and shake as if I was locked inside a commercial freezer. At this moment, I would much rather be inside a commercial freezer than waiting for these monsters find me. I hear Jesse give instructions for one of them to go inside the building, the other to go around the building and he was going to look inside the bus.

Minutes feel like decades and time moves ever so slowly – but my heart is beating double time. I feel someone lean on the van and try the handle, only to find it locked, then something hits the van and I jerk out of fear, but there are no windows on the back of the van and they cannot see me.

"Son of a bitch!" Jesse says as they reconvene in the parking lot. "Are you sure you didn't see anything?" He asks the others.

"Nothing, Sir." One of the goons answers.

"Did you show her picture to the cashier?"

"Yes, Sir. Also to the cleaning crew and the few customers inside the building. No one has seen her around here."

"Dammit!" He says and hits the van again causing my heart to jump. I realize I have stopped breathing and make myself inhale slowly.

"If she isn't here, she must be at the train station. Let's go!"

After loud doors slam, I hear the squeal of tires peeling out of the parking lot and at the same time the bus engine reeves up. I jump from behind the seat up over the driver side and quickly look out of the window – they are gone! Unlocking the door, I jump out of the cleaning van and run towards the bus moving my arms so the driver sees me right as he was getting ready to take off.

The driver opens the door and asks "Got any luggage?"

"No luggage, thanks." I climb up and start walking towards the back of the bus.

"Miss?" I hear the driver voice again and my soul jumps out of my skin, he has recognized me!

"Do you have your ticket?" Realization dawns on me as I turn around, dig inside my pocket and pull the ticket out, passing it to him. He gives me what is seems a knowing smile and I swiftly turn around and move towards the back, staying away from the windows – they were definitely not safe. Not until I leave this awful place. Finding an empty seat on the aisle next to an older lady, I sit down. Leaning back on the seat, I am able to take a deep breath. Looking up to the Heavens, I quietly whisper a thank you, and it is the first time in a long time my lips dare to give in to a tiny smile. Once my body stops trembling and my breathing returns to normal, I realize we are out of the city limits and it is the first time in at least a year that I actually feel hopeful instead of hopeless.

* * *

"You will NEVER be able to hide from me, you fucking bitch! I will find you and destroy you! I will never stop looking for you!"

Jesse's voice chases me while I run as fast as I can, leaving me no choice but to draw a huge breath of air. I feel a hand on my arm, shaking me gently. My eyes open in a panic and I look down at my arm, then up, following the hand that is touching me. My gaze stops on a pair of gentle eyes looking sadly at me.

"You were having a bad dream, dear." The old lady says to me. I nod at her and smile thanking her for waking me up. There's no telling what I have blabbered about while I was dreaming and I need to keep everything low key.

I look around carefully noticing everything for the first time. The lights are off with just a faint glow coming from the emergency exit signs. Looking out the window, I read the next road marker that we come across. It appears we are in South Carolina. The temperature inside this bus is a little chilly, and I'm thankful for the oversize sweatshirt I have on. Getting up slowly to stretch my aching muscles, I look at all the other passengers around me: everybody's head is bobbing gently following the motions of the bus. I allow myself to relax a little. Things are going good and this crazy idea is going to work out after all.

When the bus arrives at the next stop, I approach the driver and ask how long we have to use the facilities. Fifteen minutes before we head out again. I hurry to use the restroom – another dinky one, but at least smells of pine sol instead of pee – and then I head towards the vending machines. Things have gotten pricey: I slide in a dollar and a quarter for a bottle of Coke, and another dollar for a Twix bar. Can you say sugar high? Shaking my head, I head back to the bus, the driver is talking to another passenger, telling him the next stop is Atlanta, Georgia, and after that he's headed for Columbus, Georgia. I have never been too comfortable in extra large cities. I start to consider where to get off. Although my ticket says Miami, Florida, I do not want to end up there. If Jesse figures out that I left on this bus, he will follow.

Jesse is like my very own dedicated and personal bounty hunter, although I have never committed a crime, he treats me as if I had taken away everything that matters to him, when in reality he has done that to me and others. He's obsessed with owning me. Relentless. Always seeking me out. I have to come up with a plan to keep him away. If I could fake my own death I would do it, just to get rid of him, but I lack the contacts, money and access to do what's needed to carry out that plan.

Relaxing in my seat, I close my eyes again and when I wake up, I will be where life wants me to be. Long ago I made a promise to myself: When I finagle my way out, there would be no regrets and life will be lived to the fullest enjoying every day as if it was my last. I have suffered enough during my life and I am letting go of all that. Will my future be happy? Who knows, but I'm sure as hell going to give it everything I've got.

* * *

The bus driver makes the announcement that we are arriving in Columbus, Georgia. I can't help but to smile. Those three steps leading out of the bus are symbols of freedom, happiness and the possibility of dreams to be sought after – I cannot wait to leap out of this bus and into life. As the sun comes out in the horizon I look at the blazing orange, blue and yellow sky and say to myself "Happy Birthday, Brianna." Today, I am 18 years old and free.

Looking around the neighborhood makes me wonder if a bus station has ever been built in a decent area. There are questionable individuals everywhere. Thank goodness for daytime arrivals. Nothing can put a damper on my day, however, and I have tons of things to do. First and foremost I have to find a place to stay and put into motion the second part of my plan.

I notice that the old lady who sat next to me also got off the bus. I ask her if she knows of a nearby motel. She indicates that there is one about a mile down the road, I thank her and start walking. While passing a car dealership I hear a loud engine and the sounds transports me back to last night. My heart starts hammering fast, my head feels hot and heavy. I find myself tensing up and have to remember to relax

– I was not followed. No one knows my whereabouts and I need to let go of the fear. Fear can cripple you while it works its way inside your head. It creates holes filled with doubt until all your resolve is weak and sinks into nothing.

Fear is the reason one believes when people tell you that you are no good, you are ugly and that no one is ever going to want you. Fear rules you when you are treated like scum – a piece of old gum stuck on the sole of someone's shoe. You forget who you really are and the things you used to dream about accomplishing. You forget about hope and start to believe all the lies you are told and the real you crumbles into pieces. And while you are down at your lowest, the same people who hate on you start to put you back together with hate, but the pieces are mismatched and it is impossible for you to ever become whole again. You are now like a wall full of cracks, waiting for the final wrecking ball's blow that will allow you to fall apart and never recover. It makes you weak. It makes you stay. It's all you know... but now fear can kiss my ass. I will submit to it no more. I feel the resolve fill my body as I make this promise to myself: From now on I will seek fear and conquer it. Never again will I fall prey to its tangles. I refuse to give in. I refuse to live scared.

Walking into the rinky-dinky motel, I am able to secure a room. The attendant doesn't ask many questions. Actually, he doesn't even look up. I notice the faded chipped pink counter and read the prices listed on a small flyer taped onto the counter. There is a lot to be said about a place that charges by the hour. Immediately, I say a silent prayer for the mattress to be clean and the room to be bed bug free. I'm thinking I may have to sleep fully clothed.

Leaving the office I notice someone dealing by the dumpster, which confirms my suspicions about the place. This is not a very safe area. I hurry to the room, keeping my nose down to avoid "seeing" anything. I unlock the door and push it open when the smell of smoke hits my nose like a ton of bricks. One would think that after being exposed to that smell on a daily basis for-freaking-ever, that one would be used to it by now. Well, One.Is.Not.

The room has seen better days, but I didn't expect much of it, really, it would have been silly of me. It has the basics: a full size bed, a TV, small refrigerator, a microwave resting on top of the fridge, one lonely window covered by old dark drapes and an air conditioner unit below the window.

Stepping into the room, I place my backpack on the bed. With one swift motion I take off the hat and the wig I was wearing, relieving my itchy scalp. After removing all the hair pins, my long brown hair spills down all over my shoulders and my back, like running water. I take off my oversized clothes and stand there in my boy shorts and tank top. Turning the clock radio on, someone is belting out a song about freedom and new beginnings, and I think how fitting for this moment, I can't help myself as I'm listening to the beat I break out into a happy dance.

Later, I feel relaxed after a hot shower and clean clothes that are not ill fitting. The TV is on and I'm randomly changing the channels. It feels weird being on my own, as if I'm a little lost. I guess when life is planned for you day in and day out, you lose your decision making abilities. I only have enough money to cover the motel for a few weeks and then I will be on the streets.

"You will never amount to anything!"

That damned voice again. Years of being a victim of hate will continue to play inside your head even if you are long gone and far away from that situation. It's hard to believe that I was able to escape from a sadistic mother, only to unwillingly fall prey to a sadistic motherfucker like him. I would much rather be disemboweled while alive and breathing, than to ever let anyone have that power over me again. I allow myself a moment to feel sad and lonely. I don't dwell on it long. I have survived this far and will continue to do so. I can't afford to trust anyone. The friends I left behind are better not knowing what happened and it is better for me to keep it that way.

As I am deep in my thoughts trying to ignore the memories that keep oozing out of the vault inside my head, I remind myself that I have options. Life will get in the way, but I have the power to decide how to handle MY life, and I choose to survive. I choose to be happy.

In that moment, I hear it. A commercial on TV. Not any random commercial, but what is about to become my lifeline.

"There is strong, and there is ARMY Strong." The narrator says.

Wow! A light bulb turns on inside my head. The United States Army. The idea keeps playing in my head. I can join and they provide room, food, training, and financial help for school. All this and I get a paycheck! If I get lucky enough I could even be assigned at a far away post, perhaps in another country. I roll off the bed and open the nightstand drawer pulling out the phonebook at the same time. I quickly locate the telephone number and address of the nearest recruiting office. I jot it down on a piece of paper and place it inside my backpack. Since it is still early in the afternoon, I call a taxi and get ready to go. For once in my life, I know exactly what I need to do.

Chapter 2

Colton (3 years later)

"Hey doofus, stop throwing like a sissy and put some arm behind that ball!" I yell at my best friend Traxx. It is a nice day on campus. We got here yesterday and I was glad to get away from all the family drama. I don't think I will be going back anytime soon. My birthday was two weeks ago – the big 21 – and my trust fund has kicked in. If I don't blow it, I will be just fine. I am done with my parents trying to run my life and telling me what to do, who I need to hang out with, or not hang out with, who to date, what to study. Done!

"I'm ready. Anytime now, Colton!" Traxx is trying to get my attention and I realize the football is in my hand.

"You know, Traxx, I actually don't feel like doing this. Let's go get some food."

"In that case" Traxx says, "I gotta go by the house first to change into a clean shirt. Sweaty pits makes for a not so attractive quality for the girls, if you know what I mean." He winks at me with a naughty smile.

Traxx Maxwell became my best friend when we were 10 years old and he caught me breaking the glass to one of the school's fire alarms and pulling the knob just as he was coming around the corner. We looked at each other and took off running together, hiding outside behind the bushes stifling our giggles until everyone was outside, too, and we could blend back in with our classes. We have been inseparable since then.

"You are always thinking about scoring, you are such a man whore!"

"I am NOT a whore!" Traxx fakes disgust. "I'm just someone who loves to try free samples. If a girl wants to give it away, who am I to deny her?" A smile breaks across his face.

"Good thing you believe in using condoms or one day your dick would break out with some nasty warts and fall off." I smile back at him. "I don't have a problem with you sampling… 'goods'… but don't try to shove your ho-hos my way. I can get my own sampling. I'm just a tiny bit more particular about what I wrap around my dick. I want to be one hundred percent put together when we graduate. I don't want to have to carry my junk inside a pickle jar."

"Ha, ha. Really funny dorkface!" he smacks my arm. "It is not my fault that you only crave a certain type. You really need to broaden your horizons because pretty girls who don't want to run your life are quite hard to find."

"Not as hard as you think. I get plenty." I said.

"All girls end up trying to run your life."

"That's when I break it off. I have been dealing all my life with my parents trying to tell me what to do, and I'll be damned if I'm going to let some girl do the same shit. I will never commit to a girl like that. On a second thought, I will never commit to a girl. Period." I find myself getting a bit upset at the thought of living my life dependent on a girl's approval. Hell no! I get plenty of offers and go out with any girl I want. I'm just choosier than Traxx because I actually like to have "a conversation before the bedroom." During and after, they always want to please me and they think their sex is better than any other sex I've had. Wrong! It's all pretty much the same. And, I enjoy the shit out of it while it's happening and I let go the moment is over. It never fails. They always think they are the one to tame me. That I will call them back. Newsflash: I can't nor want to be tamed.

Traxx looks at me and says "Whatever makes you happy. I'm just saying maybe you are putting too much into it. You need to be more like me: Give them one night that they will never forget and don't double dip."

"Traxx you are such a class act..." We look at each other and start laughing.

Just as we are about to cross the street, we hear this roar – a motorcycle. We stop to let the guy go by. It's a nice black and white sports bike. I'm getting ready to look at the make and model when it slows down as it passes in front of us, and I realize that there's no way in hell this is a guy. The rider's chest is the size of a couple of grapefruits, followed by an impossibly small waist and the nicest ass I have seen in a while.

Traxx and I look at each other at the same time, with surprised expressions on our faces. Then we immediately frown. Our eyes follow the biker girl until she stops to park not too far away from where we are standing. I'm in a trance and so is Traxx.

"A girl on a sports bike wearing tight ass jeans! That's the hottest thing I've seen all year!" Traxx is trying to get my attention, but it's certainly not working as my eyes are fixated on that girl. I have got to see what she looks like!

As she dismounts from the bike, she pulls her helmet strap off. Her back is to me – I can't see her face. *I need to see her face.* I know if I don't hurry up and act now, Traxx is going to go for it and get the upper hand. I slam the football on his chest and I tell him I'm headed that way and to throw me the ball when I reach her. He smiles knowingly. What an ass.

I jog towards the girl and as I'm getting closer, she takes the helmet off. She places a hand around her neck under her hair, and pulls. Shiny brown hair cascades like water to the middle of her back. My breath hitches a little. Slowly – as if she knows what she's doing to me - she turns around and looks over her shoulder directly into my eyes. Suddenly I can't breathe, I know I'm staring, but I can't help myself. Sun-kissed skin, blue-green eyes, high cheekbones and full glossy lips shaped like a heart and so plump that they make a small "o" in the middle. At first her lips don't move, but then… as if she was not cute enough, I see her lips curve into a small smile ending with a dimple and a full set of bright pearly whites. I am about to say something when I hear far away someone calling my name. Next, there's a 'thud' and something hits me on the back of my head, making me lose my balance. The next thing I know, I'm eating grass. *Great! Dammit, Traxx!*

Lying on the grass, I realize the situation can't get much worse. So I'm going with it. I turn to my side first, it helps me appreciate her body. It could be confused with a guitar. I get to look at those curves and legs that go on forever. Too bad they are covered by some impossibly tight jeans. I find myself wishing that I could inspect the whole package up close and personal. That's when I felt my dick trying to get my attention. Hell! This is not the time to get a boner. I close my eyes and try to think of something else. Suddenly I hear slow, deliberate steps getting closer to me. The sunshine that hits my face is covered by a shadow. I take a deep breath and finally decide to open my eyes. When I look up, the sea within her eyes is staring at me. I feel really hot and I think I may be embarrassed. There is some type of energy going through my body while she's looking at me, and I notice there is a puzzled look in her eyes. We can't stop looking at each other, when suddenly we both shiver lightly and it ends the spell.

She decides to break the ice and smiles at me. "Wow! I didn't know I had the power to knock someone down just by *looking* at them. I must add this special skill to my resume." She winks – *winks at me!* - "You are the first guy I've met who decides to make a great and lasting first impression by falling at my feet *before* we even have a conversation." She says with a sarcastic tone. And then a little more serious she asks "Are you okay?" Me? I am mesmerized. I can't talk. All I see is that gorgeous smile with the cute dimple. It dawns on me that all I want to do in this very moment is to slowly lick and kiss that dimple. She has perfect white teeth, a small and round button nose. Long dark lashes and those plump, glossy lips. I better pull out my "A" game.

"Yes." I grunt. "Did it work?" I said, sounding a little too hopeful and giving her my best shy smile.

"Nope." She responds and extends her hand to help me up and when I give her my hand, I notice that she effortlessly and swiftly pulls me up to my feet. She's strong. Her touch makes me feel like I am on fire. I look at her questioningly and I notice she's looking at our hands, does she feel it too? Once I'm up, her hand leaves mine – it's too soon, I think. Then just as swift as she came to check on me, she turns around and starts walking away. I again notice her body's every hugging curve being held tightly by her riding gear, and those exquisite long legs covered by tall boots.

"Hey! Wait!" I call after her as she reaches to get a messenger bag that was tied to the back of her seat. "What is your name?"

She turns, looks at me with those blue-green eyes, gives me a tiny smile and says "Unfortunately for you, I don't feel like sharing today. I guess you are going to have to do some difficult, ball breaking detective work, you know, if you *really* want to know my name." And then she swiftly jogs away, across the street and into the building.

And just like that, a dare has been issued. She obviously has no idea who she's messing with. At that very moment, Traxx gets to me while I'm staring at her getting farther and farther away, creating a distance I don't want to have. "Hey Colton, what the hell happened? What was that about?"

"That my friend… is my new challenge. Come on, let's get changed and get out of here. You are lucky I won't beat your ass for knocking me down with that ball."

"That's what you get for not paying attention, bro. It ain't my fault you didn't take your eyes away from her to see the ball coming your way. I did call your name… Hey, you ummm… have grass between your teeth…" He points at where the grass is, then he proceeds to laugh his ass off, turns around and runs like hell. I clean my teeth with my index finger, find the green culprit, and shake my head in disbelief. What an idiot I must have looked like in front of her! Giving up, I run and follow Traxx to the truck.

* * *

Brianna

Well, that guy was strange and... sexy! I have met my share of good looking guys in the past, but there's just something about this one... Maybe it's the combination of that jet black hair and blue-gray eyes with thick eyelashes and a manly set of eyebrows. Maybe it was how cute and defenseless he looked while he was down on the grass. Or that one cute little crooked tooth in his lower jaw against a perfect top row. Dammit! I need to stop thinking like a dog in heat! Ugh! But... maybe it was that strong set of thighs, so muscular that all I could do was to picture myself sitting on top of them. Shit, it was probably all of the above thrown in with the body of a Greek God. He must have been, what? 6'5? A lot taller than me and I'm 5'8, which is four inches taller than the average American woman.

Stop, Brianna. There is no room in your life for that.

I came to study here with a purpose. I cannot stray away from my goal. Stop thinking about boys, they will only bring you trouble. And you need to avoid trouble. Focus. Remember your goals. That's it. Maybe I need to go to the shooting range later in order to work out some of this tension.

I have been successfully hiding away for years. I left my safe haven in the US Army only to pursue my dream of attending Shoreline University. Thanks to the Army, I was able to build my confidence, learned about self-defense, weapons, and vehicles. I found out that I was strong inside, and that I can work hard to become strong on the outside as well. I spent a lot of time with guys. Guys can only bring drama into your life if you let them get close to your heart. So I learned to have friends with benefits. I could call on any of the guys I was friends with when I needed a sexual pick me up – no strings attached. It worked for me. Drama? I have had plenty of that shit to last me a lifetime.

I stop in front of the Registrar's office, and as I walk in I put all thoughts of the grass-diving pretty boy out of my mind. *There is no time for that.*

* * *

I walk into the apartment I share with my best friend, Ciara Collins. I hear the music playing. I don't like to come home to a dead silent place. It gives me the creeps. Music soothes me, and Ciara spoils me when it comes to this. She had a surround sound system installed in the living room, and additional speakers throughout the apartment so that I can hear music anywhere within it. Right now "Pocket Full of Sunshine" by Natasha Bedingfield is playing.

Ciara and I were roommates in the Army, and we thought we were very lucky when we realized we both are huge Ocean Tides football fans and we wanted to finish our degrees here, in Pristina. This is a small town, about 15 minutes from the beach, located in the Gulf portion of Florida. Her family could not believe that she had joined the Army and left them, and it actually made them appreciate her a lot more than they used to. She's a daddy's girl and she will be the first one to tell you that. The one good thing about it is that her dad does not hesitate to give her everything she needs or wants. Luckily, she does not act like a spoiled brat. She's really down to earth and a sweet girl.

Ciara completed her Army term a few months before I did. She and I decided that after her visit home, she would go to Florida, find a job and also an apartment that we can share. She waited for me to finish my term and come to meet her. Sadly, I did not have a family to visit before I got here. I consider her my sister and imagine the bond we share is similar, if not stronger, than the love sisters would have for each other.

"Hi Brianna! How was your day? Did you accomplish everything you needed to do?" She smiles as she walks into the kitchen. She's wearing a towel on her head and a robe and has freshly applied makeup.

"What's up tramp?" I smile back at her and wink. She knows I'm kidding. I grab a cup from the cabinet and a coke from the pantry, and after a little ice I pour the soda into the cup. "Yeah, I did. I'm so ready for classes to start. The sooner they do, the sooner I can be busy. You know how antsy I get when I don't have a purpose." I pout a little to make my point stronger. I take a big swallow and walk into the living room. Ciara follows.

"Well, that is great news" She smiles.

"*What* is great news, exactly?"

"The fact that you are antsy and need something to do. Didn't you get my text? Hurry up and get in the shower. We are going out!"

"I'm really not in the mood to party today. I have to go through my school papers and get everything ready because I have an early class in the morning." I tell her while shrugging my shoulders and getting comfy on the couch.

"Oh! Did you get your schedule all fixed up? Are they going to give you credit for all the classes you took while you were in the Army?" She asks.

"Yeah, all but a couple of electives. It's okay. It doesn't affect my status as a Junior. I like that eye shadow on you." She smiles big. Ciara is my complete opposite. She's petite and I'm tall. Her eyes are like sapphires, mine are two toned: Green on the inside surrounding my pupils, and then more bluish throughout the rest of the irises. She's a natural blonde and I'm a brunette. But we follow the same principles and have been best friends for years.

"Thanks!" She smiles brightly while looking at her work of art in the mirror. "Go on, get ready!" She says. "It's a small get together. This girl, Carrie, invited us when she came to get her dog at Pet Village today." She gives me a look that means I need to get my butt off the couch and start moving. I still don't want to go, but I will do it for her. I sigh loudly and roll my eyes to the back of my head and tell her to count me in.

When she moved here to Pristina, Florida, a new business was opening, a doggy day care called Pet Village, and she managed to score a job. She really doesn't need the job because her family has plenty of money, but she likes to take care of the dogs and it gives her extra money that she can spend without having to explain things to her dad. When I finally arrived in town after months of waiting, she convinced her manager to hire me too. Ciara lets me pay rent, but I suspect she only charges me a small amount, because what I pay cannot be half of the rent this luxury complex charges. I don't like the fact that I'm not paying my share, but trying to change the terms Ciara has set for this is like arguing with a cement wall. So I go along with it in order to make her happy.

An hour later we are all dolled up – me in dark slim jeans, platform silver sandals and a tight black halter top that makes my boobs pop. My body is well defined and somewhat muscular without bulging. Ciara's is the same way. It's one of the many benefits of getting up every morning and doing push-ups, sit-ups, and a run of at least two miles. I'd like to think I have curves in all the right places. Ciara's wearing a burnt orange strapless mini dress, cinched with a dark navy belt and dark blue platform sandals. We add a little bling with jewelry: watches, necklaces and bangle bracelets. We both chose to wear our hair down in long soft waves.

"I see you chose to wear school colors – smart choice!" I tell Ciara while giving her the once over look.

"Guilty as charged! And is not even football season yet!" she replies. We both giggle as we walk out the door.

"I assume I am the designated driver?" I ask her.

"But of course!" She says in her best *Grey Poupon* commercial accent and smiles. "We need to stop by the liquor store on the way there."

"But of course!" I reply. She drives a brand new white BMW 220i Coupe convertible with all the bells and whistles. I drive a metallic blue Ford Mustang GT convertible, slightly used, but all I care is that is not an automatic and it has a V8 engine. This baby runs like hell with just a tap on the gas. Yes, I love speed. I love everything that gets my adrenaline going. I should have become a stuntwoman, and if this school business doesn't pan out like I expect, then that will become my plan B. For the moment, we take her Beemer. I love driving any vehicle, but this is certainly a smooth, sweet ride.

The radio is playing, the music is loud, and the weather is perfect. Suddenly I start thinking about the guy I saw this morning and I become really quiet. I can picture those strong arms around me, his cute smile and his mouth next to mine whispering sweet nothings against my lips. It's not long before Ciara notices I am way too far gone inside my head.

"Spill it!" She says while staring at me. I give her an annoyed look at which she responds by opening her eyes really big and extending her right arm in a circular motion, meaning I better get with the program.

"There is nothing to tell, really…" I try to dance away from the subject. It doesn't work. So I continue. "When I was going to see the advisor on campus, I noticed these 2 guys in front of the building getting ready to cross the street, so I slow down a little bit to take a good look at them… and my instincts were 100% accurate, they were so freakin' hot! Both of them were tall and buff with nice chiseled features. I guess they thought I was a guy at first, because when I passed right in front, their mouths dropped open and they were staring hard, like they could not believe what was right in front of them! It was funny, actually."

"The way that your butt lifts up when you are on that bike, really suits you! Didn't I tell you? Uh! And you were wearing those tight jeans you love so much!" She says all that while wiggling her eyebrows up and down.

"I know, right? Well, then I parked not too far away from where they were, and I hear a guy running towards me and getting closer. I see him in my peripheral vision, so I prepare myself to knock the shit out of somebody. I was getting ready to reach for my steel nunchucks from the inside of my boots, but I didn't feel any threat, so I waited to see what was going to happen. I took a look over my shoulder to let him know I am onto him and he completely freezes in place and stares me down! He was the epitome of a god – Gor-ge-ous! Black messy hair, a bit long but not too much. Blue-gray eyes, scruffy face, tall, tanned and buffed. Oh… and his lips, they were not thin or big, just the right size – made me want to sample, know what I mean?" I show her a huge grin.

"Yes! And then, what happened?"

"You are not going to believe it." I turn my head with the most straight face I can muster and her facial expression becomes a serious one.

"What??? Spill it, you are killing me, Knuckles!" I roll my eyes at the term of endearment. Our friends started to call me 'Knuckles" when I used brass knuckles to beat up a guy who tried to sexual assault me. He failed. I rearranged his face before I called the cops. No one other than Ciara knows that I never go anywhere without some kind of weapon. "Fine! I'm spilling. He got hit with a football in the head, lost his balance and fell face first on the grass." We look at each other and bust out laughing.

"Are you for real?" She giggles.

"Real."

"Did he say anything after that?" She asks me.

"I went to check on him, biting my tongue so I didn't laugh out loud. I helped him up and then he tried to get my name, but I turned around and left him chowing down on some grass. I ran to my appointment, and by the time I came back out they were gone." I shrugged.

We continued to laugh and joke while at the liquor store and all the way to the party. Even though I know my past is too complicated and that I don't need to be with anyone, I silently wondered if I would see that guy again soon.

Made in the USA
Charleston, SC
22 May 2015